THE
SILVER WELL

M KENELM RINGSTEAD

BLOXWICH
2022

THE
SILVER WELL

TRUE
SCIENCE FICTION
IN THE
PAST AND FUTURE
ANNALS OF SPYING

M Kenelm Ringstead

MIDLAND TUTORIAL PRODUCTIONS
BLOXWICH

AGWELL
RINGSTEAD

DEDICATED WITH RESPECT AND ADMIRATION TO THE BRAVE THE LATE

MAGAWA

Magawa was a Giant African Pouched Rat
whose sense of smell was keener than a dog's.
He successfully detected sixty-seven hidden explosive devices
in Cambodia and died in retirement in January 2022.
He was awarded the PDSA Gold Medal for Gallantry in 2020.

TABLE OF CONTENTS

CHAPTER ONE
ROMANS

This is not how I remembered it. The last I saw of High Rochester was on a wan evening of statue-still serenity in the late September of 1978, as I drove a hired Escort to board the night at Jedburgh. As I sped through the windless calm of a Northumberland evening wisps of coal smoke drifted from the chimneys of the lone roadside terrace of miners' cottages into the still and melancholic sky. It was a scene then commonplace, but of indescribable beauty, never to be forgotten, not even by a young man in a hurry.

This is not how I remembered it. Puffing obesely in diabetic senility up a shapeless lane lined with recent retirement bungalows, as I made my way from the bus stop to Bremenium. From a very prosaic, very British streetscape into the eerie heights of a very eerie country, heights not so much adjacent as coeval.

I remembered my days of hope as a young doctoral student at Chesters House in Glasgow, a hostel named for the Wall of Antoninus Pius that traced its buried way immediately to the North.

I remembered how the great Italian poet Dante Alighieri had expressed his mid-life crisis in the opening stanzas of his great *Inferno*[R1.1] that I had read at Chesters. It was one of the three great Books that changed my life.

Ahi quanto a dir qual era è cosa dura	Ah me! how hard a thing it is to say
esta selva selvaggia e aspra e forte	What was this forest savage, rough, and stern,
che nel pensier rinova la paura!	Which in the very thought renews the fear.
Tant' è amara che poco è più morte;	So bitter is it, death is little more;
ma per trattar del ben ch'i' vi trovai,	But of the good to treat, which there I found,
dirò de l'altre cose ch'i' v'ho scorte.	Speak will I of the other things I saw there.
Io non so ben ridir com' i' v'intrai	I cannot well repeat how there I entered
tant' era pien di sonno a quel punto	So full was I of slumber at the moment
che la verace via abbandonai.	In which I had abandoned the true way.
Ma poi ch'i' fui al piè d'un colle giunto,	But after I had reached a mountain's foot,
là dove terminava quella valle	At that point where the valley terminated,
che m'avea di paura il cor compunto,	Which had with consternation pierced my heart,

<table>
<tr><td>guardai in alto e vidi le sue spalle</td><td>Upward I looked, and I beheld its shoulders,</td></tr>
<tr><td>vestite già de' raggi del pianeta</td><td>Vested already with that planet's rays</td></tr>
<tr><td>che mena dritto altrui per ogne calle.</td><td>Which leadeth others right by every road.</td></tr>
<tr><td></td><td></td></tr>
<tr><td>Allor fu la paura un poco queta,</td><td>Then was the fear a little quieted</td></tr>
<tr><td>che nel lago del cor m'era durata</td><td>That in my heart's lake had endured throughout</td></tr>
</table>

But at the age of seventy-five this was for me not so much a mid-life crisis as a pilgrimage of expiation, inchoate and incondite, hardly conscious though planned with scientific deliberation.

Sensible readers will indulge me when I write that even at this remote time there are only some things that I may say. I am not a signatory to The Official Secrets Act 1911 or any similar British or Foreign compact. My brief and undistinguished spying career was very junior and did not officially exist. I was paid to do a job which as far as I know harmed no man, woman or beast, although the job itself may reasonably be thought pointless or even farcical. I do not fear the sanction of the State nor private litigation. Nevertheless I feel a continuing loyalty to My Country and to the individuals I knew of old times, friend and foe, some of whom are still alive. Such a fidelity must persist even when my World and my Country are no more and the aged are at rest. Therefore I name no man or woman whom I know to live, unless by their *nom de guerre*. I name institutions and corporations that I know to have ceased activity. Some traders or academic foundations or similar that I know to persist I name, but only in neutral contexts essential to the technical aspects of this disquisition.

Suddenly, from abaft my sinister beam, materialised a smirking apparition with a shock of red hair.

"Good evening, Sir", said this person in a non-descript Continental accent, "May I walk with you a while?"

I was discomfited, I admit a bit nervous, with some nameless dread, accosted by a lone man, solid enough in the broad daylight, or rather the bright but setting sun of autumn, a stage set like a frame for grief and guilt.

He had that smarmy fixed grin and over-familiar air of a certain type of European, common enough in the last century but rare in this, somehow solicitous, somehow treacherous, somehow having too much time on his hands.

I gazed fixedly at a portable manger, just to the side of the track, a hundred meters further up the hill.

"What is your name, Sir", enquired my insolent companion. I glanced left into his face, somewhat ill-temperedly, my own beginning to redden, not with exertion, but if with sweat, then it was a cold pallor.

My full name is Marjerry Kenelm Ringstead. I do not know what vanity, what streak of malice or narcissism prompts parents to award children provocative or fatuous names. I understand the practice is long illegal in France. My heart goes out to the many Evelyns, Francises and Florences who have tried to live the lives of men. School was a hell for them, and remains such, even for those for whom it is only a recollection of the last century. The boys (or sometimes girls) would make sure to use a suitable diminutive and masters use the appellation in full at every suitable or unsuitable opportunity. Of course I was called "Marge" or "Margery". Any desire to be called "Jerry" was sorely mis-placed and swiftly disabused.

Most people think Kenelm is a brand of furniture but I take great pride in the name. St Kenelm was the first Christian king of my country, who as a sixteen-year-old, was murdered and martyred somewhere in the Clent Hills by his Pagan elder sister. The Clent Hills retain an unholy reputation to this day. I encourage friend and foe alike to address me as "Ken" or "Kenny" and most are glad to do so, though usefully I have noticed that real enemies always address me as "Dr Ringstead".

"Who is asking?" I responded abruptly. The man's face changed a little slightly to a rictus of injured pride, striving to retain the mask of amity.

"Oh, Dr Ringstead, do you not remember me?"

I racked my brains. As I remarked when opening this tale, I had not stopped here on my last and only passage so long ago. Was he one of the many foreigners I had known at Chesters? The lonely place, the setting sun, the still silence, the unwelcome comrade, the remorse of an early promise dissipated, a thousand caitiff thoughts and yearnings, and the apprehension of a freezing night unsheltered: All converged to recall the many evil histories of these eldritch moors of England's Debatable Land.

Was this creepy man (if such he was) an emissary of Satan, or a reiving revenant, risen of the humic ground or the Roman tombs ahead?

"I am Nicolas Bourbaki"

I was now convinced I was mocked. "Nicolas Bourbaki" is the pseudonymous appellation affected by French mathematicians and scientists, when upon citation in some learned publication, they wish, for whatever reason, to remain unrecognised.

There followed a tense lacuna, mutually-sensible. All pretence at civility was now suspended.

Then the stranger resumed his laconic smirk, or rather now a sneer of recognition that I recognised the reference, and that it disturbed me.

"I am the moving Spirit of Disinterest", my companion clarified.

What the hell did he mean?

Disinterest is a curious thing: Like atheism a privative, notoriously difficult to prove, and even dubious of existence, for as the Ancients said Nature abhors a vacuum, yet the poor are always with us.

I am told that the atom is almost entirely an empty void, that any seeming solid is only a nimbus of probability, and that each cubic meter of outer space (assuming cubes exist in the vicinity of matter, and that a meter has any relevance to the unthinkably remote) contains at least a few hundred jittering protons, orbited at extreme range to them, by an each electron.

I suspected Bourbaki of being a Catholic. Catholics, of course, believe in ghosts. I am not talking about Sunday Catholics who read Camus and Sartre and worship at the charcuterie on Fridays: I am talking about *real* Catholics, the sort you get down the Bogside, or in the case of my fellow traveller, the literal bog side.

I suppose I am a good Protestant. I believe in demons and suspected Bourbaki of being one, come to plague me for sure, but innocent of all but imagined violence. I am not especially psychic. I rarely encounter the supernatural, and have only encountered demons thrice. They are not very frightening, but are decidedly repellent. The first two appeared strikingly like faceless black, smooth shop-window mannequins that shared my bed in a very static, dummy-like way, the first kneeling on the edge and the second (was it the first revisiting?) actually lying beside me. I swore at them in a way of which I did not know I was capable, but they remained silent and stupid, leaving in their own time. I later developed the idea that these were beings trying to materialise from another universe, and failing to do so in an entire way. The third apparition was much more skilful, succeeding in the simulation of a woman long dead but very close to me, before briefly reverting to his archetype. I was unable to answer him back in any way.

The details of the latter manifestation are only mildly offensive, but I am reluctant to describe the very real but incredible details in a fictional short story which is mostly "about" applied radiology and the problems of parallax. It would not be "appropriate" as they say nowadays, and there would be a danger of readers thinking that that encounter also was made-up.

Of course, the Great Myth of our culture and our civilisation (whatever that is) is that Science is disinterested. We naturally hope, knowing that hope a pious esperance, that football referees and High Court judges are disinterested, tracing the arguments and contentions with a pure and intense, but dispassionate, intellectual interest. Our hope extends to scientists. The opposite of disinterest, I suppose, is interest, in the vulgar, pecuniary sense, looking for the personal advantage of profit. And yet disinterest is not necessarily congruent with justice, or even mercy, because it can too easily be perfunctory, mechanical, idle or even self-satisfying, and the latter is not disinterested. And the handing down of judgment, always blasphemous, is the very epitome of sectional interest, if only vicariously, as in the man who says "I do this because I am the guardian of the commonwealth, and I serve the public, so don't take it personally, old boy".

So given this cold and god-like equity of disinterest, how can it be that disinterest is a spirit, and much less move? For we think that Spirit is somehow static, or even immovable, even unto the proverbial ghost that walks, or the Unmoved Mover in his empyrean. How bloodless and lifeless a thing is disinterest, and how lively and active a spirit? Even an evil, selfish, sensually-interested spirit?

According to the ancient formula for congress with spirits I quietly said to Bourbaki:-

"In the name of Our Holy Savior Jesus Christ, state your business"

Bourbaki failed to disappear.

Instead he instinctually missed a step to fall back slightly on the incline, and adopted a silly, nervous sniggering. His visage was now as ruddy as mine, and distinctly unspiritual.

"Very well, my friend", said Bourbaki with icy control, "I shall state my business".

"You travelled this road before, as a scientist. You sought fame, respect and vindication, all vanities of the self. You sought such at the cost of your soul. And now you travel again, seeking Knowledge that you know is inaccessible to mortal man, knowing the only knowledge as can be known, that your wages is Conjecture and confoundment, for the peace you crave could only have ensued the blessings of those you spurned".

"And your business is...?" I replied ungraciously.

"Enlightenment"

As if in self-confutation at length Bourbaki added:-

"My public reason for my presence, and that I declared on the new visa-application, is the measurement and classification of the remaining blocks of ashlar about the West Gate. I hope to contribute to *The Annals of Masonry*".

My interest was piqued. I too, in idle retirement, had measured Roman masonry, in my case on the ancient quayside of the Roodee at *Deva* (Chester). But amid interesting suggestions about Roman dimensioning there was too little exposure for justified statistical analysis.

Could this person read my mind?

Was Bourbaki sending an arcane signal, his idea of a funny handshake? *The Annals of Masonry* is on the face of it a plausible name for a learned periodical but of course Masonry, colloquially-understood, is a well-known vulgar heresy, more attractive to traders than thinkers. In any case the title *The Annals of Masonry* is far too frank and informative an appellation to appeal to scientific editors. *Hebdomadal Proceedings of the Society of Tectonic Dimensioning* would be more their style.

And if Bourbaki was an EU citizen, then so long as his stay in the UK was less than ninety-one days, he required no visa. I decided to probe, however crudely, this aspect of his provenance.

"Are you an EU citizen?" I asked baldly.

Taken aback, Bourbaki resumed his girlish giggle before answering:-

"What kind of a question is that!? I would say I was Hungarian, but my folk have lived in Rosario for eighty odd years".

I suppose I was expected to know where Rosario was, unless the word had some symbolic meaning lost on my dull apprehension.

Where the tarmacadam had given way to dirt, and then to grass our Hungarian diverged without valediction to the ruins of Bremenium. I was glad to see him leave and hoped not to meet him again, either on the Street, or at the Tombs where I knew there were traces of ashlar for him to ponder, if such was his whim and such his intelligence.

It was well into autumn and the weather of the high moors of Britain very fickle. An icy breeze was already gathering its breath for Vespers, and little flecks of snow guided it south.

I was dressed in an alpinist's Goretex® storm suit of the kind that people wear in the "death zones" of the highest Himalayan peaks. Foreign readers in particular will think this quite excessive, but it is better for a sick old man to sweat, strip and chill rather than perish of hypothermia in a high place, by altitude and latitude.

On my feet I wore Goretex-lined synthetic hiking boots with Vibram® soles, and within long Goretex® oversocks, with a spare pair in my sack.

Besides my cloth cap and my two sticks I carried a Goretex® rucksack for water, snap and the all-important geochemical sample tubes. At my chest I packed a light waterproof bivvy bag, large enough to enclose my kit as well as my person. This provided extra protection during the falls to which I am prone (no risible pun intended), as well as an extra layer of insulation, if necessary.

By the way I am not a Gore shareholder or dealer: It is just that in fifty years of walking the steeping British hills it is this particular brand I have found the most reliable.

I afforded the weight also of an ordinary motorcyclist's crash helmet, with visor and chinguard, a protection for the head certainly, but mostly a defence against driving rain and hail.

All of my kit was woodland camouflage including the normally bright orange helmet, to which I had fixed camo tape.

I suppose I looked the part of a rural spy, and certainly was not especially protected from shot or shrapnel, stray or straight, but I believe in being inconspicuous.

Shortly I reached the Tombs. Roman Law forbade the inhumation of bodies within the walls of settlements. Accordingly the entitled poor were buried in extramural cemeteries and the rich or esteemed in masonry tombs that flanked the thoroughfares outwith the gates. There was little above the surface except in the case of one: It showed two courses of a nearly perfect circle of ashlar. I was too stupid to study the lithology of this stone, but I presume it felsite, or siliceous freestone or something a little more obdurate than Dinantian limestone. Whatever it was it was almost certainly the same as the stone that built the West Gate of Bremenium, if not its other walls.

For some morbid or maudlin reason I had decided to bivouac upon Lamb Crag, slightly East of Dere Street and on the opposite side to the known tombs. At this point Dere Street was not a modern road and was little more than a tussock-flanked linear depression. I am not much of a sky expert and was not aware that a full moon was rising as the gloom gathered and I prepared my lonely, fireless camp upon the hill. A camp I hoped would be no vigil.

As I lay I looked up at the youthful Pleiades gambling gaily across their frozen firmament as the Ancients saw and loved the girlish passengers so many years ago. I hoped against hope that these virginal blue lucky sisters of the spring would somehow be auspicious in a World and a Planet in stark need of remission. I prayed. I slept.

At 0234 I woke and became aware that there was movement around me, though I had selected a spot unlikely to feel the tread of man or beast. A light wind sighed darkly in two stunted mountain ash trees that kept a couple's company in the treeless tracts about.

There was a bright moon. Dark shadows appeared aimlessly to patrol the tombs before me. Somehow they were too low for men. Were they demons? There was no luminosity about them. I have written elsewhere about the possibility that some dimly luminous apparitions may arise from the slow combustion of phosphoric gases in still air, but this air was not quite still and the shapes in no manner lit, not even by the moon. In any event, the remains entombed here, if not mummified by the peat, would have decayed far beyond the stage at which gas might generate. It crossed my mind that badgers or foxes might be at play, risen from their lairs in the ptomathalomi, but if so then they would share their homes with the bony remains of many generations of ancestors, theirs and ours.

It is weird indeed, not that there are inexplicable things, but that the human mind seeks a supposedly rational explanation for any perplexity. Even at the expense of attracting a potentially lethal attention, not from ghosts or even demons, but from very living marksmen.

Accordingly I took out my powerful torch and shone it in the direction. Twenty sets of bobbing red eyes shone, shimmered and occulted in the near distance: Sheep or maybe feral goats, I surmised. Maybe hostile soldiers or policemen. And yet one set of eyes, if that is what they were, differed. They shone *blue*. I was used to the idea that retinae often reflected white light red or brilliant white, or perhaps occasionally green, but blue was entirely new and to which species it may pertain, zoological or theological, I had no idea.

As I gazed fascinated in this eerie fastness the blue eyes *parted*. What was going on? Were these not a creature's two eyes? Then I realised. They were coming toward me at pace!

I fainted or I fell asleep. I know not which.

As it dawned I awoke. I brushed myself down, re-packed my oversack, took a swig of sparkling water and a bite of snap. I forbore insulin and other drugs. Today they would be neither necessary nor desirable.

Who or what had danced the tombs in the moonlight had
gone.

It was time myself to depart.

<u>Reference for Chapter One</u>

R1.1   **The Opening Verses of the Inferno by Dante Alighieri**
Thought,Co
https://www.thoughtco.com/inferno-canto-i-4092995

AGWELL
RINGSTEAD

There is in the far North of England, set in a desolate, wind-blasted wilderness of blanket peat and Boreal tussock-grass, a lonely water source called The Silver Spring. To be precise, in a story in which nothing is what it seems in a land of shadows, the Silver Well is situated at 55° 19′ 06″ N, 2° 17′ 13″ W or in terms of the British National Grid system NT 81889 02732[R2.1].

In an old-fashioned idiom, we might say that Britain is a Temperate Maritime environment similar to British Columbia or the southernmost parts of Chile and New Zealand. Any former servicemen or others who know The Falkland Islands (Islas Malvinas) will instinctively understand The Cheviot Hills of Britain's Debatable Lands. The British climate is especially fitful at altitude: Five minutes of brilliant sunshine can succeed an hour of snow or hail and succumb to a few seconds of torrential rain at any half-hour of the four astronomical seasons. And literally above all the wind: Virtually relentless it was the wind that quite literally brought Britain its world-wide wealth, and today the English generate twenty percent of their electric power using it, hardly possible in any other densely-inhabited place.

The Debatable Lands are an exception to the national demographic realities. Like Picardy and similar frontier lands anywhere they are depopulated and impoverished. In days gone by they were notorious for their murders and arsons, and the depredations of the Border Reivers, opportunistic clans of nominally English or Scottish bandits and cattle thieves who would not be decisively suppressed until the eighteenth century. Their names read like the character list (or come to that the cast list) of some Hollywood soap about rivals in the oil trade: Ewing, Armstrong, Scott, Kerr, Carmichael, Maxwell, Bell, Geddes, Thomson, Eliot. Like politicians in every age and clime, the kings and emperors of Europe's past favored great rivers or narrow icy ridges to delimit the limes of their barely lawful realms, and the kings of Scotland and England were not exceptions. But the Cheviot Hills, whilst bleak, monotonous and soul-destroyingly lonely rarely exceed a thousand feet and whilst boggy and treacherous, are nevertheless rangeable.

Some time prior to AD140 Roman strategists and statesmen crystallised the idea that they would like to add Scotland to their already enormous empire. Perhaps they were tempted by the mineral and human wealth of England and Wales (Britannia) to surmise that Scotland was similar. We know that the emperor Antonius Pius ordered the construction of a turf rampart across the waist of Scotland in AD142. Somehow associated with this is the Roman military road of Dere Street which led the two hundred miles or so from the Legionary Capital of York to a place now called Cramond, at the Eastern terminus of the Antonine Wall, well within Scotland.

We do not know what, if anything, the Romans called this road. The phrase "Dere Street" is definitely a later Anglo-Saxon term, a "street" being any surfaced, engineered road, especially a long-distance one. The meaning of "Dere" is obscure but may be connected with the territorial appellation "Deira". The famous Ninth Legion marched up Dere Street and into Scotland, into legend, lost from history. From the outset Dere Street was an Army road built by the Army for the Army. Two thousand years later, it is an Army road today.

The Silver Well, whatever and whyever it is, sits in the moss one hundred meters East and some twenty-five vertical meters below Dere Street, now a tarmacadamised single-track lane direct as a broken arrow through the hills. The road is adequate to occasional traffic with vehicles that have pneumatic tires. Much of modern Dere Street embeds the A68 Darlington to Edinburgh trunk road, but this particular stretch is prohibited to civil traffic, except that it is a public footpath when artillery training is suspended. The Silver Well itself appears to be secured within a modern roofed cubical or small concrete bunker, set within a square fenced enclosure.

I do not think that drinking water is abstracted. I do not know the mean discharge of the spring, or whether that fluctuates. I do not know if the water is toxic to livestock. I do not, indeed, know whether it contains silver, and if it does, then how or why.

Angus Lunn in his *The Northumberland Wildlife Trust: A History*[R2.2] briefly adverts to a Silver Nut Well "near Otterburn", which is a chalybeate (i.e. iron-infused) well that coats organic detritus with silvery marcasite. Marcasite is basically "white pyrite", FeS_2, with an orthorhombic crystal structure, rather than common "yellow pyrite", or Fool's Gold, which has a cubic structure. Thus pyrite and marcasite are chemically-identical, but very different in appearance. Marcasite could readily be mistaken for the silver minerals pyrargyrite (Ag_3SbS_3), argentite (Ag_2S), acanthite (also a form of Ag_2S), native silver (Ag), several exotic silver-metallic sulphides, and even the lead mineral galena (PbS).

Meanwhile, on page 77 of her book *Forbidden Rites: Your Complete Introduction to Traditional Witchcraft*[R2.3], Jeanelle Ellis writes

"At Silver Well near Otterburn in Northumberland if you threw pine cones into the well, they would be changed to silver for you." To the peasant folk of Redesdale two hundred and more years ago this would definitely qualify as witchcraft, but we will examine the topic more scientifically later in our long and hopefully edifying thought-experiments.

Maps

The general situation of the Silver Well is defined in Figure 2.1, an excerpt of a mid-twentieth century 6-inch-to-one-mile map. The scale of this maplet is therefore 1 in 10560. But re-scaling has rendered this unreliable. The entire image represents 830.3 meters East to West and 577.4 meters North to South.

Whilst the Silver Well is at about (0.45, 0.5) in terms of relative image co-ordinates note that there is another spring at the same altitude but on the opposite side of the valley at roughly (0.87, 0.85). This is the Golden Well. The Silver Well is about a hundred meters from the Roman road.

I have added the blue arrows to represent the general direction of surface or subsurface superficial drainage toward the Silver Well.

The Sills Burn is a small stream (creek) and the thin blue watercourses are no more than spade-width slits cut in the peat which I know from painful experience are invisible on the ground and very easy to fall into, standing suddenly in water at the bottom. The parallel pecked black lines are sheep-runs beaten by sheep, rabbits and feral goats.

At this point it is helpful to study a second map: A 6-inch-to-one-mile Victorian map of the environs. (There are no twenty-first century public large-scale maps available in the UK though reliable American satellite pictures are obtainable and professional cartographers use these to facilitate planning, building construction and soforth). The entire image represents 840.39 meters East to West and 585 meters North to South.

The Victorian map is superior in many ways to its twentieth century debasements, and the thousand foot contour is boldly and clearly demarcated.

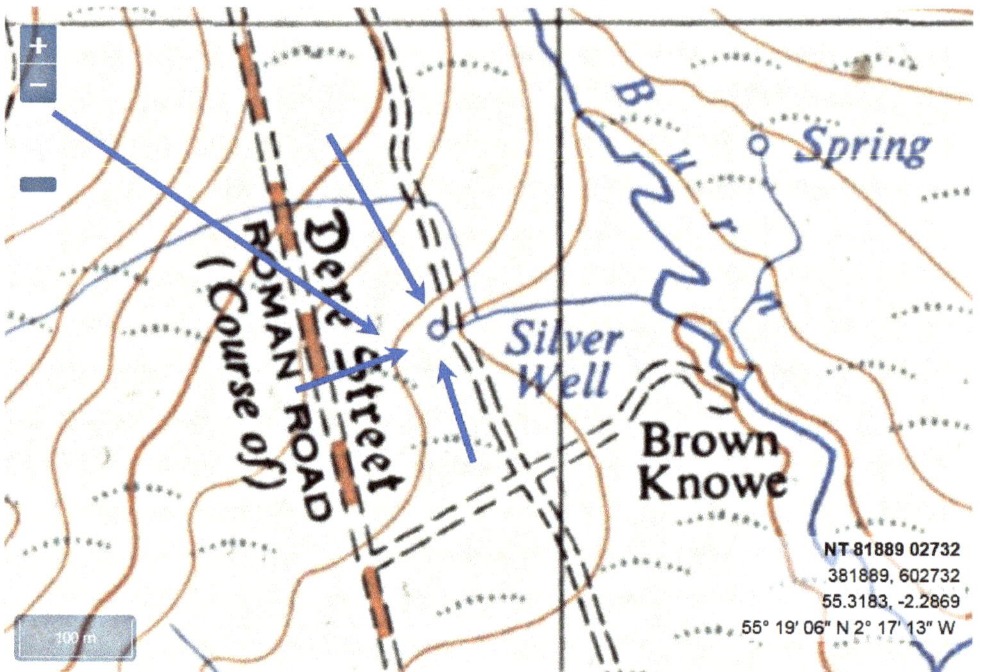

Figure 2.1
The Silver Well with Dere Street and the Sills Burn

On this map the Silver Well is at about (0.45, 0.5) in terms of relative image co-ordinates.

The green-labelled red circles center upon water sampling points A through K at which water may be sampled to ascertain the presence or absence of silver, or indeed other minerals in solution or colloidal suspension. Note the strategy of sampling. For source water one location is indicated. For stream water three locations are chosen immediately below a confluence and immediately above on the two affluents.

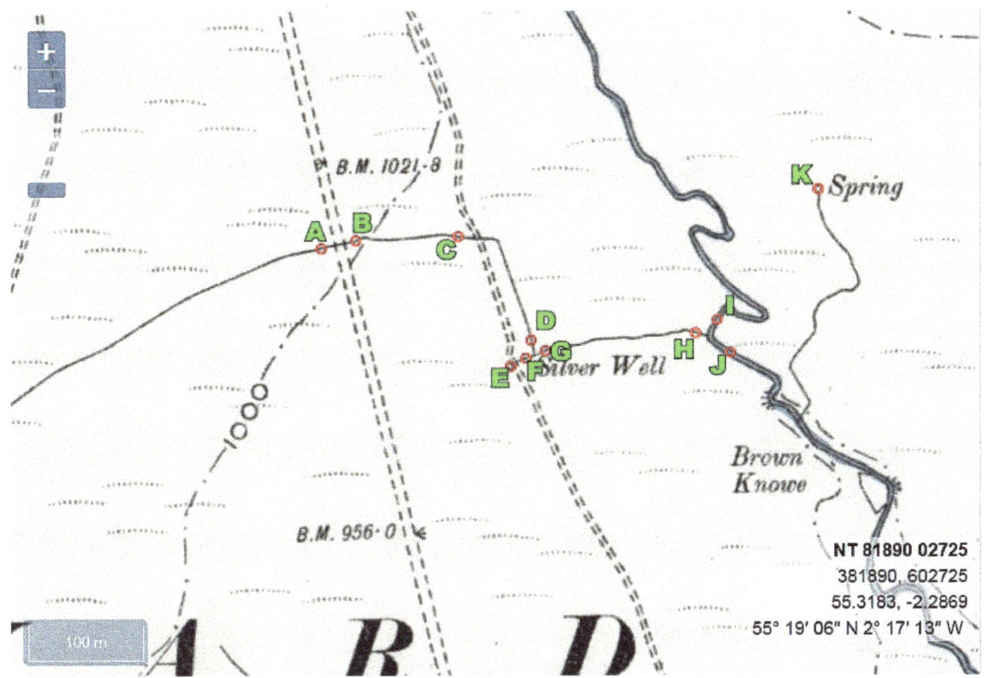

Figure 2.2
The Silver Well with Dere Street and the Sills Burn

<u>Assumptions</u>

My working hypothesis is that:-

(a)	Something Visible Coats Vegetable Matter in the Silver Well
(b)	That something *Continues* to Coat Matter
(c)	That Coating Agent Precipitates from the Spring Water
(d)	That Coating Agent moves some Short Distance under Gravity, probably through the Peat-Cover, which Overburden does not of itself remove or contribute Coating Agent in such a way as to frustrate appearance at The Silver Well

(e)   The Coating Agent is either:-
  (i)   Geological
          Naturally sourced from the country rock
  (ii)   Cultural
          Artificially Placed in or Topographically above the Well by the Hand of Man

We need critically further to discuss these sub-assumptions.

(a)   We need to be sure that the "coating" is not surficially-trapped air or water on the one hand, or mineralogical displacement in the manner of pyritised fossils and the like.

(b)   We need to know that the target substance *still* remains in the target placement: Otherwise we find ourselves in an ongoing Oak Island situation.

(c)   We cannot ordinarily be sure that the visible change does not arise from some autochthonous degradation of the organic deposit itself, such as oxidation, or such as bacterial attack ("rotting").

(d)   We need determinately to establish that the well itself is not contributing the material (perhaps because Iron Age people or modern Pagans have sunk votive silver in the spring propitiously).

Sampling Strategies

The naive eleven-site strategy at Figure 2.2 is inherently wasteful and expensive as logic determines that only five sampling sites are essential, and perforce the other six redundant.

Please note that the Number of Presence Configurations, $Q_{(n)}$, for the n Sampling Sites of Figure 2.2 is given by:-

$$Q_{(11)} = O_{(11)}^{\ n} = 2^{11} = 2048$$

Equation 2.1

Where $O_{(n)}$ is the Number of Available Option States in our problem. ($O_{(n)}$ is 2 because our Option is Silver found present (1) or silver found absent (0)).

In particular, $Q_{(n)}$ is **not** the Number of Permutations of $O_{(n)}$ in n, $P_{(n)}$, **nor** is it the Number of Combinations of $O_{(n)}$ in n.

$Q_{(n)}$ is always larger that $P_{(n)}$ or $C_{(n)}$ and becomes exponentially bigger with n.

These facts are illustrated by Table 2.1:-

Serial	$O_{(n)}$	n	Number of Perms	Number of Combs	$O_{(n)}^n$
1	2	3	6	3	8
2	2	11	110	55	2048
3	2	5	20	10	32

Table 2.1
Relations Between $O_{(n)}$, $P_{(n)}$, $C_{(n)}$ and $Q_{(n)}$
when $O_{(n)}$ is Two (Binary Option)

To simplify the logic of site exploration for silver metal (Ag) we will initially consider, for a given sampling site, A through K, whether silver is present (1) or absent (0).

In this predicament this leads immediately to three existential Conditions:-

(α) Culvert
Ag detected at Site B but not at Site A

B&¬A

Someone at some time, most likely at the end of Roman occupation or during the age of Viking raids deposited a hoard of silver treasure in the Roman drainage culvert mapped under Dere Street between Sites A and B.

Several Roman and Viking hoards have been disclosed in Great Britain, and some are internationally important.

Discoveries were particularly common during the intensive military construction and agricultural deep-ploughing campaigns of the Second World War; and again in the post-1990 fashions for hobbyist metal-detection.

         (β)   Springs
                      Ag detected at Site E or Site K or Both

E.or.K

Someone at some time has been placing or dumping silver into one or both of the springs identified on the map.

This is most likely votive behavior on the part of Ancient Iron Age peoples, Romans or conceivably modern Pagans.

         (χ)   Geology
                      Ag detected at Site A or Site I

A.or.I

The silver found in or about The Silver Well arises naturally from the weathering of country rock at or above one or both of the two Sites A or I.

*Note that these conditions are **not** mutually exclusive, except where silver is absent everywhere.*

Now the above logic indicates that of the eleven proposed Sampling Sites A through K only five Sites, A, B, E, I and K are actually relevant to the testing of Existential Conditions α, β, and χ.

This pruned five-site selection is shown in the revised plan of Figure 2.3

As can be seen from Table 2.1 $Q_{(n)} = O_{(n)}^n = 32$ for this five-site scheme, and conventionally Selection $S_{(n)}$ serial starts at zero (no target anywhere) and counts through to 2^n-1 (target everywhere).

The thirty-two Selection States $S_{(32)}$ for this economised five-site scheme are given in Table 2.2, together with the attendant thirty-two Existential Condition configurations of Conditions α, β and χ.

It is immediately obvious that whilst some target-presence outcome applies to S-1 of the available S Selection States, the available three Outcome Reasons, α, β and χ are by no means equal.

If Existential Condition α is considered (silver in the culvert) then the *a priori* Probability p(α) is only 8/52 = 0.1538 whilst the Probabilities of p(β) (silver in the springs) and p(χ) (silver in the rocks) is each 22/52 = 0.4231. The probability of all three ExC (silver is everywhere) is $1/S = 1/2^n = 1/32$. This arises when S = 11.

At a scientific level, silver might of course be everywhere notwithstanding, because silver is in the rocks over, or through, which all local water passes.

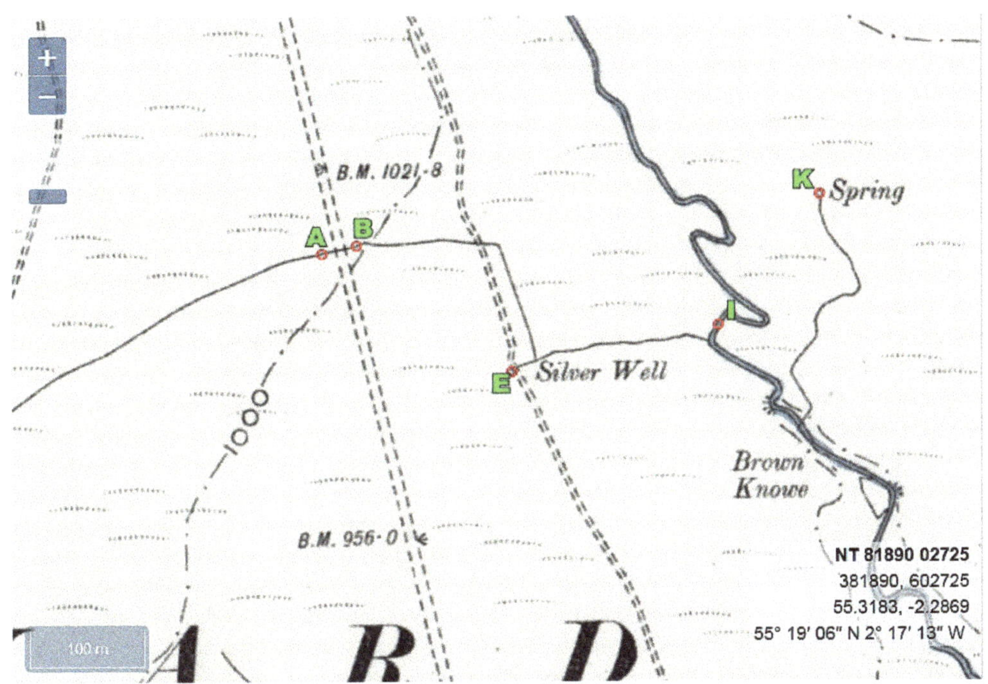

Figure 2.3
The Five Sampling Site Revised Plan

Whatever your views about the relevancy or intellectual-interest of the English silver wells it is most essential that you learn these very basic principles of tactical and strategic decision planning. They are especially applicable to spying and security applications generally. Please note that the normal rules of mathematical statistics are not naively applicable.

Naive thinking has led and shall lead to unnecessary injuries and fatalities.

Binary Places	5						Point Serial	Culvert B&¬A α	Condition Springs E.or.K β	Geology A.or.I χ
						Totals	52	8	22	22
						p	1	0.1538	0.4231	0.4231
Selection Serial	Binary Form	1	2	3	4	5				
		A	B	E	I	K				
0	00000	0	0	0	0	0	0	0	0	0
1	00001	0	0	0	0	1	1		1	
2	00010	0	0	0	1	0	1			1
3	00011	0	0	0	1	1	2		1	1
4	00100	0	0	1	0	0	1		1	
5	00101	0	0	1	0	1	1		1	
6	00110	0	0	1	1	0	2		1	1
7	00111	0	0	1	1	1	2		1	1
8	01000	0	1	0	0	0	1	1		
9	01001	0	1	0	0	1	2	1	1	
10	01010	0	1	0	1	0	2	1		1
11	01011	0	1	0	1	1	3	1	1	1
12	01100	0	1	1	0	0	2	1	1	
13	01101	0	1	1	0	1	2	1	1	
14	01110	0	1	1	1	0	2	1	1	
15	01111	0	1	1	1	1	2	1	1	
16	10000	1	0	0	0	0	1			1
17	10001	1	0	0	0	1	2		1	1
18	10010	1	0	0	1	0	1			1
19	10011	1	0	0	1	1	2		1	1
20	10100	1	0	1	0	0	2		1	1
21	10101	1	0	1	0	1	2		1	1
22	10110	1	0	1	1	0	2		1	1
23	10111	1	0	1	1	1	2		1	1
24	11000	1	1	0	0	0	1			1
25	11001	1	1	0	0	1	2		1	1
26	11010	1	1	0	1	0	1			1
27	11011	1	1	0	1	1	2		1	1
28	11100	1	1	1	0	0	1			1
29	11101	1	1	1	0	1	2		1	1
30	11110	1	1	1	1	0	1			1
31	11111	1	1	1	1	1	2		1	1

Table 2.2
Existential Condition Outcomes for
The Essential Five Sampling Station Scheme
ABEIK

Students may wish to consider whether Sampling Site I is dispensable.

In fact I will talk you through it. The outcome is instructive.

In the four-station model ABEK, the participation of Geology, Existential Condition χ, in the formation of the pattern of silver distribution is proven by the presence of silver at Sampling Site A only (i.e. above the culvert).

The number of Selection States S is now only $2^4 = 16$.

If Existential Condition α is considered (silver in the culvert) then the *a priori* Probability $p(\alpha)$ is now slightly increased to $4/24 = 0.1667$ whilst the Probabilities of $p(\beta)$ (silver in the springs) is $12/25 = 0.5000$ and $p(\chi)$ (silver in the rocks) is $8/24 = 0.3333$. The probability of all three ExC (silver is everywhere) is $1/S = 1/2^n = 1/16$. This arises when in no instance.

In Bayesian terms these constitute *a posteriori* probabilities of the three conditions α, β, and χ: *Given that the distribution of the target in the field has not changed.*

Therefore if you lower the availability of observed data you favor inherently improbable interpretations of objective "facts".

At the expense of being tedious I need once more to assure my younger or less experienced readers of two or three points. In order to prove a thesis with certainty you need to *minimise* the available evidence, *whether or not it bears out your argument*. The forgoing logico-mathematical exercise and its "Bayesian" principles clearly illustrate this most important lesson.

Geology, physiology, and even spying are diverse and most difficult sciences, because whilst rocks and bodies lie all about us, their nature and origin, beyond the obvious, are historical and obscure. Virtually anything could be true of these phenomena and theory perilous, because one man's self-evident fact is another's utter balderdash.[R2.4]

Lawyers and politicians seem to know these principles by instinct (or some of them may be trained: I do not know).

Binary Places: 4

Point Serial

Selection Serial	Binary Form	1 (A)	2 (B)	3 (E)	4 (K)	Totals	Culvert B&¬A (α)	Springs E.or.K (β)	Geology A (χ)
Totals						24	4	12	8
p						1	0.1667	0.5000	0.3333
0	0000	0	0	0	0	0	0	0	0
1	0001	0	0	0	1	1		1	
2	0010	0	0	1	0	1		1	
3	0011	0	0	1	1	1		1	
4	0100	0	1	0	0	1	1		
5	0101	0	1	0	1	2	1	1	
6	0110	0	1	1	0	2	1	1	
7	0111	0	1	1	1	2	1	1	
8	1000	1	0	0	0	1			1
9	1001	1	0	0	1	2		1	1
10	1010	1	0	1	0	2		1	1
11	1011	1	0	1	1	2		1	1
12	1100	1	1	0	0	1			1
13	1101	1	1	0	1	2		1	1
14	1110	1	1	1	0	2		1	1
15	1111	1	1	1	1	2		1	1

Table 2.3
Existential Condition Outcomes for
The Reduced Four Sampling Station Scheme
ABEK

<u>The Geological Setting</u>

Figure 2.4 reproduces the National Library of Scotland archival map image that presents the small-scale regional geology of the relevant part of the Cheviot Igneous Complex and Dinantian Redesdale.

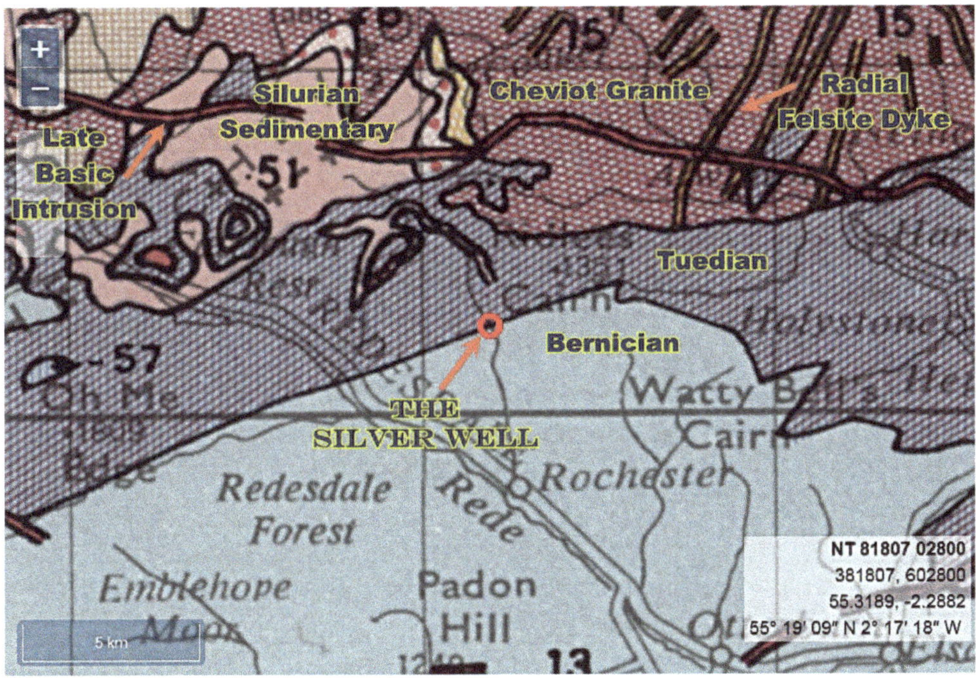

Figure 2.4
The Small-Scale Geological Context of The Silver Well
in the Redesdale Cheviot Hills of England

GS 10inch 1955 map coloring key

Facies Number	Color	Surface Habit	Description	Comments
57	turquiose	areal	Bernician Carboniferous Limestone	Northerly Contact
15	sienna	linear	Felsite, Trachite,etc	Acid Dykes
56	purple	areal	Tuedian Carboniferous Limestone	Southerly Contact
13	rust	linear	Basalt, Dolerite, Camptonite, etc	Basic Dykes or Sills
51	pink	areal	Ludlow and Wenlock Silurian Sediments	Limestone?
12	red	aerial	Granite, Syenite, etc.	Cheviot intrusion

The geological setting of the Silver Well is very similar to the Grangemill-Bonsall area of the White Peak.
Therefore I speculate that the silver may result from the acid weathing of galena.

Table 2.4
Ten-Inch Geological Map Tinting Scheme

The red circle marks the position of The Silver Well at the junction of the Bernician and Tuedian beds within the Lower Carboniferous (Dinantian) limestones.

The Silver Well and its sister spring at the same elevation on the opposite side of the Sills Burn valley appear to be at the meeting-plane of the Tuedian and Bernician facies of the Dinantian Carboniferous Limestone, perhaps better described as a carbonaceous calc-sandstone at this place. (By the way, these nomenclatures are deprecated by twenty-first century geologists).

These two facies are separated by the 3-inch (75 mm) Oakshawford Coal Horizon.

The Tuedian lower member comprises algal limestones with cementstone. The Bernician is the upper (younger). The Lower Bernician incorporates several thicker coal horizons and carbonaceous shales, many of which are highly pyritic and could potentially have contributed to marcasite formation in reducing conditions.

Victorian or Edwardian geologists described the Oakshawford Coal as having a "microsporidial" fossil assemblage. (In my opinion, the pre-war palaeontologists who described this horizon meant to refer to the spores of primitive Carboniferous tree-ferns). In Scottish terms I believe this to be a "Cannel Coal".

I do not know if the Tuedian-Bernician interfacial planes have either trapped, conducted or precipitated metalliferous liquors.

I know no evidence of the Lead-Zinc-Fluorspar mineralisation so characteristic of the Dinantian North Pennines in the Cheviot Hills.

Whilst the bedrock geology has considerable variation, the surface of the land is monotonous and presents few surface bedrock exposures. I have no knowledge of borehole prospecting in The Cheviots whether for water, coal or metals.

The proprietary mobile telephone (cellphone) applications program what3words® is intended to be a voice-notification method of imparting an exact location on the Earth's surface. It is often said that it is "human-friendly" and especially useful for emergency use, as for example when amateur hill-walkers get lost or injured in remote places and need to summon Emergency Services.

Table 2.5 summaries the approximate co-ordinates of the Cheviot Hills' Silver Well in a diversity of numerical conventions basically involving latitude and longitude on the surface of the ellipsoid of revolution, together with the relevant what3words code ///fabricate.crowns.suspect

Alpha Code		Easting	Northing	Sexagesimal						Decimal	
				Latitude			Longitude			Latitude	Longitude
				Degrees	Minutes	Seconds	Degrees	Minutes	Seconds		
UK Ordnance Survey		NT 81890	02725	55	19	6	-2	17	18	55.3183	-2.2869
What3Words®	///fabricate.crowns.suspect										

Table 2.5
The Geographical Co-Ordinates of the Silver Well

The principal of what3words® is that the Earth's surface is divided into three-meter square patches and each patch is awarded a definite three word permutation code that can be written or voiced. This is mathematically possible because if there are $W = 171476$ words in the English language, then the number of Permutations of Three Words Without Repetition is given by:-

$$P(3) = W \times (W - 1) \times (W - 2) = 5.042 \times 10^{15}$$
Equation 2.2

Now the Surface Area of the Earth, S, is 5.10×10^{14} square meters and hence there are 5.67×10^{13} three-meter square patches.

Therefore, there are more than enough permutations of three English words to specify three-meter patches on the surface of this particular planet. To be pedantic, the Fractional Redundancy, FR, is given by:-

$$FR = 1 - \frac{T}{P(3)} = 0.988757$$

Equation 2.3

So we have about eighty-nine times more three-word permutations than we need.

Therefore this concept has a very great intellectual appeal to pure mathematicians, statisticians and other theorists.

But hold on a minute.

You are shouting in a thick Coatbridge accent into a capacitive microphone with no wind muff on a cellphone in a Force Nine gale with driving hail. Is that "crown" or "crowns" or even "rowans"? Is that "fabricate" or "falcate" or even "imbricate"?

The arithmetic facts are summarised in Table 2.6.

Surface Area of the Earth (square meters)	5.10E+14
Area of a Patch (square meters)	9
Number of Patches on Earth Surface (P)	5.67E+13
Number of English Words (W)	171476
Permutations of Three Objects without Repetition	6
Permutations of Three Objects with Repetition	27
Permutations of Three Objects abstracted from W Objects without Repetition	5.042E+15
Permutations of Three Objects abstracted from W Objects with Repetition	1.82E+41
Fractional Redundancy (T)	0.988757

Table 2.6
The Arithmetic Basis of what3words®

<u>References for Chapter Two</u>

R2.1   **The National Library of Scotland Side-by-Side Map Archive**
https://maps.nls.uk/geo/explore/side-by-side/#zoom=5&lat=56.00000&lon=-4.00000&layers=1&right=BingHyb

R2.2   **The Silver Nut Well**
"The Northumberland Wildlife Trust: A History"
Angus Lunn
https://www.nwt.org.uk/sites/default/files/2018-05/Angus%20Lunn%20-%20NWT%20History.pdf)

R2.3   **Witchcraft (the esoteric believe system)**
"Forbidden Rites: Your Complete Introduction to Traditional Witchcraft"
Jeanette Ellis
O Books; 1st Edition (31 Aug. 2009)
ISBN-13 : 978-1846941382
636 pp
p77
(https://books.google.co.uk/books?id=Gr_BaAPVhMQC&pg=PA77&lpg=PA77&dq=the+silver+well+story+northumberland+otterburn&source=bl&ots=JmMUx079gR&sig=ACfU3U18VPqJ5Q-9EIJFs839rdWhQg1RqQ&hl=en&sa=X&ved=2ahUKEwi3-8GQy5buAhU0Q0EAHUGmAqk4ChDoATADegQIARAC#v=onepage&q=the%20silver%20well%20story%20northumberland%20otterburn&f=false), Jeanelle Ellis

R2.4   **Existential Paradox of Knowledge**
KJV Ecclesiastes 1:18, 2:13

AGWELL
RINGSTEAD

CHAPTER THREE
SILVER AND HER SHINING SIBLINGS

Context

In 1869 the great Russian genius Dmitri Mendeleev published his Periodic Table of the Elements, one of the key principles of modern science. This concept organised the eighty or so known chemical elements into seven horizontal Periods of listing, and, within that structure, eighteen shorter vertical Groups of similar substances.

This idea was not original with the Russian, but, and this is crucial, his developed pattern enabled him to *predict* the physical and chemical characteristics of elements that scientists did not as yet know existed. These attributes included physical properties such as atomic mass, gravimetric (mass) density, melting point, boiling point, chemical valency and even the formulae and aqueous solubility of compounds.

The elements within the groups proved uncannily similar.

In particular, in 1871 Mendeleev was able to specify Element 31 which he dubbed "eka-aluminium". Four years later the magnificently-monikered French chemist Paul-Émile Lecoq de Boisbaudran identified the rare metal spectroscopically in a sample of sphalerite zinc ore. De Boisbaudran named the metal Gallium in honor of his country, which is perhaps more than, as a Huguenot, his country had honored him. Of course, cynics and enemies were quick to point out to us lesser intellects that Le Coqs are gallinaceous...

Also, Mendeleev predicted the existence and indeed the character of "eka-silicon", a metalloid. In 1886, the German chemist Clemens Winkler studied a galena-like mineral called argyrodite (Ag_8GeS_6) which he had found in the Himmelsfürst Mine in Saxony. He successfully isolated eka-silicon, Element 32, which not to be outdone by the eminent foreigners, he christened Germanium.

Mendeleev forecast that his eka-aluminium would have a low melting point. It proved upon isolation to be very low: 29.767°C. Human blood temperature is 37°C. Accordingly, gallium, a solid at room temperature, will easily melt in your hand.

When the British and the Germans fueled heavy industries with coal they recovered gallium from the flue-soot. Today the World's supply is mainly a by-product of bauxite refining, for as the Russian predicted many moons since, gallium and aluminum are blood-brothers, and like to go together. The modern secondary source is zinc ore.

Take a look at Figure 3.1, a modern Periodic Table of the Elements downloaded from Wikipedia[R3.1]. Gallium (Ga), Germanium (Ge) and Arsenic (As) are next-door-neighbors respectively at 31, 32, and 33 (by the way, 31 is my address in Bloxwich).

In the summer of 1964 I was a lad of twelve. I developed a consuming interest in metals and the winning of metals, an interest that has never wholly remitted. I sent away to the long-defunct chemical laboratory suppliers, Hopkins and Williams which was based at Chadwell Heath in the far East of London. They offered five grams of Gallium for £10, then more than a week's wages for most men. I sent a postal order and received my gallium. I watched fascinated as the button of metal fused in my palm and formed a bright mercurial pool. On pouring it back into its glass vial it quickly re-solidified, albeit with a disgusting organic scum that the brilliant metal expelled with contempt.

(Five grams of Gallium can be visualised volumetrically as a cube with a side length of 9.46 millimeters).

It was in that year that I was honored to meet the late Mr Don Braggins of Clare College, Cambridge. Don was at that time an eminent metallurgist in the prime of his career, working for Metals Research Ltd in their garret premises above the long-gone Percival's Garage in King Street, Cambridge. The firm specialised, and in 2021 still specialises, in the growth of lattice-perfect large metal crystals, suited to the engineering of quantum-physical electronic microassemblies. I did not understand such things as a twelve-year-old, and neither come to that did most educated adults, but I wrote to Mr Braggins offering to buy some metal specimens for my collection.

Don wrote back inviting me to a guided tour of his factory, and gifted me a splendid assortment of off-cuts and used test specimens, some perfect crystals on the scale of tens of grams, all very valuable albeit used. One item, a large pyramid of metallic bismuth, still had the remains of a very expensive iridium thermocouple embedded in its fabric.

This was one of the major impetuses to science and scholarship that graced my adolescence, and I have harbored a lifelong and unrequited gratitude to Don for his kindness, especially at a time when most of my elders thought I had grim prospects.

It seemed that Don had no gallium to hand, and of course he had far too much intelligence to give a boy a lump of arsenic, but he did give me some silicon, and a shining off-cut of germanium. I was especially proud of this germanium, knowing that in the Britain of 1964, such a thing was almost as inaccessible as plutonium, and much rarer. So I foolishly put it in a matchbox by itself and biroed "Ge" on the yellow Bryant and May label. It subsequently disappeared. Doubtlessly it was found by an adult and thrown out in the trash.

Amongst these other specimens, Don gave me a tiny block of Silver illustrated in Photograph 3.1. The red radial lines are 10mm apart, as are the parallel blue graticule lines of the scale paper. The steel rule is of course similarly calibrated. So you can judge that the block is very nearly one centimeter long and about five millimeters wide. Over the years, the block has developed the black patina of silver because kept in an industrial atmosphere.

Needless to add, even for my lay-readers, gallium, germanium, arsenic, aluminum and silicon are today all staples of the global microelectronics industries, the foundation of modern industrial practice. Don and his colleagues were great pioneers, and applied photo-physics, computer photography and solid-state display owe them everything.

Have another look at the Periodic Table. The nonad of elements centered upon germanium at 32 are related, whether in their properties, their geological ore associations, their crystal habits, or whatever. The central Group-wise vertical Silicon-Germanium-Tin is especially striking, and this is a subset of Group 14, the tetravalent Carbon homologs: Carbon, Silicon, Germanium, Tin, Lead, and Flerovium. The first five Group 14 elements are chemically and structurally very similar. Since the remotest Palaeolithic ages the economic survival of my country has hinged upon these five elemental commodities. At first, the men who dwelt in crevices in the ground fashioned silex, silicon dioxide, to make tools and weapons. Much later lead roofed the great churches and houses of the Middles Ages, and lead and tin were smelted together to form pewter for the table. Coal, mostly carbon, fueled our First Industrial Revolution, and near-neighbors Aluminum and Copper a Second, whilst a Third revolution has implicated silicon, germanium and tin.

Photograph 3.1
The Silver Block given to me by Mr Don Braggins

But what about the promised silver? you understandably wonder.

So let us look at the nonad centered upon silver (Ag), as shown in Figure 3.2.

Copper and Gold are the blood-brothers of Silver. They have been known and esteemed for as long as men have known value, or have bedecked Woman. Copper and Gold are the tanned rangers, the only distinctly-colored metals. Unoxidised, for example when freshly-cut, copper is pink, and gold is yellow. On the other hand, silver is the whitest and most reflective substance, notwithstanding that a whiff of sulfur will turn it the deepest black. The triad are the ancient emblems of goddesses, and their deathless propitiants.

Copper, silver and gold are the best conductors of heat and electricity and therefore firm favorites with electricians and thermal engineers. They are ductile and resilient, slow to corrode and heavy enough for their absence to go noted: Victorian chemists, even before Mendeleev, knew them collectively as the "Coinage Metals". Further back in time they were the incorruptible "Noble Metals". Today we call them Group Eleven.

Silver also has sisters. Flanking her is Palladium (Pd) at 46 and Cadmium (Cd) at 48. Palladium is an even less reactive white metal, related to the similar Platinum. All three are financial bullion metals, though all bullion purchase except for gold is still taxed at 20% in the UK. On the Other hand Cadmium looks, sounds and smells like Zinc, its very close relative, and with whose ores, especially sphalerite ("blende") it is intimately combined. Notwithstanding, a dash of zinc is essential to human health, and cadmium fatal, for cadmium is chemically a near-perfect impostor, but as ineffectual as such usually are.

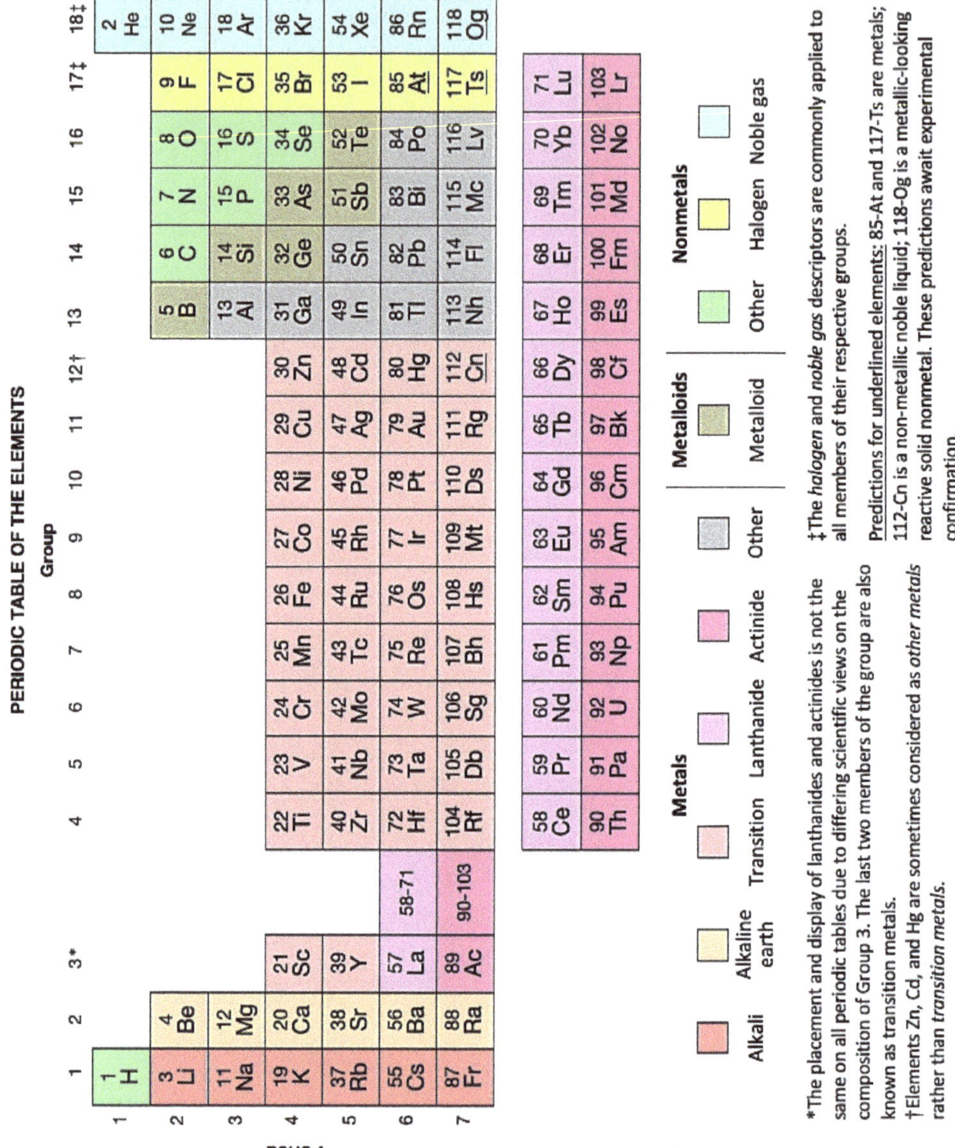

Figure 3.1
The Periodic Table of the Elements[R3.1]

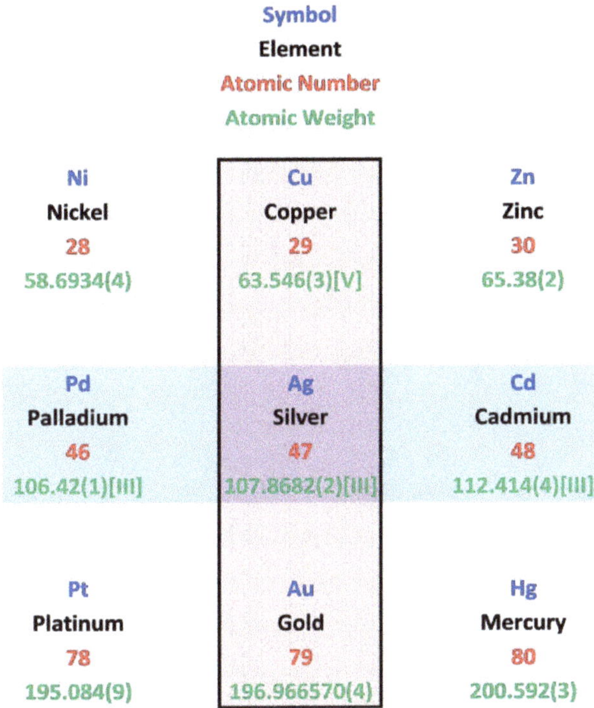

Figure 3.2
The Silver Nonad: An Extract from the Periodic Table

Silver also has cousins, and her relations with them are as interesting as germane relations tend to be. For example, Nickel, Zinc, Platinum and Mercury all show some similarity to Silver as well as distinctions. Jewelers know that the Coinage Metals are miscible in the solid state in all proportions to found a gold alloy of any cost and caratage. Notoriously, mercury, a liquid element related to both Silver and Gold will dissolve both.

On occasion My Late Mother worked as a laboratory technician during the last century, as separately did I. Both of us had occasion to handle mercury (thankfully discouraged by current legislation, and current economics). Unfortunately, a spill deprived Mother of most of her wedding ring.

Because of the underlying facts of atomic sizes and the geometrical realities of the cubic crystallographic system, metallic silver is also very soluble in (solid-state) lead sulphide (PbS; Galena) lead ore, at least at the sorts of temperatures and pressures within a few hundred fathoms of the Earth's surface. Indeed, the vast majority of silver throughout human history has been refined as a by-product of lead smelting. Until about 1830AD this was done by cupellation: Blowing a draft of air across a shallow bath of molten lead to skim off the lead oxide formed as a powder, eventually leaving a small residue of liquid silver which could separately be tapped and cast. That was the way the Romans did it, with limitless forests and limitless slaves. As you doubtless discern, this was very slow, and fuel and labor expensive, even when unpaid. Around 1829 the English introduced the much more economical Pattinson Process: Successive crystallisations of cooling lead that concentrated silver in the residual liquors, which nevertheless voided much costly heat as repeated losses of the latent heat of lead crystallisation. In 1850 this was superseded by the very much cheaper Parkes Process that mechanically mixed molten zinc into molten lead. Any silver in the lead "preferred" to dissolve in the zinc. Silver is three thousand times more soluble in zinc than it is in lead. The mixing was stopped, *the zinc and its compounds segregated themselves into a floating sheet*, the lead was tapped, and the zinc re-used. When the zinc was adjudged economically argentiferous it was allowed separately to cast and then cheaply electrolysed, whereupon pure silver would be "thrown down" as an "anode slime".

It is very difficult to quantify the respective costs of these three processes. The matter is highly empirical and conditioned by feedstock impurities, local fuel costs, automation, and especially local labour cost. As well of course as the point in history. I had to resort to the 1870 monograph of John Percy[R3.2] MD FRS in order to attempt an assessment as the comparison related to the German smelting and refining practices of the eighteen-sixties..

Table 3.1 clearly shows the way in which the Pattinson Process halved the cost of extracting silver from lead, or more than half if one moves from the preparation of litharge to the fine-stage refining of the silver and the recovery of lead metal. The apparent advantage of Parkes over Pattinson is only around 10%, but bear in mind that the latter was a very immature technology at the time and further savings could be effected with automation and other refinements.

CUPELLATION TO LITHARGE

£	s	d	Decimal Pounds Sterling	Centner as Metric Tonne	£/Tonne
0	1	0	0.05	0.05	0.999992

PATTINSON'S PROCESS

	£	s	d	Decimal Pounds Sterling	Metric Tonne	£/Tonne
Freiburg	0	10	7	0.529166667	1	0.529167
Stolberg	0	9	6.6	0.4775	1	0.4775
Tarnowitz	0	12	9	0.6375	1	0.6375
						0.548056 **Mean**

PARKES PROCESS

£	s	d	Decimal Pounds Sterling	Long Ton as Metric Tonne	£/Tonne
0	10	1	0.504166667	1.016047	0.496204

Table 3.1
Absolute Total Costs of Cupellation, Pattison and Parkes
Lead Desilverisation Processes
As Practiced in Germany in the Eighteen-Sixties

To paraphrase Umberto Eco in his novel *The Name of the Rose*, the relevancy of this obscure disquisition shall manifest in due course.

<u>The Concept of the Reducing Agent</u>

A reducing agent is a chemical, elemental or compound, that donates a distantly-orbital valency electron or electrons to an oxidising agent, which accepts electrons. Whether a particular chemical behaves as a reducing agent or an oxidising agent depends upon context, but in everyday circumstances Alkali Metal (Group 1) and Alkaline Earth metals (Group 2) are reducing agents, as are Hydrogen (monatomic or diatomic) and Carbon (e.g. coal, charcoal).

The tendency of this atomic orbital electron passage process is to bind a positively-charged cation to a negatively-charged anion to form an electrically-neutral molecule whose behaviour simulates that of a Group 18 noble gas such as Xenon: In a phrase it is chemically inert, at least until its components are re-separated by added energy. The anion has an excess of (negatively-charged) electrons which it donates to a cation.

Ammonia, NH_3, is also a reducing agent, including its aqueous form, $(NH_4).OH$, Ammonium Hydroxide.

You can generate Hydrogen, a gaseous reducing agent, by putting metallic Zinc (potentially another reducing agent) in the liquid oxidising agent Sulphuric Acid.

$Zn + H_2SO_4(dil) \rightarrow ZnSO_4 + H_2$
Zinc + Sulphuric Acid (diluted in water)
Gives
Zinc Sulphate + Hydrogen

You, or preferably a robot, can put Silver Sulphide (Argentite, or Acanthite $= Ag_2S$) in a porcelain "boat" in a silica tube and roast the mineral over a Bunsen burner. If you then pass the reducing agent hydrogen, perhaps from the flask containing your zinc in the sulphuric acid, through the hot tube the silver sulphide will reduce to metallic silver and the hydrogen will form the waste toxic gas hydrogen sulphide H_2S from the mineral's sulfur content.

$Ag_2S + H_2 \rightarrow Ag_2 + H_2S$
Argentite + Hydrogen
Gives
Silver + Hydrogen Sulphide

Readers, never do this. The results of this experiment are very well-known, but the exercise itself is highly dangerous. I personally have known men, professionals, blinded or killed by similar tasks.

I recollect my first term at Manchester University many decades ago, I was as happy as Larry. I took chemistry as a subsidiary subject, but was considerably more interested in the circumjacent women than in sensitive, tedious, filthy and occasionally dangerous chemical experiments. One negligent winter's afternoon I poured ammonia into a solution of silver nitrate in a test tube. Instantly a beautiful roiling cloud of sparkling silver flecks precipitated, writhing intestinally like surprised sardines shimmering in a shoal.

Now I am a very poor chemist but (with the benefit of Wikipedia) I think the three-stage chemical reaction went something like this:-

$$2\ AgNO_3 + 2\ NaOH \rightarrow Ag_2O(s) + 2\ NaNO_3 + H_2O$$
2.Silver Nitrate + 2.Caustic Soda
Gives
1.Silver Oxide + 2.Sodium Nitrate + 1.Water

then

$$Ag_2O(s) + 4\ NH_3 + 2\ NaOH + H_2O \rightarrow 2\ [Ag(NH_3)_2]OH +$$
2 NaOH

1.Silver Oxide + 4.Ammonia + 2.Caustic Soda + 1.Water
Gives
2.Diaminesilver Complex + 2.Caustic Soda

then

$$2\ [Ag(NH_3)_2]^+ + RCHO + H_2O \rightarrow 2\ Ag + 4\ NH_3 + RCOOH$$
+ 2 H$^+$

2.Diaminesilver ions + Alkyl Aldehyde + Water
Gives
2.Silver + 4.Ammonia + Alkyl Carboxylic Acid +
2.Hydrogen Ions

The R stands for an Alkyl radical (essentially monovalent) of which the simplest is Methyl Aldehyde commonly called Formaldehyde.

If the lovely recollection is so then things are not quite as I remember them since Caustic Soda (Sodium Hydroxide = NaOH) must have been present *ab initio*. We may have been testing for glucose via the Tollen's Reaction. After fifty years the memory I thought I remembered was probably mis-remembered all along.

There are plenty of organic radicals that function as reducing agents in the right setting. Oxalic Acid, Formic Acid and Ascorbic Acid (Vitamin C) are all well-known examples. Gallic Acid and Tannic Acid can also function as reducing agents and these later are suspected of precipitating copper and silver from aqueous solutions in the natural environment.

As a boy of fourteen I borrowed a book from my local library in Ware, a town just North of London. It was *Mining for Metals in Wales* by FJ North[R3.3]. I read it avidly and planned to visit the old mines of mountain Wales when I was old enough and rich enough to buy a motorcycle. I was especially intrigued by the copper and gold mines of the Coed y Brenin (King's Forest) of Merionethshire, and most especially by a strange copper mine at Dol Frwynog. I quote from North:-

"The mines already described were worked on traditional lines by methods applicable to ores that occur in lodes, but a mine of an unusual kind was worked at Dol Frwynog where peat on the floor of a small valley had been impregnated with copper bearing solutions. The bog received the drainage of a hill on the southern side of the Mawddach valley, and included two beds of peat consisting largely of decomposed grass and decayed wood, separated by a thin layer of stones.

The body of the peat was richly impregnated with carbonate of copper, whilst leaves, fragments of wood, and nuts had been largely replaced by metallic copper. The peat, or turf as it was called, was cut in the usual way and after being dried by exposure to the air was burnt in heaps. As the pile smouldered fresh material was added, care being taken to prevent the peat from bursting into flame lest the heat should result in the formation of slag from which the metal could not be readily extracted. After 8 to 10 days the ashes were sent to Swansea to be smelted. In one year 2,000 tons of ashes valued at £20,000 were recovered from the "Turf" mine. Parts of the lower layers of the peat were so richly impregnated with copper salts that they were cut into blocks and sent away for smelting with no more treatment than air-drying to reduce the water content.

Extensive search was made, without success, in the hope of finding a rich lode from which the copper had been derived, but the peat rests upon slaty rocks that contain small crystals of iron pyrites and specks of copper pyrites and it is more likely that, instead of being derived directly from a lode like that which has been worked in the small Dol Frwynog mine about half a mile away, the metalliferous compounds in the peat were carried in water that percolated through the local rocks and rose as springs feeding the rivulets that drained into the bog."

I have quoted at length because this most obscure report is central to the technical and scientific aspects of our story.

This report of the reduction of cuprous liquors by vegetable debris is corroborated by a more recent discovery in a bog at Cooke, Montana (*Organic Precipitation of Metallic Copper* by TS Lovering: USGS Bulletin 795-C: 1927)[R3.4].

The Concept of Electronegativity

Closely allied to the Concept of the Redox Reaction involving the passage of orbital electrons from one atom to another is the Concept of Electronegativity, usually discussed with reference to the behaviour of hydrogen or a pure metal with respect to the salt (i.e. neutral compound) of another metal dissolved in water, or occasionally an acid.

For example, if you put pure Iron in a solution of (hydrous) Copper Sulphate the Iron will enter the solution and pure Copper will be precipitated: This is because Iron is more *electropositive* than Copper. The greater the difference in terms of electropositivity between the two elements then the faster and stronger the exchange with the proviso that the original metal (or indeed the product metal) is not physically protected from further corrosion by a coating of the (insoluble) product salt.

The relevant chemical equation is:-

$$Fe + CuSO_4 \rightarrow FeSO_4 + Cu$$

Iron + Copper Sulphate
Gives
Iron Sulphate + Copper

Note that because Iron is capable of being both divalent Fe^{2+} and trivalent Fe^{3+} the actual reactant ratios may differ from the above, which is written for the simple, divalent Fe^{2+} reaction.

When I was nine my grandparents bought me a Merit Chemistry Set, which was the most formative toy I ever had. I went out onto the lawn in the Cadgwith sunlight and, placing some copper sulphate and water in a test tube provided, I immersed an old-fashioned 78rpm iron gramophone (phonograph) needle. A rough rust of metallic copper soon covered the iron.

The same displacement process was frequently used in Wales, notably at Parys Mountain late in the eighteenth century, to displace valuable copper from the mine drainage liquors. The iron was in the form of scrap cast iron brought by sea. The copper was used at Soho in South Staffordshire to make "cartwheel" pennies.

Another possibility involves zinc and silver nitrate. You could write this reaction:-

$$Zn + 2AgNO_3 \rightarrow 2Ag + Zn(NO_3)_2$$
Zinc + Silver Nitrate
Gives
Silver + Zinc Nitrate

In general, zinc will "throw down" metal from any silver salt dissolved in water, but exasperatingly silver can also form a metal colloid in water ("nanoparticals") which is not subject to chemical manipulation in this way.

The chemical reactions are called Displacement Reactions and the most electronegative of the metals is called the most reactive.

An interesting aspect of electronegativity is the fact that hydrogen, a gas at standard temperature and pressure, in many ways behaves as a metal. Indeed, because of this any metal more electropositive than hydrogen will dissolve in water: Caesium explosively, Magnesium quite slowly and Iron very slowly. On the other hand, metals less electropositive than hydrogen can never dissolve in ordinary water. Such more electronegative metals include Copper, Silver and Gold. Note that Aluminum would dissolve in lakes and rivers rather briskly if it was not for the fact that it forms a protective coat of aluminum oxide which is very coherent and protects the otherwise naked metal from further corrosion. This protective coat forms upon several other metals too, notably Vanadium and Tantalum.

Atomic Number	Symbol	Element	Electro-negativity	Atomic Number	Symbol	Element	Electro-negativity	Atomic Number	Symbol	Element	Electro-negativity
87	Fr	Francium	0.70	21	Sc	Scandium	1.36	51	Sb	Antimony	2.05
55	Cs	Caesium	0.79	92	U	Uranium	1.38	52	Te	Tellurium	2.10
19	K	Potassium	0.82	73	Ta	Tantalum	1.50	42	Mo	Molybdenum	2.16
37	Rb	Rubidium	0.82	91	Pa	Protactinium	1.50	33	As	Arsenic	2.18
56	Ba	Barium	0.89	22	Ti	Titanium	1.54	15	P	Phosphorus	2.19
88	Ra	Radium	0.90	25	Mn	Manganese	1.55	1	H	Hydrogen	2.20
11	Na	Sodium	0.93	4	Be	Beryllium	1.57	44	Ru	Ruthenium	2.20
38	Sr	Strontium	0.95	41	Nb	Niobium	1.60	46	Pd	Palladium	2.20
3	Li	Lithium	0.98	13	Al	Aluminium	1.61	76	Os	Osmium	2.20
20	Ca	Calcium	1.00	81	Tl	Thallium	1.62	77	Ir	Iridium	2.20
57	La	Lanthanum	1.10	23	V	Vanadium	1.63	85	At	Astatine	2.20
70	Yb	Ytterbium	1.10	30	Zn	Zinc	1.65	86	Rn	Radon	2.20
89	Ac	Actinium	1.10	24	Cr	Chromium	1.66	45	Rh	Rhodium	2.28
58	Ce	Cerium	1.12	48	Cd	Cadmium	1.69	78	Pt	Platinum	2.28
59	Pr	Praseodymium	1.13	49	In	Indium	1.78	74	W	Tungsten	2.36
61	Pm	Promethium	1.13	31	Ga	Gallium	1.81	79	Au	Gold	2.54
60	Nd	Neodymium	1.14	26	Fe	Iron	1.83	6	C	Carbon	2.55
62	Sm	Samarium	1.17	82	Pb	Lead	1.87	34	Se	Selenium	2.55
63	Eu	Europium	1.20	27	Co	Cobalt	1.88	16	S	Sulfur	2.58
64	Gd	Gadolinium	1.20	14	Si	Silicon	1.90	54	Xe	Xenon	2.60
65	Tb	Terbium	1.20	29	Cu	Copper	1.90	53	I	Iodine	2.66
39	Y	Yttrium	1.22	43	Tc	Technetium	1.90	35	Br	Bromine	2.96
66	Dy	Dysprosium	1.22	75	Re	Rhenium	1.90	36	Kr	Krypton	3.00
67	Ho	Holmium	1.23	28	Ni	Nickel	1.91	7	N	Nitrogen	3.04
68	Er	Erbium	1.24	47	Ag	Silver	1.93	17	Cl	Chlorine	3.16
69	Tm	Thulium	1.25	50	Sn	Tin	1.96	8	O	Oxygen	3.44
71	Lu	Lutetium	1.27	80	Hg	Mercury	2.00	9	F	Fluorine	3.98
72	Hf	Hafnium	1.30	84	Po	Polonium	2.00	2	He	Helium	–
90	Th	Thorium	1.30	32	Ge	Germanium	2.01	10	Ne	Neon	–
12	Mg	Magnesium	1.31	83	Bi	Bismuth	2.02	18	Ar	Argon	–
40	Zr	Zirconium	1.33	5	B	Boron	2.04				

Table 3.2
An Ordered Table of Elemental Electronegativities
with the most
Electropositive Elements
At the Top Left

Concentration

Concentration, z, is ordinarily expressed as (mass) parts per million (grams/tonne). In some contexts, never ours, concentration is volumetrically expressed as milliliters per cubic meter.

For example, if in a certain sample of one kilogram of water there is 1.4 grams of silver then z = 1.4g/kg = 0.0014 =1400 ppm (parts per million).

Note that by this reckoning the kilogram is of *any* material, that is to say we are speaking of 1.4 grams of silver and 998.6 grams of water.

Unfortunately for our argument, but perhaps fortunately for our world, there are never as much as 1.4 grams of silver in natural water. In fact in any typical sample of river water there are 6.5×10^{-10} parts of silver which we can write out as 0.00000000065, or let us say 0.00065 ppm.

Now a certain analytical machine, let us call it an x-ray spectrometer, can measure to a theoretical 1ppm of any heavy element sitting in a matrix, and the solvent water might qualify as a matrix. Equally a lump of rock might be the matrix. Or a pad of damp felt. We do not necessarily concern ourselves whether the matrix is solid or liquid. We are not yet interested in the *amount* of silver present or indeed the amount of anything else, only in the *concentration*.

Then adequately to assess, discriminate and compare the concentrations of silver found in different containing specimens we need our machine accurately to measure concentrations about a hundred times bigger than the 1ppm minimum, let us say around 400ppm.

This is of course about three orders of magnitude bigger than one part per million and around seven orders larger than the typical concentration of silver in river water.

Therefore, if we are going reliably to measure the silver in a sample we need to amplify the concentration of silver in the sample medium by some 10^7 times or seven orders of magnitude, say 10 million times.

This is a tall order but not impossible because plants and animals, including humans, massively concentrate heavy metals all their lives.

For example, the tiny tunicate animal of the *Ascidiacea* class can concentrate vanadium from seawater by a factor of 10^7, storing the very rare metal in special blood proteins.

On land, the dwarf juniper *Juniperus Procumbens* has been found to have up to 200ppm of silver in its tissue, and comparable concentrations occur in other conifers. The typical concentration of silver in soil is around 0.5ppm.

Table 3.3 lists the elements in the Earth's Crust in terms of their Abundance in mg/kg (i.e. ppm):-

Atomic Number	Symbol	Element	Abundance in Earth's Crust (mg/kg)	Abundance in Earth's Crust $\log_{10}$ (mg/kg)	Abundance in Earth's Crust $4+\log_{10}$ (mg/kg)
8	O	Oxygen	461000	5.663700925	9.663700925
14	Si	Silicon	282000	5.450249108	9.450249108
13	Al	Aluminium	82300	4.915399835	8.915399835
26	Fe	Iron	56300	4.750508395	8.750508395
20	Ca	Calcium	41500	4.618048097	8.618048097
11	Na	Sodium	23600	4.372912003	8.372912003
12	Mg	Magnesium	23300	4.367355921	8.367355921
19	K	Potassium	20900	4.320146286	8.320146286
22	Ti	Titanium	5650	3.752048448	7.752048448
1	H	Hydrogen	1400	3.146128036	7.146128036
15	P	Phosphorus	1050	3.021189299	7.021189299
25	Mn	Manganese	950	2.977723605	6.977723605
9	F	Fluorine	585	2.767155866	6.767155866
56	Ba	Barium	425	2.62838893	6.62838893
38	Sr	Strontium	370	2.568201724	6.568201724
16	S	Sulfur	350	2.544068044	6.544068044
6	C	Carbon	200	2.301029996	6.301029996
40	Zr	Zirconium	165	2.217483944	6.217483944
17	Cl	Chlorine	145	2.161368002	6.161368002
23	V	Vanadium	120	2.079181246	6.079181246
24	Cr	Chromium	102	2.008600172	6.008600172
37	Rb	Rubidium	90	1.954242509	5.954242509
28	Ni	Nickel	84	1.924279286	5.924279286
30	Zn	Zinc	70	1.84509804	5.84509804
58	Ce	Cerium	66.5	1.822821645	5.822821645
29	Cu	Copper	60	1.77815125	5.77815125
60	Nd	Neodymium	41.5	1.618048097	5.618048097
57	La	Lanthanum	39	1.591064607	5.591064607
39	Y	Yttrium	33	1.51851394	5.51851394
27	Co	Cobalt	25	1.397940009	5.397940009
21	Sc	Scandium	22	1.342422681	5.342422681
3	Li	Lithium	20	1.301029996	5.301029996

Table 3.3a
Elements in Descending Order of Crustal Abundance

Atomic Number	Symbol	Element	Abundance in Earth's Crust	Abundance in Earth's Crust	Abundance in Earth's Crust
			(mg/kg)	$\log_{10}$ (mg/kg)	$4+\log_{10}$ (mg/kg)
41	Nb	Niobium	20	1.301029996	5.301029996
7	N	Nitrogen	19	1.278753601	5.278753601
31	Ga	Gallium	19	1.278753601	5.278753601
82	Pb	Lead	14	1.146128036	5.146128036
5	B	Boron	10	1	5
90	Th	Thorium	9.6	0.982271233	4.982271233
59	Pr	Praseodymium	9.2	0.963787827	4.963787827
62	Sm	Samarium	7.05	0.848189117	4.848189117
64	Gd	Gadolinium	6.2	0.792391689	4.792391689
66	Dy	Dysprosium	5.2	0.716003344	4.716003344
18	Ar	Argon	3.5	0.544068044	4.544068044
68	Er	Erbium	3.5	0.544068044	4.544068044
70	Yb	Ytterbium	3.2	0.505149978	4.505149978
55	Cs	Caesium	3	0.477121255	4.477121255
72	Hf	Hafnium	3	0.477121255	4.477121255
4	Be	Beryllium	2.8	0.447158031	4.447158031
92	U	Uranium	2.7	0.431363764	4.431363764
35	Br	Bromine	2.4	0.380211242	4.380211242
50	Sn	Tin	2.3	0.361727836	4.361727836
63	Eu	Europium	2	0.301029996	4.301029996
73	Ta	Tantalum	2	0.301029996	4.301029996
33	As	Arsenic	1.8	0.255272505	4.255272505
32	Ge	Germanium	1.5	0.176091259	4.176091259
67	Ho	Holmium	1.3	0.113943352	4.113943352
74	W	Tungsten	1.3	0.113943352	4.113943352
42	Mo	Molybdenum	1.2	0.079181246	4.079181246
65	Tb	Terbium	1.2	0.079181246	4.079181246
81	Tl	Thallium	0.85	-0.07058107	3.929418926
71	Lu	Lutetium	0.8	-0.09691001	3.903089987
69	Tm	Thulium	0.52	-0.28399666	3.716003344
53	I	Iodine	0.45	-0.34678749	3.653212514
49	In	Indium	0.25	-0.60205999	3.397940009

Table 3.3b
Elements in Descending Order of Crustal Abundance

Atomic Number	Symbol	Element	Abundance in Earth's Crust	Abundance in Earth's Crust	Abundance in Earth's Crust
			(mg/kg)	$\log_{10}$ (mg/kg)	$4+\log_{10}$ (mg/kg)
51	Sb	Antimony	0.2	-0.69897	3.301029996
48	Cd	Cadmium	0.159	-0.79860288	3.201397124
80	Hg	Mercury	0.085	-1.07058107	2.929418926
47	Ag	Silver	0.075	-1.12493874	2.875061263
34	Se	Selenium	0.05	-1.30103	2.698970004
46	Pd	Palladium	0.015	-1.82390874	2.176091259
83	Bi	Bismuth	0.009	-2.04575749	1.954242509
2	He	Helium	0.008	-2.09691001	1.903089987
10	Ne	Neon	0.005	-2.30103	1.698970004
78	Pt	Platinum	0.005	-2.30103	1.698970004
79	Au	Gold	0.004	-2.39794001	1.602059991
76	Os	Osmium	0.002	-2.69897	1.301029996
44	Ru	Ruthenium	0.001	-3	1
45	Rh	Rhodium	0.001	-3	1
52	Te	Tellurium	0.001	-3	1
77	Ir	Iridium	0.001	-3	1
75	Re	Rhenium	7.00E-04	-3.15490196	0.84509804
36	Kr	Krypton	0.0001	-4	0
54	Xe	Xenon	3.00E-05	-4.52287875	-0.52287875
91	Pa	Protactinium	1.40E-06	-5.85387196	-1.85387196
88	Ra	Radium	9.00E-07	-6.04575749	-2.04575749
43	Tc	Technetium	3.00E-09	-8.52287875	-4.52287875
89	Ac	Actinium	5.50E-10	-9.25963731	-5.25963731
84	Po	Polonium	2.00E-10	-9.69897	-5.69897
86	Rn	Radon	4.00E-13	-12.39794	-8.39794001
87	Fr	Francium	1.00E-18	-18	-14
61	Pm	Promethium	2.00E-19	-18.69897	-14.69897
85	At	Astatine	3.00E-20	-19.5228787	-15.5228787

Table 3.3c
Elements in Descending Order of Crustal Abundance

Logarithmic Forms of Concentration

You can see that in Tables 3.3a, b and c the Concentrations z are additionally quoted as their Base Ten Logarithms and as the base ten logarithms augmented by an additive Shift Constant, s, which in this case is four.

These relations may be formalised as:-

$$\zeta = s + log_{10}(z)$$
Equation 3.1

where ζ is the Adjusted Logarithmic Transform of Concentration.

A convenience of this form is that it scales and shifts very different orders of magnitude into sizes convenient for comparison, especially graphical comparison.

Another number control stratagem is to define:-

$$\zeta' = \frac{1}{-log_{10}(z)}$$
Equation 3.2

This form vastly reduces the numerical dispersion whilst preserving the relational order of magnitudes.

Table 3.4 shows the crustal abundance data for the eleven nonad and associated metals, together with sulfur which is of interest to analyses that assess the presence of pyrite (cubic FeS_2), marcasite (orthorhombic FeS_2), galena (PbS) or indeed any of the several silver sulphide minerals.

Table 3.5 shows the average abundance of relevant metallic elements in various media including seawater, river water and vegetation (typically algal matter in the form of seaweed).

<u>Assessment of Sulfur in River Water</u>

Most reporters cite the presence of sulfur in freshwater in terms of the sulfate ion SO_4^{2-}. Because the atomic weight of sulfur is 32.06 and that of oxygen 15.999 it is obvious that the weight fraction of S in this ion is 0.500968811.

The World Health Organisation[R3.5], estimated that the average global concentration of sulfate in river water was some 315 mg/liter which indicates an average sulfur content of around 157 mg/liter or some 157ppm. It has to be said, however that this figure is extremely variable, depending upon the upstream presence or absence of pyrite, gypsum and other very common sedimentary sulfur minerals, as well as pollution and leaf decay.

Marcasite

The presence of both Iron and Sulfur in river water is relatively very high and likely to "swamp" heavy metal analyses unless suitable chemical and number control methods are applied.

The weight proportion of Fe to FeS_2 in pyrite and marcasite is 0.465510774 and the proportion of Iron to Sulfur is 0.870945103. Thus the reciprocal of this latter figure is 1.148. Accordingly if any analytical peak for Fe is 1.148 or thereby as tall as the peak for S then one may strongly suspect the decomposition of pyrite as a mechanism for the ferrugination of the water sample.

Graphical Representation of Typical Heavy Metal Concentrations

Figure 3.1 is a plot of the Transformed Mean Concentrations typical for Sulfur, Iron and Heavy Metals in Seawater, River Water and Dried Vegetation exposed to environmental water, usually algae.

Atomic Number	Symbol	Element	Group	Period	Atomic Weight (Da)	Density (g/cm^3)	Melting point[6] (K)	Boiling Point (K)	Specific Heat Capacity $(J/g \cdot K)$	Electro -negativity	Abundance in Earth's Crust z_{EC} (mg/kg)	Abundance in Earth's Crust $\log_{10}$ (mg/kg)	Abundance in Earth's Crust $z_{EC} = s+\log_{10}(z) = 4+\log_{10}(z)$ (mg/kg)	Selection Serial
16 S		Sulfur	16	3	32.06	2.067	388.36	717.87	0.71	2.58	350	2.544068044	6.544068044	1
26 Fe		Iron	8	4	55.845	7.874	1811	3134	0.449	1.83	56300	4.750508395	8.750508395	2
28 Ni		Nickel	10	4	58.6934	8.912	1728	3186	0.444	1.91	84	1.924279286	5.924279286	3
30 Zn		Zinc	12	4	65.38	7.134	692.88	1180	0.388	1.65	70	1.84509804	5.84509804	4
29 Cu		Copper	11	4	63.546	8.96	1357.77	2835	0.385	1.9	60	1.77815125	5.77815125	5
82 Pb		Lead	14	6	207.2	11.342	600.61	2022	0.129	1.87	14	1.146128036	5.146128036	6
48 Cd		Cadmium	12	5	112.414	8.69	594.22	1040	0.232	1.69	0.159	-0.79860288	3.201397124	7
80 Hg		Mercury	12	6	200.592	13.5336	234.43	629.88	0.14	2	0.085	-1.07058107	2.929418926	8
47 Ag		Silver	11	5	107.8682	10.501	1234.93	2435	0.235	1.93	0.075	-1.12493874	2.875061263	9
46 Pd		Palladium	10	5	106.42	12.02	1828.05	3236	0.244	2.2	0.015	-1.82390874	2.176091259	10
78 Pt		Platinum	10	6	195.084	21.46	2041.4	4098	0.133	2.28	0.005	-2.30103	1.698970004	11
79 Au		Gold	11	6	196.96657	19.282	1337.33	3129	0.129	2.54	0.004	-2.39794001	1.602059991	12

Table 3.4
Earth's Crust Abundance and
Logarithmically-Transformed Abundances for Twelve Selected
Elements

Atomic Number	Symbol	Element	Wikipedia Atomic Weight	Mean Fractions			$\log_{10}$(Mean Fractions)			$\zeta'=1/-\log_{10}$(Mean Fractions)		
				Sea Water	River Water	Dry Organic*	Sea Water	River Water	Dry Organic*	Sea Water	River Water	Dry Organic*
16 S		Sulfur	32.06	9.09E-04	3.15E-04	2.20E-03	-3.041359202	-3.5016894	-2.65758	0.3288	0.285576	0.376283
26 Fe		Iron	55.845	1.03E-08	7.50E-07	1.10E-04	-7.988302712	-6.1249387	-3.95861	0.125183	0.163267	0.252614
28 Ni		Nickel	58.6934	1.25E-09	3E-10	0.0000055	-8.903089987	-9.5228787	-5.25964	0.112321	0.10501	0.190127
29 Cu		Copper	63.546	1.75E-08	5.4E-09	7.85E-06	-7.756961951	-8.2676062	-5.10513	0.128916	0.120954	0.195881
30 Zn		Zinc	65.38	2.8E-09	7.5E-09	0.00036	-8.552841969	-8.1249387	-3.4437	0.11692	0.123078	0.290386
46 Pd		Palladium	106.42	4.45E-14	1.12E-11	3.5E-10	-13.35163999	-10.950782	-9.45593	0.074897	0.091318	0.105754
47 Ag		Silver	107.8682	5.1E-11	6.5E-10	5.5E-07	-10.29242982	-9.1870866	-6.25964	0.097159	0.108848	0.159754
48 Cd		Cadmium	112.414	3.1E-10	5.05E-08	8E-08	-9.508638306	-7.2967086	-7.09691	0.105168	0.137048	0.140906
50 Sn		Tin	118.71	5.5E-12	2.3E-11	1.2E-08	-11.25963731	-10.638272	-7.92082	0.088813	0.094	0.12625
78 Pt		Platinum	195.084	1.845E-13	3.65E-10	2E-10	-12.73400363	-9.4377071	-9.69897	0.07853	0.105958	0.103104
79 Au		Gold	196.96657	2.2E-08	3.3E-12	1.225E-10	-7.657567449	-11.481486	-9.91186	0.13059	0.087097	0.100889
80 Hg		Mercury	200.592	4.5E-12	1.25E-09	3.7E-07	-11.34678749	-8.90309	-6.4318	0.088131	0.112321	0.155478
82 Pb		Lead	207.2	1.6E-11	1.65E-08	0.0000075	-10.79588002	-7.7825161	-5.12494	0.092628	0.128493	0.195124
Total			1432.87417	4.394E-08	8.25E-08	0.0003819	-112.1594779	-101.59307	-75.7093	1.114072	1.214125	1.763652
Mean			130.261288	3.994E-09	7.5E-09	3.471E-05	-10.19631617	-9.2357339	-6.88267	0.101279	0.110375	0.160332
Pop SD			56.2638607	7.533E-09	1.443E-08	0.0001029	1.820612113	1.28738524	2.048378	0.018187	0.015197	0.05362

Concentrations
(mg/L)
where L = 1027.3 grams

"CRC Handbook of Chemistry and Physics"
"1st Student Edition"
Robert C Weast PhD, Editor-in-Chief
CRC Press Inc. of Boca Raton
1988AD
Library of Congress Card Number 0-8493-0740-6
ISBN 0-8493-0740-6

Anomalous Entries:-

34 Se   Selenium

* Usually Dry Phytoplankton or Seaweed Concentration z_{alg}

Table 3.5
Element Concentrations in Seawater, River Water and Vegetation

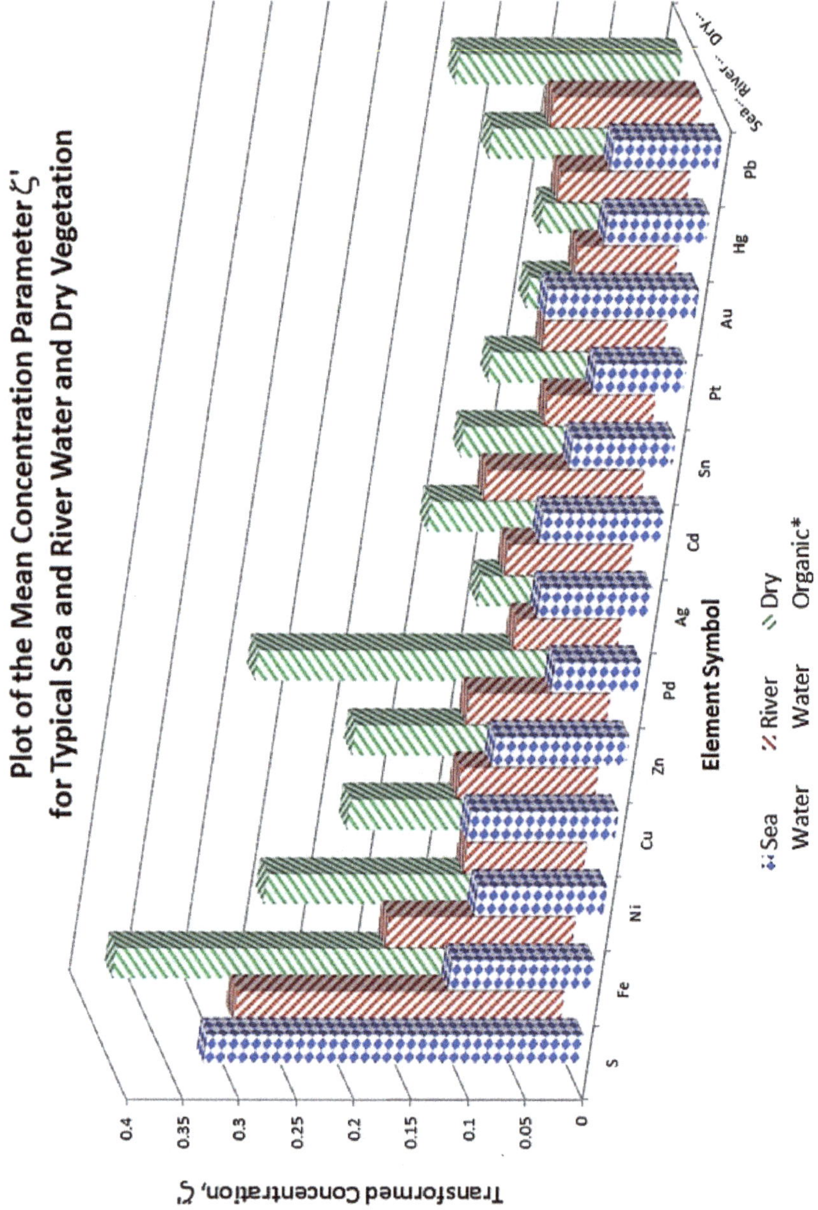

Figure 3.1
**The Transform Concentration Parameter ζ' for the
Selected Elements**

<u>Molarity</u>

Most metals can only exist as a salt in solution. This does not happen invariably to apply in the case of silver, which can permeate water as an ionised salt, say in the form Ag^{2+} and CO_3^{2-}; or alternatively as a colloid which comprises tiny particles of the element held in a suspended state by molecular kinesis.

To illustrate the molar case we will consider only the dissolved salt Silver Carbonate, Ag_2CO_3.

Now each (whole or ionically separated) molecule of silver carbonate clearly comprises two atoms of silver, one atom of carbon and three atoms of oxygen. Reference to appropriate tables discloses that Silver (Ag) has an Atomic Weight of 107.8682; Carbon 12.011 and Oxygen 15.999. Therefore the Molecular Weight of Silver Carbonate Ag_2CO_3 is given by:-

$$MW_{Ag2CO3} = 2 \times a_{Ag} + 1 \times a_C + 3 \times a_O$$
$$= \sum n_x a_x$$
$$= 2 \times 107.8682 + 1 \times 12.011 + 3 \times 15.999$$
$$= 275.7444$$

Equation 3.3

Now in theory a 1N or 1 normal solution of Ag_2CO_3 has 275.7444 grams of the salt dissolved in each liter of water, and a 2N solution $2 \times 275.7444 = 551.4888$.

However, we know this is impossible because the maximum amount of silver carbonate that can be dissolved in a liter of water is 31 grams.

Notwithstanding, if we know the weight fraction of silver carbonate in water to be 0.00830817 we can compute the Molarity of the Solution as:-

$$Mol_{Ag2CO3} = \frac{F_{Ag2CO3}}{MW_{Ag2CO3}} = \frac{0.00830807}{275.7444} = 0.000030129968$$

Equation 3.4

where F_{Ag2CO3} is the Weight Fraction of the Ag_2CO_3 in the solute, and MW_{Ag2CO3} is the Molecular Weight of Ag_2CO_3.

Therefore this particular dilution of silver carbonate is 0.000030129968 normal. (Technically speaking, molarity is the number of moles in a standard volume of solution, and normality the concentration of a *reactive species*. For our purposes the two are synonymous).

Table 3.6 expands the calculation of molarity for reference.

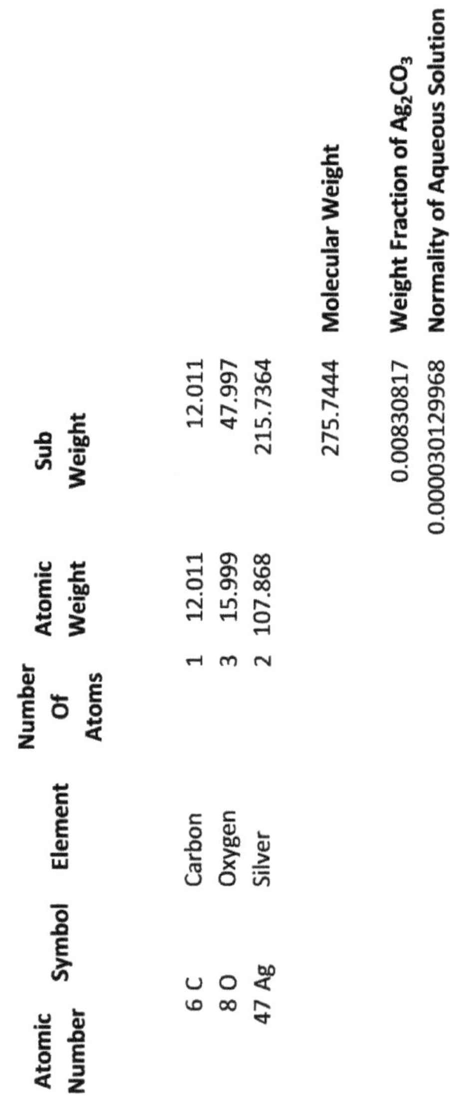

Atomic Number	Symbol	Element	Number Of Atoms	Atomic Weight	Sub Weight		
6	C	Carbon	1	12.011	12.011		
8	O	Oxygen	3	15.999	47.997		
47	Ag	Silver	2	107.868	215.7364		
					275.7444	Molecular Weight	
						0.00830817	Weight Fraction of Ag_2CO_3
						0.000030129968	Normality of Aqueous Solution

Table 3.6
The Calculation of the Molarity of Silver Carbonate, Ag_2CO_3

CHAPTER FOUR
THE X-RAY FLUORESCENCE ANALYSER

The Scope and Limitations of the Portable X-Ray Fluorescence Analyser

An X-Ray Fluorescence Analyser is a machine designed to characterise and quantify the chemicals in a sample. Such a device, that interprets patterns of reflected, transmitted or emitted light received is called a spectroscope, because it processes a spectrum of electromagnetic radiation (light) in order to do its job.

There are many different kinds of spectroscope. Newton's Prism was a primitive one, and transmission spectroscopes using flames to analyse chemical make-up started to be developed in the nineteenth-century.

All light travels in some kind of wave pattern and waves, as you know, can have both height and length, or more technically amplitude and frequency (because frequency is reciprocal wavelength). Light, including very high-energy light such as x-rays, betrays the make-up of a mixed chemical sample because the *frequency* of the light discloses the *quality* of the underlying chemical in terms of elemental atomic number, whilst the *intensity* discloses the *quantity* of the element present. Of course, samples can be very mixed and sophisticated mathematical post-processing is often needed to translate the received analog information into meaningful tabulations.

Classically, x-rays were made by bombarding a piece of copper with high-velocity electrons in a vacuum, but today very localised and finely-shone x-rays can be made using modern solid-state electronics together with precision optical collimation. This has made it practical for x-rays to be produced by a hand-held "gun" that can be employed by scientists in the field, as, for instance, they undertake routine surveys.

In the particular method of X-ray Fluorescence, a weak x-ray of very finely controlled frequency is shone on a target to make the target's atoms fluoresce, meaning to answer the exciting x-ray by producing their own frequency-shifted radiation which can then be picked up by analysing instruments and interpreted to provide information about the nature and amounts of the responding atoms.

A well-known feature of x-rays is that they can shine through apparently opaque matter, but excitation x-rays are typically weak and fluorescence-exciting x-rays accordingly have these "limitations":-

(a)	They only penetrate (and excite) the first one or two millimeters of the target

<table>
<tr><td>thirteen</td><td>(b)</td><td>They cannot excite an atom of less than twelve or</td></tr>
</table>

	protons.

In other words, they are useless for assessing the

presence

or amounts of elements lighter than Atomic Numbers

13 or 14,

i.e. constituents lighter than Magnesium or

Aluminum.

This last "limitation" is not hard-and-fast and largely
arises because it is impossible to eliminate the thin

film of air

that interposes itself between the analyser's window

and the

target sample: And that film of gas mostly is

comprised of

the offending lighter atoms.

Now like all weaknesses, the limitations of hand-held x-ray machines can be inverted to become a strength.

For example the shallow penetration of the excitation rays makes them ideal for assessing the composition of thin films of heavy metal compounds, such as the glaze on pottery, or perhaps the delicate layers of mineral paint applied by an Old Master artist. All without interference by irrelevant material such as the underlying clay or impregnated canvas.

The very fact that common gases or other light elements like Carbon, Hydrogen, Nitrogen and Oxygen are invisible to x-ray fluorescence devices means that common organic substances like organic tissues, oils and life-debris do not significantly mask or distort the excited return readings, so that desired heavy metal markers can reliably be received and compared. This means that the fluorescence rays are ideal for inspecting the composition of alloys, fabricated products and of course geological samples in or out of the field. These significant markers may well, however, be definite organometallic chemical complexes themselves informative about the nature and origin of the target sample.

The x-ray fluorescence "gun" used by geologists looks like a chunky plastic pistol, garishly colored in case it is lost or mis-laid, and having a sealed and protected window at the business end to let excitation rays out, and measurable excited rays in. This window is typically one centimeter square, or in some models 2.5 cms square. Care should be taken to make sure that the end of the instrument is held in contact with the sample surface, both to ensure strong readings and for the safety of persons. Expect to pay between £15000 and £20000 if you want a hand-held x-ray analyser (2021). Modern machines are wholly solid-state and powered by rechargeable lithium batteries.

Let us imagine that we could take our "gun" to near space, and hold its x-ray window against a continent to analyse the composition of the Earth's Crust.

We may expect to receive a fluorescence spectrum something like Figure 4.1

Clearly, this rendition for all 92 or so elements, arranged in increasing order of atomic number is a bit unselective and confused, especially since there are such profound differences in the abundance of chemical elements on a rocky planet.

What we would *like* to see is something more like Figure 4.2

Or even for preference something that emphasises the relations of the three fair sisters of Group Eleven, perhaps something like Figure 4.3

Note that because of the extreme orders-of-magnitude differences in the concentrations of elements in the natural environment, in order to visualise their relative standings we must transform their raw fractions, perhaps by taking logarithms.

For Figures 4.2 and 4.3 I have constructed:-

$$\zeta' = \frac{1}{-log_{10}(F_\mu)}$$

Equation 4.1

where ζ' is the Inverse Logarithmic Elemental Concentration Function; and F_μ is the Fractional Mass Concentration (z).

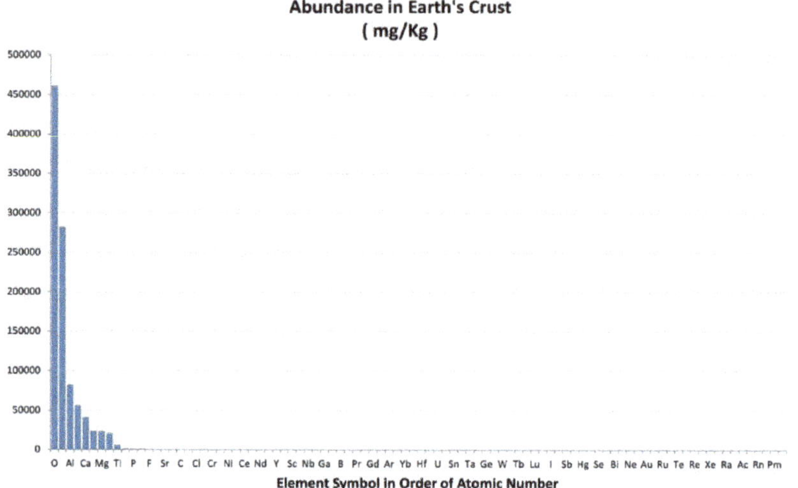

Figure 4.1
A Hypothetical Fluorescence Spectrum of the Earth's Crust

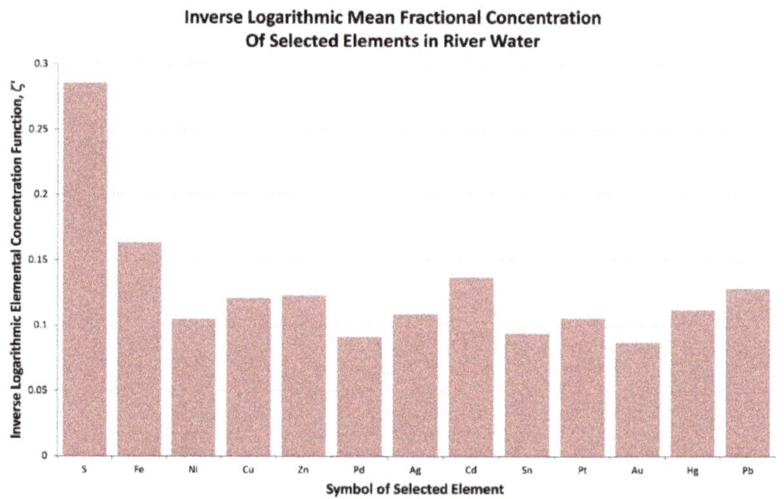

Figure 4.2
A Hypothetical Fluorescence Spectrum of Selected Elements
(Mean Fresh Water)

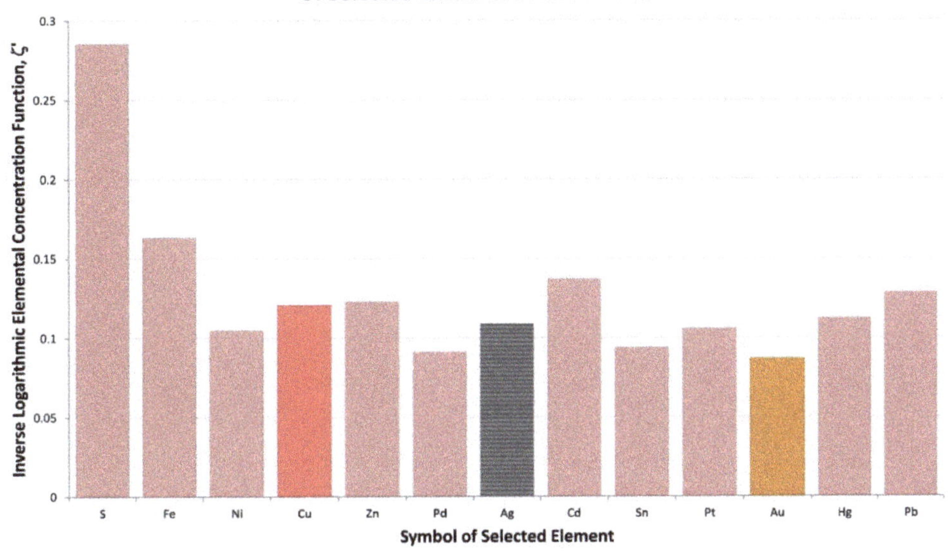

Figure 4.3
A Hypothetical Fluorescence Spectrum of Selected Elements
(Mean Fresh Water)

For example, if the Mean Fraction of Silver (Ag) in ordinary river water is $6.5×10^{-10}$ or 0.00000000065 and that of Copper (Cu) is $5.4×10^{-9}$ or 0.0000000054 then their respective ζ's are 0.108848435 and 0.120953995, which clarifies that copper is relatively more abundant than silver by a factor of:-

$$a_{Cu,Ag} = \frac{F_{Cu}}{F_{Ag}} = \frac{10^{\frac{1}{\zeta_{Ag}}}}{10^{\frac{1}{\zeta_{Cu}}}} = 10^{\left(\frac{1}{\zeta_{Ag}}-\frac{1}{\zeta_{Cu}}\right)} = 8.307692308$$

Equation 4.2

where $a_{Cu,Ag}$ is the Relative Abundance of Copper with regard to Silver; F_x is the Fraction of Element x and ζ_x is the Inverse Logarithmic Elemental Concentration Function for Element x.

What we are *actually going to see* is rather something like Figure 4.4

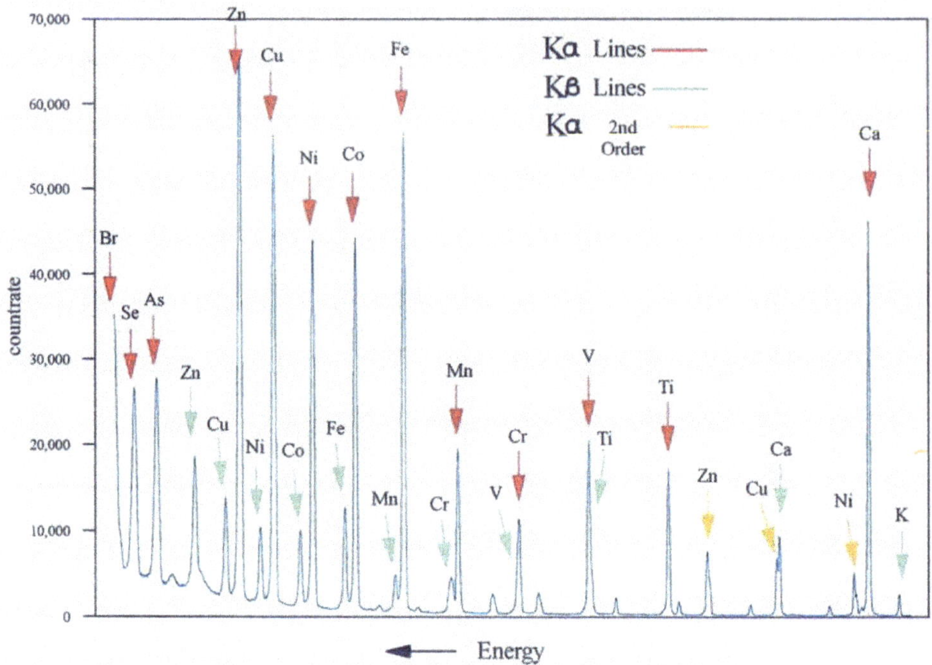

Figure 4.4
An Actual Analog X-Ray Fluorescence Spectrum[R4.1]

   This is because the fluorescence spectrum is a real-life analog phenomenon subject to perturbations, especially Rayleigh and Compton scattering effects that we shall briefly discuss later.

   Indeed, the spectrum looks like a series of overlapping Gaussian distributions ("Bell Curves") *which it is not*. The machine has to be programmed to clean this submission by filtering-out confounding or superfluous collected frequencies and adjusting the residue to assign measuring intensities appropriately before an arithmetically-correct analysis of elemental proportions can be reported.

   I hope that you will indulge me whilst I counsel younger readers that this and all other information is a *construct* not an actuality, a construct built and interpreted by the human brain including its linguistic and software media-of-interpretation. And constructs do not exist, so to say, in The Mind of God. All human "knowledge" is therefore defective: A lesson on which lives hinge, and must be well learnt and learnt now.

<u>Preferred Fluorescence Frequencies</u>

Most of the frequencies of atomically-emitted radiation are too weak or too overlapping to be reliable indicators of the amounts of chemical elements in a sample.

Therefore, scientific convention has identified a roster of acceptable frequencies to be isolated by instrumental circuitry and software. These Preferred Frequencies are usually the Kα spectral lines, caused by a particular electron quantum leap within the shells of orbiting atomic electrons. (The Lα lines are used above Cadmium at Atomic Number 48).

Wavelength is of course inverse frequency, and the preferred *wavelengths* of excited radiation are listed in Table 4.1

<u>Compton and Rayleigh Scatter</u>

Figure 4.4 exemplifies the way in which the returned radiation is diffused across adjacent frequencies blurring the purity of the quantitative signal.

This is due to phenomenon of scattering in which radiation is perturbed by the matter through which it passes.

Rayleigh Scattering arises when the incident radiation is of much longer wavelength than the size of the interacting particles, which are excited into elastic electric polarity and emit slightly-shifted sympathetic radiation.

Compton Scattering, on the other hand, occurs at the sub-atomic level and is due to the scattering of a photon by an incident high-energy electron, that is an electron which has a quantum short-wave (The Compton Effect).

Both effects interplay when very high-energy electromagnetic radiation, such as x-rays, is shone.

Rayleigh Scattering is described by Equation 4.3:-

$$f(\theta)_{Rayl} = K(1 - cos^2\theta)$$
Equation 4.3

where K is an Arbitrary Constant; f(θ)Rayl is the Degree of Rayleigh Scattering; and θ is the Scattering Angle.

Compton Scattering is described by Equation 4.4:-

$$f(\theta)_{Comp} = \lambda' - \lambda = \frac{h}{m_e c}(1 - \cos\theta) = \kappa(1 - \cos\theta)$$

Equation 4.4

where λ is the Initial Wavelength; λ' is the Scattered Wavelength; h is Planck's Constant; m_e is the Rest Mass of the Electron; c is the Celerity of Light and κ is the Grouped Quantum Physical Constant. $f(\theta)_{Comp}$ is the Degree of Compton Scattering.

Clearly, any x-ray instrument that is going to quantify the amount of an element in a sample has to be programed to compensate for the Rayleigh and Compton Effects, amongst other things.

Figure 4.5 illustrates the contrasting behaviors of the Rayleigh and the Compton Effects.

Table 4.1
Preferred Emitted X-Ray Wavelengths

Atomic Number	Symbol	Element	Preferred XRF Line	Preferred λ (nm)	Atomic Number	Symbol	Element	Preferred XRF Line	Preferred λ (nm)	Atomic Number	Symbol	Element	Preferred XRF Line	Preferred λ (nm)
1	H	Hydrogen			32	Ge	Germanium	$K\alpha_1$	0.1254	63	Eu	Europium	$L\alpha_1$	0.2121
2	He	Helium			33	As	Arsenic	$K\alpha_1$	0.1176	64	Gd	Gadolinium	$L\alpha_1$	0.2047
3	Li	Lithium	$K\alpha$	22.8	34	Se	Selenium	$K\alpha_1$	0.1105	65	Tb	Terbium	$L\alpha_1$	0.1977
4	Be	Beryllium	$K\alpha$	11.4	35	Br	Bromine	$K\alpha_1$	0.104	66	Dy	Dysprosium	$L\alpha_1$	0.1909
5	B	Boron	$K\alpha$	6.76	36	Kr	Krypton	$K\alpha_1$	0.09801	67	Ho	Holmium	$L\alpha_1$	0.1845
6	C	Carbon	$K\alpha$	4.47	37	Rb	Rubidium	$K\alpha_1$	0.09256	68	Er	Erbium	$L\alpha_1$	0.1784
7	N	Nitrogen	$K\alpha$	3.16	38	Sr	Strontium	$K\alpha_1$	0.08753	69	Tm	Thulium	$L\alpha_1$	0.1727
8	O	Oxygen	$K\alpha$	2.362	39	Y	Yttrium	$K\alpha_1$	0.08288	70	Yb	Ytterbium	$L\alpha_1$	0.1672
9	F	Fluorine	$K\alpha_{1,2}$	1.832	40	Zr	Zirconium	$K\alpha_1$	0.07859	71	Lu	Lutetium	$L\alpha_1$	0.162
10	Ne	Neon	$K\alpha_{1,2}$	1.461	41	Nb	Niobium	$K\alpha_1$	0.07462	72	Hf	Hafnium	$L\alpha_1$	0.157
11	Na	Sodium	$K\alpha_{1,2}$	1.191	42	Mo	Molybdenum	$K\alpha_1$	0.07094	73	Ta	Tantalum	$L\alpha_1$	0.1522
12	Mg	Magnesium	$K\alpha_{1,2}$	0.989	43	Tc	Technetium	$K\alpha_1$	0.06751	74	W	Tungsten	$L\alpha_1$	0.1476
13	Al	Aluminium	$K\alpha_{1,2}$	0.834	44	Ru	Ruthenium	$K\alpha_1$	0.06433	75	Re	Rhenium	$L\alpha_1$	0.1433
14	Si	Silicon	$K\alpha_{1,2}$	0.7126	45	Rh	Rhodium	$K\alpha_1$	0.06136	76	Os	Osmium	$L\alpha_1$	0.1391
15	P	Phosphorus	$K\alpha_{1,2}$	0.6158	46	Pd	Palladium	$K\alpha_1$	0.05859	77	Ir	Iridium	$L\alpha_1$	0.1351
16	S	Sulfur	$K\alpha_{1,2}$	0.5373	47	Ag	Silver	$K\alpha_1$	0.05599	78	Pt	Platinum	$L\alpha_1$	0.1313
17	Cl	Chlorine	$K\alpha_{1,2}$	0.4729	48	Cd	Cadmium	$K\alpha_1$	0.05357	79	Au	Gold	$L\alpha_1$	0.1276
18	Ar	Argon	$K\alpha_{1,2}$	0.4193	49	In	Indium	$L\alpha_1$	0.3772	80	Hg	Mercury	$L\alpha_1$	0.1241
19	K	Potassium	$K\alpha_{1,2}$	0.3742	50	Sn	Tin	$L\alpha_1$	0.36	81	Tl	Thallium	$L\alpha_1$	0.1207
20	Ca	Calcium	$K\alpha_{1,2}$	0.3359	51	Sb	Antimony	$L\alpha_1$	0.3439	82	Pb	Lead	$L\alpha_1$	0.1175
21	Sc	Scandium	$K\alpha_{1,2}$	0.3032	52	Te	Tellurium	$L\alpha_1$	0.3289	83	Bi	Bismuth	$L\alpha_1$	0.1144
22	Ti	Titanium	$K\alpha_{1,2}$	0.2749	53	I	Iodine	$L\alpha_1$	0.3149	84	Po	Polonium	$L\alpha_1$	0.1114
23	V	Vanadium	$K\alpha_1$	0.2504	54	Xe	Xenon	$L\alpha_1$	0.3016	85	At	Astatine	$L\alpha_1$	0.1085
24	Cr	Chromium	$K\alpha_1$	0.229	55	Cs	Caesium	$L\alpha_1$	0.2892	86	Rn	Radon	$L\alpha_1$	0.1057
25	Mn	Manganese	$K\alpha_1$	0.2102	56	Ba	Barium	$L\alpha_1$	0.2776	87	Fr	Francium	$L\alpha_1$	0.1031
26	Fe	Iron	$K\alpha_1$	0.1936	57	La	Lanthanum	$L\alpha_1$	0.2666	88	Ra	Radium	$L\alpha_1$	0.1005
27	Co	Cobalt	$K\alpha_1$	0.1789	58	Ce	Cerium	$L\alpha_1$	0.2562	89	Ac	Actinium	$L\alpha_1$	0.098
28	Ni	Nickel	$K\alpha_1$	0.1658	59	Pr	Praseodymium	$L\alpha_1$	0.2463	90	Th	Thorium	$L\alpha_1$	0.0956
29	Cu	Copper	$K\alpha_1$	0.1541	60	Nd	Neodymium	$L\alpha_1$	0.237	91	Pa	Protactinium	$L\alpha_1$	0.0933
30	Zn	Zinc	$K\alpha_1$	0.1435	61	Pm	Promethium	$L\alpha_1$	0.2282	92	U	Uranium	$L\alpha_1$	0.0911
31	Ga	Gallium	$K\alpha_1$	0.134	62	Sm	Samarium	$L\alpha_1$	0.22					

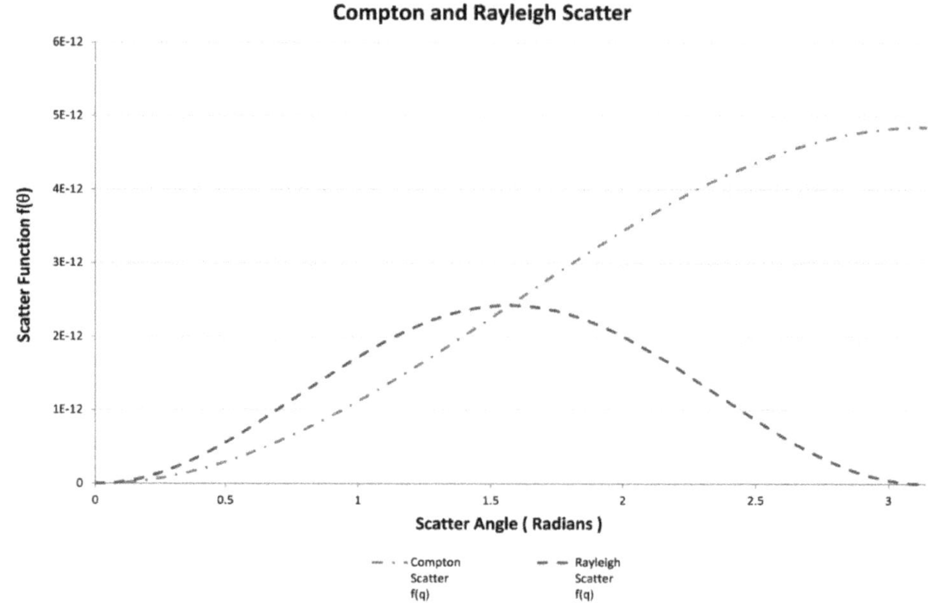

Figure 4.5
The Rayleigh and Compton Scatters Compared

References

R4.1   Wikipedia contributors. (2021, January 14).
X-ray fluorescence.
In Wikipedia, The Free Encyclopedia. Retrieved 16:00, February 24, 2021,
from
https://en.wikipedia.org/w/index.php?title=X-ray_fluorescence&oldid=1000381618

Picture Description
English: Historical note: this was run as a pressed powder on the scanning channel of the
Siemens MRS404 at Blue Circle Cement, Atlanta Plant, in 1995. We had no scandium, gallium   or germanium!
Date   24 December 2006 (original upload date)
Source   Transferred from en.wikipedia to Commons by Pieter Kuiper using CommonsHelper.
Author   LinguisticDemographer at English Wikipedia

I do admire craftsmen.

They seem to have every virtue I lack. Patience, dexterity, taste and discretion.

As a boy I went to a neighbourhood secondary modern school where they tried to teach us woodwork and metalwork, and not a great deal else except Rugby and Anglicanism. I loathed it. But I enjoyed the woodwork though I was no good at it. I was even allowed to keep my little projects. I am unfair: The geography and history masters were excellent and I owe to Mr "Hairy" Hurrell whatever aptitude for higher mathematics I possess.

I digress.

About twenty years ago I was already many years without a job and I had a fad of attempting woodwork. I would drive to high-class joiners' workshops in the South Staffordshire locality to bargain for scrap British and Foreign hardwood offcuts. These I would take home to my shed and transform into Calvary crosses or small boxes. On one occasion I was privileged to visit the works of Linwood and Company, the long-departed church furnishers of Lichfield where I drove a hard bargain thinking that only the shareholders would benefit from my trade. The foreman who discussed the price for the lot I had selected agreed a figure and then casually mentioned that the cash would go to the works Benevolent Fund. I gave him the balance of my £35 budget there and then. Within the year, Linwood had joined all the other splendid British factories in the sky.

A certain craftsman in the workshop overheard this exchange and buttonholed me as I loaded my car. He asked if I would consider joining the Lichfield Institute. If so he would propose me and see if he could persuade a seconder. I had no idea who or what the Lichfield Institute was but for some reason I said "Yes". We exchanged email addresses and I drove off and forgot the matter.

A couple of weeks later the President of the club sent me an email letter saying that I had been proposed by a Mr Norbert Farmer and seconded by his friend, retired silversmith Arthur Armstrong. I was invited to subscribe and did so.

There are still a number of so-called gentlemen's clubs in England, though they are rare outside Central London. Almost all now admit women. Some are biased toward science, the performing arts, gambling or whatever but all collaborate fraternally and the Lichfield

Institute has a "special relationship" with the Forester. Hence a number of Lichfield members are interested in matters spiritual.

Most people think that "Clubmen" sit around reading the Telegraph, complaining of modern youth and swilling whisky. This is far from reality. Beside their charitable functions the clubs support their members and each other *inter alia* by offering cheap accommodation if you happen to be in the relevant location. Food, drink and shelter are all cheap or subsidised, though the overnight arrangements can be spartan in the older or poorer establishments. Indeed, many clubs argued for decades that they could not accommodate ladies because they did not have separate dormitories or lavatories. There is no hocus-pocus and this is definitely *not* Freemasonry.

Many men prefer accommodation in clubs to hotels, because in hotels, though they are far more numerous and convenient, you have to pay commercial prices, not a trifling consideration if you want to visit Central London, especially Circusland.

I drew sketch diagrams of several pieces of laboratory apparatus I required, and knowing my limitations approached Mr Armstrong for advice. He very kindly agreed to help. Arthur is an experienced and very expert turner and fitter and my confidence proved well-placed.

First of all he re-drew my sketches to proper draftsman standards, and discussed these plans with me.

He identified many problems with my original conceptions and recommended adjustments, which I invariably agreed. Though I naturally paid for the materials Arthur was so kind as to undertake all the necessary carpentry and machining of which I was so signally incapable.

To illustrate my ineptitude take a look at Figure 5.1, an attempted isometric drawing of a pellet compressor for manual use on a laboratory bench. Remember that an x-ray fluorescence analyser measures the *relative proportions* of elements in a mixed sample, not the *absolute amounts*, so if you compress your sample, let's say a wad of damp leaves, by hammering it into the bottom of a tube using your trusty Brummagem screwdriver it hardly matters that you have not used a precision hydraulic press controlled by load cells.

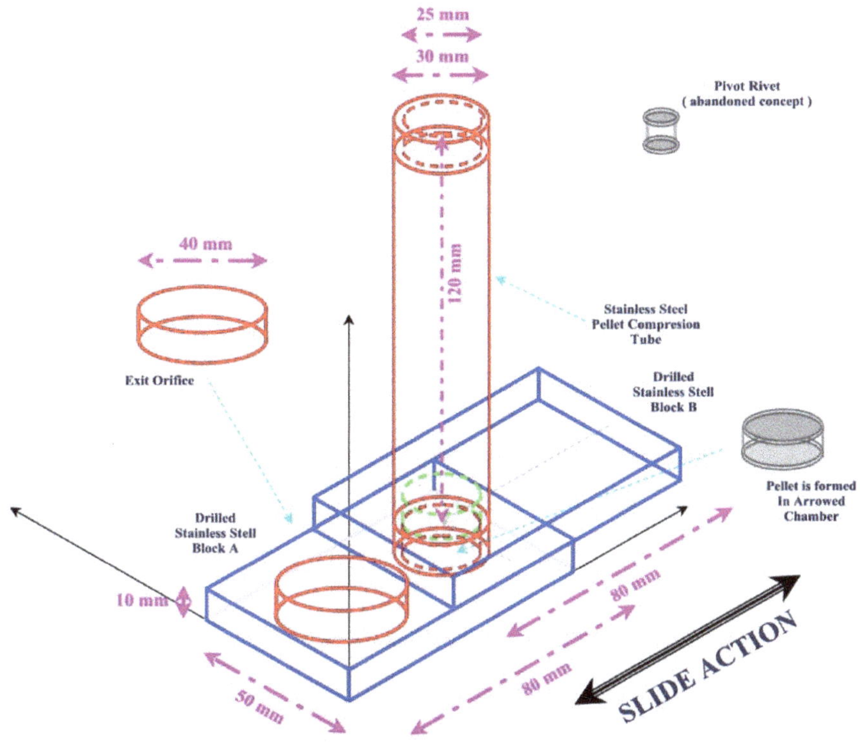

Figure 5.1
A Weird if not Surreal Attempt at a
Pellet Compressor Design

At first I thought the thing to do was to rotate the upper plate (presumably some kind of steel) over the lower plate, to expel the formed pellet, then I thought a sliding action was better, without taking into account that at compression the upper plate would overhang and require the support of a rigid step like a carpenter's bench stop.

Mr Armstrong was rightly critical of this design and suggested we allow the upper plate to be freely-rotated by hand between the compressive and expulsive phases of knocking.

So we got our heads together, and prepared orthographic drawings of the apparatus desired.

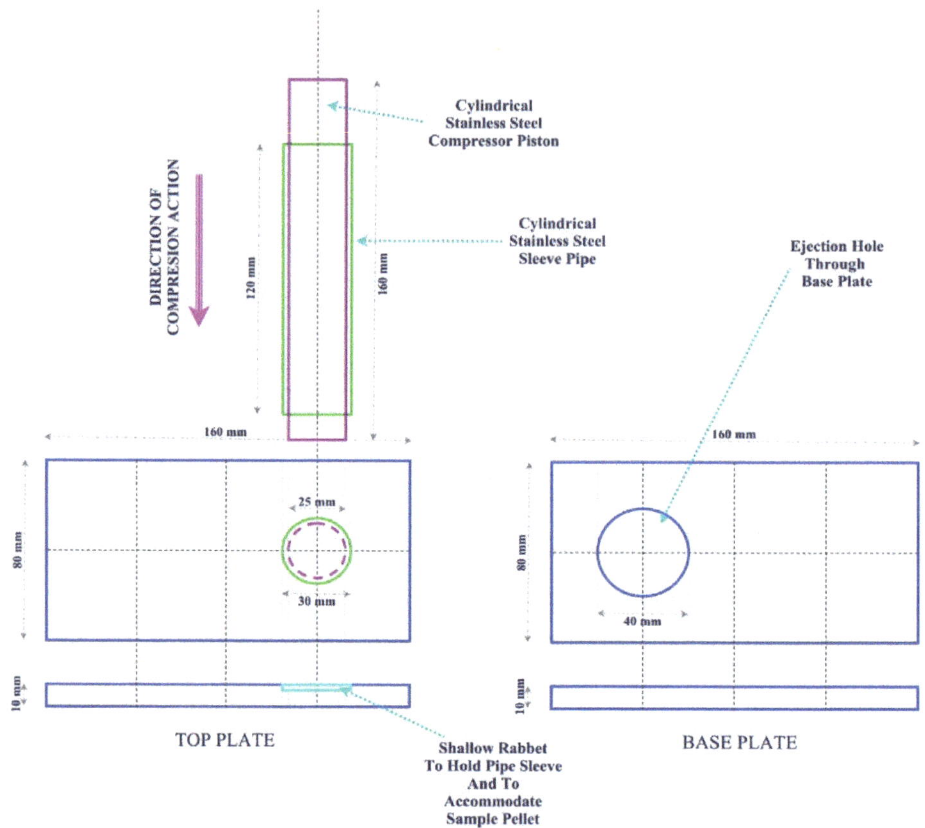

**Figure 5.2
A Workable Design for a
Pellet Compressor**

We decided to use Stainless Steel 304 for the Pellet Compression apparatus: The rod, the tube and the two flat plates. This was because 304 gave good resistance to corrosion, for example by organic acids and tannins, as well as good machinability.

A further consideration, besides of course cost, is that the absence of apparatus corrosion helps to safeguard delicate samples with trace metals from any experimental contamination.

There is a slight mismatch between the diameter of suitable commercially-available rod and the pellet-forming tube in which it is supposed to travel. We thought long and hard about this problem and decided that rather than have Arthur carefully and tediously bore a large-diameter rod to fit the thinner rod snugly, or trim a tube internally, it was better to use off-the-shelf rod and tube and tolerate the millimeter or so play that would persist between. Not only would this policy prevent accidents but it would also forestall jamming caused or promoted by wet materials, as well as corrosion. The use of glycerine or mineral lubrication was thought most inadvisable, whilst the employment of gum arabic as a binder was a distinct possibility during sample pellet production.

The clearance was not critical, but creating and preserving the competency of pellets from loose materials was. That consolidation of the sample would have to permit the free expulsion of air and water at compression-time.

Due to the superficial penetration of x-rays as used and excited in fluorescence applications, it is not necessary for a pellet produced to be more than one or two millimeters thick, whilst it's actual thickness is not critical.

The specifications, costs and amounts of these materials as well as the cabbage shall be separately addressed in a General Bill of Materials.

AGWELL
RINGSTEAD

CHAPTER SIX
THE WEIGHING MACHINE AND ANCILLARIES

I thought at first that I could use a relatively cheap jeweller's electronic balance accurate to a milligram. Then I realised that the synthesis of river water necessary to reagent testing would require much more refined standards, optimistically at the nanogram level.

It is of course impossible to use such a nice machine in ordinary laboratory conditions if only because the breath of a spider hiding in the cabinet will set the pan bouncing to its own destruction.

Whilst a superior balance is clearly called for, a more realistic approach to laboratory practice must be attempted.

Imagine, for instance that the mean fraction of silver in river water is 6.5×10^{-10} or $z = 0.00000000065$, which it is. Then the necessary amount of silver carbonate in a kilogram of otherwise silver-free water may be set to $z \times 275.25/(2 \times 107.8682) = 0.00000000065 \times 1.278180224 = 8.30817 \times 10^{-10}$ or 0.000000000830817.

The trick here is to weigh out 0.00830817 kg of silver carbonate (i.e. 8.30817 grams of Ag_2CO_3) and dissolve it in one kilogram of water (the saturation concentration of Ag_2CO_3 is 31 grams per liter). (Strictly the amount of solvent ought to be $1 - 8.30817 = 991.69183$ grams of water). Pipette one milliliter of the well-mixed and thoroughly-dissolved solution into 0.999 kilograms of silver-free water. This reduces the concentration of Ag_2CO_3 to 0.00000830817. A repetition of this process gives $z(Ag_2CO_3) = 0.00000000830817$. Now pipette a milliliter of this solution into nine milliliters of silver-free water and you bring the z to 0.000000000830817 of Ag_2CO_3 or in other words 0.00000000065 grams per kilogram of silver. In practice you may have to weigh out 8.3082 grams of Ag_2CO_3 because you will be lucky to find a chemical balance accurate to less than 10^{-5} grams. (And if you do find one you will have to pay for it, and take both financial and operational precautions).

Note that in situations where you are composing a test liquor that contains thirteen metals you will need to scale up each concentration in the single liter by thirteen so that when the individual liters are combined to make thirteen liters of combined test liquor the mix settles to the representative proportions. This is not necessarily as straight forward as it sounds because saturation may well be exceeded and suitable adjustments therefore necessary. For example, 8 grams of Ag_2CO_3 in a liter of water multiplied by thirteen gives 104g/L whilst the saturation concentration of Ag_2CO_3 at STP is as aforenoted 31g/L.

I selected two machines: The Kern ABT 220-5DNM Chemical Balance (10mGram), and the Kern ABS 3204N Precision Analytical Balance: 0.32kg in 0.0001 grams.

To assist substance management I further purchased three pure nickel spatulas and a one milliliter pipette: SP1000-ECO 100-1000μL SciPette Digital Pipette BASIC. Obviously, various beakers and other containers were also necessary, but have not been costed.

CHAPTER SEVEN
SAMPLE TUBES

The sample tubes were made of commercially-available PVC plastic tubing, gray in color, and intended for plumbers' use in the fitment of waste water piping.

The pipes were cut to the requisite lengths by Mr Arthur Armstrong, as were bright yellow Perspex® square end-caps intended for the use of builders and other tradesmen. These end-caps were drilled with holes for stream and spring water entry and egress, and glued perpendicular to the pipe axes using ordinary hardware-store superglue.

Figure 7.1 is a drawing showing the dimensions of the sample tubes and illustrating the way in which one pipe includes the other.

Each sample tube was marked with a letter code to indicate its Contents; Location of Deposition; and Time and Date of Deposition.

For laboratory test purposes, five identical sample tubes were prepared for each of the six test scavenging substrates making of course thirty tubes in all. Each group of five tubes for a given substrate were then immersed in separate containers of representative river-water test liquor (SRW: Simulated River Water).

The sample substrate was placed or loosely-packed into the smaller tube and the larger tube then passed over the smaller tube. The two tubes were then firmly sealed together using fluorescent gaffer tape. Although the test liquor of simulated river water was usually stagnant in laboratory containers, in flowing water in the field it was intended to place them parallel to any flow so that water would gently flush through the perforations.

The tube and end-cap materials employed were: 25 mm Grey PVC Pipe PN10, 32 mm Grey PVC Pipe PN10, 0.75" Grey PVC Pipe Class E and Yellow Gloss 250 Perspex Sheet. Some of the tubing was not in the event used.

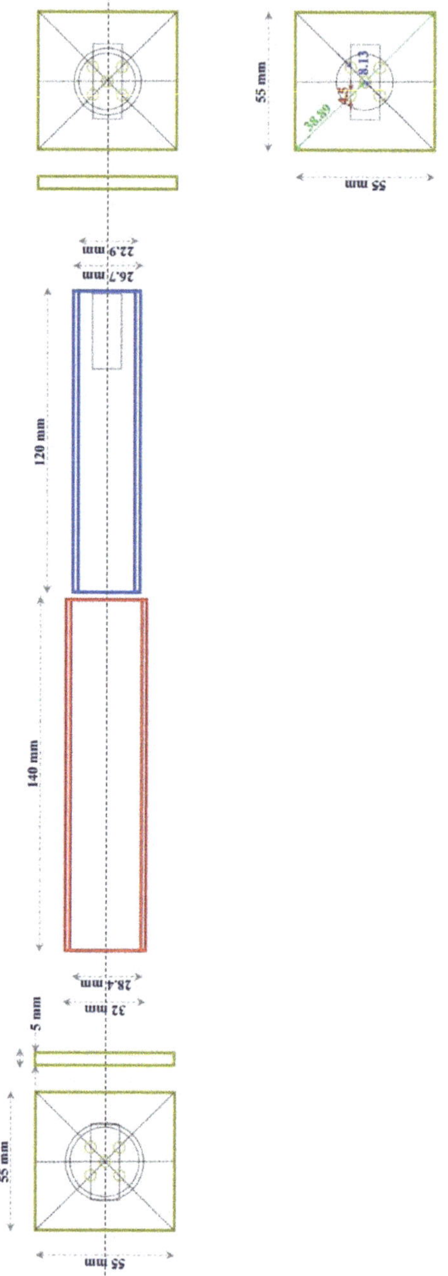

Figure 7.1
The Structure and Dimensions of a Sample Tube

CHAPTER EIGHT
THE GENERAL BILL OF MATERIALS

The General Bill of Materials lists the laboratory equipment and equipment constructional materials that were required for laboratory sample substrate test and selection purposes as applied in Mr Armstrong's workshop and by myself at the Forester Club laboratory in Northumberland Avenue, Westminster.

Table 8.1 defines the Notation used in the General Bill of Materials and its various subsections whilst Table 8.2 is the Bill of Materials for Apparatus and for Components to Manufacture Apparatus. Table 8.3 is a Summary for the Cost of All Consumable and Durable Supplies. Lastly Table 8.4 shows the Cabbage of Apparatus Component Supplies. The chemical's cabbage is very much greater: In the nineties of percent in many cases, indicating that more judicious supply may effect very large savings.

It is clear that once travel and accommodation costs are added there is little change from £30000.

All Dimensions in Millimeters

NS	Number of Supplied Items
NP	Number of Fabricated Items
L	Length
W	Width
D	Depth
T	(Wall) Thickness
OD	Outside Diameter (tubing)
ID	Inside Diameter (tubing)
VAT	Value Added Tax (%)

Table 8.1
Notation for the General Bill of Materials

Product	Amount (m = Kg; V = L)	Website	Supplied								Cost (ex VAT)	Cost (cum VAT)
			NS	L	W	D	T	OD	ID	VAT		
1.6 Liter Really Useful Box		aplaceforeverything.co.uk	6	190	130	110				20	£2.50	£3.00
25 mm Grey PVC Pipe PN10		plasticpipeshop.co.uk	1	2400	25		1.25	25	22.5	20	£2.39	£2.87
32 mm Grey PVC Pipe PN10		plasticpipeshop.co.uk	1	2400	32		1.8	32	28.4	20	£3.39	£4.07
0.75" Grey PVC Pipe Class E		plasticpipeshop.co.uk	1	5000	19.1		1.9	26.7	22.9	20	£5.64	£6.77
Yellow Gloss 250 Perspex Sheet		perspexsheet.uk	1	5500	5500		5			20	£23.49	£28.18
Zinc Foil		metaloffcuts.co.uk	5	100	100		1.2			20	£15.60	£18.72
Iron Foil		rapidmetals.co.uk	1	1000	1000		1			20	£14.85	£17.82
Lovering's Solution as Constituted	1.482734											
Simulated River Water as Constituted	16.302											
Kern ABT 220-5DNM Chemical Balance (10mGram)		sciquip.co.uk	1	330	330	340				20	£1,654.00	£1,984.80
Kern ABS 3204N Precision Analytical Balance: 0.32kg in 0.0001 grams		sciquip.co.uk	1								£973.00	£1,167.60
XRF Portable Spectrometer (Olympus Vanta)		olympus-ims.com	1							20	£18,000.00	£21,600.00
Drying Oven SQ-4600 (to 120+°C)		sciquip.co.uk	1	750	490	470				20	£715.00	£858.00
Pure Nickel Spatula		coleparmer.co.uk	3							20	£28.47	£34.16
SP1000-ECO 100-1000µL SciPette Digital Pipette BASIC	0.11	sciquip.co.uk	1								£174.00	£208.80
-10 to +200 Laboratory Thermometer	0.045	amazon.co.uk	1									£6.45
Waterproof Flourescent Tape		amazon.co.uk	1	10000	15							£6.99
Stainless Steel 304 Rod	1.92	themetalstore.co.uk	1	500	25					20	£28.17	£33.80
Stainless Steel 304 Tube		rapidmetals.co.uk	1	1000	30		1.5	30	27	20	£10.35	£12.42
Stainless Steel 304 Flat Slab		rapidmetals.co.uk	1	1000	80	10				20	£33.55	£40.26
Vermiculite (Insulation: Dupre Micafil)	100L	fluesupplies.com	1							20	£20.99	£25.19
Oak Dowel		diy.com	1	2400				12	12	20		£6.34
Wilko Water Butt with Tap Green 210L	210L	wilco.com	1	970	570	570						£30.00
PG Tips Everyday One Cup Pyramid Tea Bags Bulk Pack		amazon.co.uk	1100									£18.98
TOTAL											£21,705.39	£26,115.23
Laboratory Durables											£21,544.47	£25,866.80
Consumables (not Compositional Chemicals)											£160.92	£248.42

Table 8.2
The General Bill of Materials
as it relates to
Apparatus and Components to Manufacture Apparatus

	Cost (ex VAT)	Cost (cum VAT)
TOTAL for Apparatus and Apparatus Materials	£21,705.39	£26,115.23
Laboratory Durables	£21,544.47	£25,866.80
Consumables (not Compositional Chemicals)	£160.92	£248.42
Lovering's Solution Chemicals		£113.85
Metallic Salts for Simulated River Water (SRW) Make-up		£799.92
Chemicals' Total		£913.77
GRAND TOTAL FOR MATERIALS AND EQUIPMENT		£27,029.00

Table 8.3
Summary of the Costs
of
Durable and Consumable Supplies

Product	Cabbage (Fraction)
1.6 Liter Really Useful Box	
25 mm Grey PVC Pipe PN10	
32 mm Grey PVC Pipe PN10	0.125
0.75" Grey PVC Pipe Class E	0.28
Yellow Gloss 250 Perspex Sheet	
Zinc Foil	
Iron Foil	0.95
Lovering's Solution as Constituted	
Simulated River Water as Constituted	
Kern ABT 220-5DNM Chemical Balance (10mGram)	
Kern ABS 3204N Precision Analytical Balance: 0.32kg in 0.0001 grams	
XRF Portable Spectrometer (Olympus Vanta)	
Drying Oven SQ-4600 (to 120+°C)	
Pure Nickel Spatula	0.67
SP1000-ECO 100-1000µL SciPette Digital Pipette BASIC	
-10 to +200 Laboratory Thermometer	
Waterproof Flourescent Tape	
Stainless Steel 304 Rod	0.84
Stainless Steel 304 Tube	0.88
Stainless Steel 304 Flat Slab	0.68
Vermiculite (Insulation: Dupre Micafil)	0.98507266
Oak Dowel	0.9375
Wilko Water Butt with Tap Green 210L	
PG Tips Everyday One Cup Pyramid Tea Bags Bulk Pack	0.93181818

Table 8.4
Cabbage of Apparatus Component Supplies

CHAPTER NINE
PREPARATION OF CONCENTRATION APPARATUS

<u>Metallic Passive Displacement</u>

We have seen that so long as oxidation coats do not interpose an electropositive metal may displace a more electronegative one from an aqueous solution. We expect the latter to form a coat or slime on the surface of the electropositive displacer.

We have not studied the activity of colloids (important in the case of silver), and neither the activity of palladium black or other hydrogen-absorptive media when permeated with the electropositive gas hydrogen.

We have confined ourselves to the displacement of metal from dissolved salts. These salts are of course represented by charged ions in solution.

Criteria

When a specimen of active electropositive metal is immersed it must fulfil certain criteria. First of all it must obviously not explode or spontaneously catch fire, and neither dissolve so quickly that there is little left to handle after a few days in a stream.

Equally, the active metal must not be more electronegative than hydrogen, otherwise it will behave like gold, remaining untarnished and failing to work as a displacement agent.

It is desirable also that the metal is not damaging to life, so we must be careful not to introduce cadmium, lead or mercury to environmental water, even in metallic form.

We may list the formal criteria of submerged displacive metal as:-

(a)	Not unduly Rare
(b)	Not unduly Reactive with Water at 10°C
(c)	Not unduly Expensive
(d)	Not having a Known Tendency to form a Protective Oxidation Coating

Many radioactive elements, some Rare Earths, and some plantinoid metals are too scarce to provide enough sheets or shot to place in a sample holder and leave in the field, or they are insufficient for the one centimeter square XRF portal, or they have electromagnetic self-activity that would question or compromise XRF readings.

All elements with an electronegativity less than 1.3 (Thorium) are too reactive with water to be a viable substrate for displaced metal deposition.

Many of the elements of sufficient electronegativity are too costly to be a sensible sample substrate.

Many of the remaining candidates are known to form protective patinas in water or aerated water. These include copper, vanadium, aluminium, tantalum and several others.

Finally, any substance more electronegative than nickel, including silver itself, is obviously not applicable to displacive chemistry.

Table 9.1 lists, in order of electronegativity, the 118 known elements in terms of their satisfaction of these criteria.

Table 9.2 is an abstract of Table 9.1 that isolates viable active displacement metals only.

Magnesium is arguably unsuitable, at least for more than a day or two's submersion in fresh water. It is rather too reactive and it has a tendency to coat either with oxide or hydroxide. Also, any attempt to heat-treat the substrate in air is highly dangerous.

Uranium (presumably depleted) is potentially usable, and natural uranium may have the further advantage of being detectable with radiation counters. One the other hand, it has a high melting point.

Zinc is truly viable. It is cheap and common, just electropositive enough without dissolving in water. A disadvantage, however, is its tendency to form large crystals upon solidifying from melt, as can readily be seen on galvanised iron. Indeed, galvanised iron is a possibility for a displacive substrate. Sheets of zinc can shatter upon bending, but this problem can substantially be mitigated by heating a thin sheet to above 100°C. Additionally, zinc can be melted for homogenisation at low temperature, though I am not greatly in favor of heat-treating samples before XRF analysis as this can reduce the mass of, or sensibly eliminate, trace volatiles.

Iron is another good choice. It is cheap and common, readily workable as thin sheets, resilient and sectile. It is not, however, readily fusible.

I am less happy with cobalt. It has some tendency to corrode, and has a high melting point.

Zinc and Iron are the best metals to scavenge silver salts in environmental water, though the scavenging of colloidal silver remains an open question.

Forms

10cm square sheets or foils of Zn and Fe were selected, of a maximum 1mm thickness. If XRF tests required thicker foils, such sheets could readily be folded by hand.

Products

Zinc sheets of what we used to call ANALAR® grade can easily cost £160.

For example, alfa.com[R9.1] 10436 Zinc foil, 0.25mm (0.01in) thick, 30cm (12in) wide, 99.98% (metals basis) costs £36.10 in the UK and this is clearly not analytic grade material. On the other hand a 100mm×100mm patch of 11915 Zinc foil, 1.0mm (0.04in) thick, Puratronic®, 99.9985% (metals basis) would set you back £697 plus VAT in the UK.

11448 Iron foil, 1.0mm (0.04in) thick, Puratronic®, 99.995% (metals basis) is £1146 + VAT in the UK.

But of course this all begs the question, if you have an XRF spectrometer capable of microfraction accuracy, then why bother with high-purity analytic materials? Why have a dog and bark yourself? Why not use any old iron (literally, perhaps) and have your machine dutifully find out whatever most likely irrelevant impurities are there for you?

We are only interested in the relative abundances of silver in the water of one ditch in comparison to another ditch a few meters away. And perhaps the presence or absence of pyritic constituents such as iron and sulfur.

Therefore we would be happy with metaloffcuts[R9.2] Natural Zinc Sheet 1×100×100mm for £3.00 +VAT, or indeed 1×1000×1000mm at £66.48 plus VAT giving a hundred 10cm by 10cm sheets that we could cut out for ourselves.

From the same firm, Grade s355w Corten Mild Steel Sheet, Weathering Steel, good as iron, would cost £2.91 plus VAT for a 1×100×100mm sheet or £42.32 for 1×600×1200mm.

Atomic Number	Symbol	Element	Rare	Reactive	Expensive	Known Oxidation Coat	Too Electro-Negative
87	Fr	Francium	Y	Y	Y	N	N
55	Cs	Caesium	Y	Y	Y	N	N
19	K	Potassium	N	Y	N	N	N
37	Rb	Rubidium	Y	Y	Y	N	N
56	Ba	Barium	N	Y	N	N	N
88	Ra	Radium	Y	Y	N	N	N
11	Na	Sodium	N	Y	N	N	N
38	Sr	Strontium	Y	Y	Y	N	N
3	Li	Lithium	N	Y	N	N	N
20	Ca	Calcium	N	Y	N	N	N
57	La	Lanthanum	Y	Y	Y	N	N
70	Yb	Ytterbium	Y	Y	Y	N	N
89	Ac	Actinium	Y	Y	Y	N	N
58	Ce	Cerium	Y	Y	Y	N	N
59	Pr	Praseodymium	Y	Y	Y	N	N
61	Pm	Promethium	Y	Y	Y	N	N
95	Am	Americium	Y	Y	Y	N	N
60	Nd	Neodymium	Y	Y	Y	N	N
62	Sm	Samarium	Y	Y	Y	N	N
63	Eu	Europium	Y	Y	Y	N	N
64	Gd	Gadolinium	Y	Y	Y	N	N
65	Tb	Terbium	Y	Y	Y	N	N
39	Y	Yttrium	Y	Y	Y	N	N
66	Dy	Dysprosium	Y	Y	Y	N	N
67	Ho	Holmium	Y	Y	Y	N	N
68	Er	Erbium	Y	Y	Y	N	N
69	Tm	Thulium	Y	Y	Y	N	N
71	Lu	Lutetium	Y	Y	Y	N	N
94	Pu	Plutonium	Y	Y	Y	N	N
96	Cm	Curium	Y	Y	Y	N	N
72	Hf	Hafnium	Y	Y	Y	N	N
90	Th	Thorium	Y	N	N	N	N
97	Bk	Berkelium	Y	N	Y	N	N
98	Cf	Californium	Y	N	Y	N	N
99	Es	Einsteinium	Y	N	Y	N	N
100	Fm	Fermium	Y	N	Y	N	N
101	Md	Mendelevium	Y	N	Y	N	N
102	No	Nobelium	Y	N	Y	N	N
103	Lr	Lawrencium	Y	N	Y	N	N
12	Mg	Magnesium	N	N	N	N	N
40	Zr	Zirconium	N	N	Y	Y	N
21	Sc	Scandium	Y	N	Y	N	N
93	Np	Neptunium	Y	N	Y	N	N
92	U	Uranium	N	N	N	N	N
73	Ta	Tantalum	Y	N	Y	Y	N
91	Pa	Protactinium	Y	N	Y	N	N
22	Ti	Titanium	N	N	N	Y	N
25	Mn	Manganese	N	N	N	Y	N
4	Be	Beryllium	N	N	Y	N	N
41	Nb	Niobium	Y	N	Y	N	N
13	Al	Aluminium	N	N	N	Y	N
81	Tl	Thallium	Y	N	Y	N	N
23	V	Vanadium	N	N	Y	Y	N
30	Zn	Zinc	N	N	N	N	N
24	Cr	Chromium	N	Y	N	Y	N
48	Cd	Cadmium	N	N	Y	Y	N
49	In	Indium	Y	N	Y	N	N
31	Ga	Gallium	Y	N	Y	N	N
26	Fe	Iron	N	N	N	N	N
82	Pb	Lead	N	N	N	Y	N
27	Co	Cobalt	N	N	N	N	N
14	Si	Silicon	N	N	N	Y	N
29	Cu	Copper	N	N	N	Y	N
43	Tc	Technetium	Y	N	Y	N	N
75	Re	Rhenium	Y	N	Y	N	N
28	Ni	Nickel	N	N	N	Y	N
47	Ag	Silver				Y	
50	Sn	Tin				Y	
80	Hg	Mercury				Y	
84	Po	Polonium				Y	
32	Ge	Germanium				Y	
83	Bi	Bismuth				Y	
5	B	Boron				Y	
51	Sb	Antimony				Y	
52	Te	Tellurium				Y	
42	Mo	Molybdenum				Y	
33	As	Arsenic				Y	
15	P	Phosphorus				Y	
1	H	Hydrogen				Y	
44	Ru	Ruthenium				Y	
46	Pd	Palladium				Y	
76	Os	Osmium				Y	
77	Ir	Iridium				Y	
85	At	Astatine				Y	
86	Rn	Radon				Y	
45	Rh	Rhodium				Y	
78	Pt	Platinum				Y	
74	W	Tungsten				Y	
79	Au	Gold				Y	
6	C	Carbon				Y	
34	Se	Selenium					Y
16	S	Sulfur					Y
54	Xe	Xenon					Y
53	I	Iodine					Y
35	Br	Bromine					Y
36	Kr	Krypton					Y
7	N	Nitrogen					Y
17	Cl	Chlorine					Y
8	O	Oxygen					Y
9	F	Fluorine					Y
2	He	Helium					Y
10	Ne	Neon					Y
18	Ar	Argon					Y
104	Rf	Rutherfordium					Y
105	Db	Dubnium					Y
106	Sg	Seaborgium					Y
107	Bh	Bohrium					Y
108	Hs	Hassium					Y
109	Mt	Meitnerium					Y
110	Ds	Darmstadtium					Y
111	Rg	Roentgenium					Y
112	Cn	Copernicium					Y
113	Nh	Nihonium					Y
114	Fl	Flerovium					Y
115	Mc	Moscovium					Y
116	Lv	Livermorium					Y
117	Ts	Tennessine					Y
118	Og	Oganesson					Y

Table 9.1
A Tabulation of Candidate Displacement Agents

Table 9.2
Selected Candidate Displacement Agents

Atomic Number	Symbol	Element	Atomic Weight	Density	Melting Point	Boiling Point	Specific Heat Capacity	Electro-Negativity	Abundance In The Earth's Crust	Rare	Reactive	Expensive	Known Oxidation Coat	Too Electro-Negative
			(Da)	(g/cm3)	(K)		(J/g · K)		(mg/kg)					
12	Mg	Magnesium	24.305[VII]	1.738	923	1363	1.023	1.31	23300	N	N	N	N	N
92	U	Uranium	238.02891(3)[IX]	18.95	1405.3	4404	0.116	1.38	2.7	N	N	N	N	N
30	Zn	Zinc	65.38(2)	7.134	692.88	1180	0.388	1.65	70	N	N	N	N	N
26	Fe	Iron	55.845(2)	7.874	1811	3134	0.449	1.83	56300	N	N	N	N	N
27	Co	Cobalt	58.933194(3)	8.86	1768	3200	0.421	1.88	25	N	N	N	N	N

<u>Vermiculite Impregnated with Lovering's Solution</u>

Speaking of the homologous metal copper TS Lovering[R9.3] stated in his important USGS paper of 1927, *Organic Precipitation of Metallic Copper*:-

"The writer modified the Maillard procedure in the following manner: Two parts (molecular) of an aqueous amino-acid solution such as glycocoll) were added to four parts of a sugar solution (levulose or xylose); the liquid was then covered with petrolatum to exclude air, and one part of cupric sulphate was added to it. As the reaction proceeds slowly in the cold, temperatures of 60° to 70° C. were maintained. The solution changed from deep blue through dark green to black, and metallic copper was slowly precipitated. The time required for the reaction varied with temperature, reagents, and the hydrogen ion concentration (pH), ranging from a few minutes to 48 hours. Precipitation did not occur in moderately alkaline or acid solutions but took place readily in faintly alkaline, neutral, and faintly acid solutions. The copper precipitated was identified by both chemical and physical tests. In the presence of sugar, air being excluded, other reagents, not amino acids, such as gallic acid, phloroglucin, and tannic acid, were found to precipitate copper with varying degrees of speed and completeness. A faintly alkaline solution was found to give the best results. It was also discovered that simple ketones such as acetone can be substituted for sugar."

On the page marked 52 in his report Lovering continues:-

"From this work the writer concludes that free sulphuric acid is formed during the reduction of the copper and tentatively suggests the following type of reaction :
$$Cu^{++}SO_4^{--} + 2H^+(OH)^- + R' \leftrightarrow Cu^0 + H_2^+SO_4^{--} + R''(OH)_2^- + R'''$$
where R, R', R", and R''' are organic compounds."

All of which is clearly most suggestive.

I should remind readers that of course our problem concerns silver, which is somewhat more electronegative than copper, and also that we do not require a precipitation of actual metallic silver for our purposes, only some silver product insoluble in water. Such a product as Silver Sulfide (Ag_2S) would be ideal as its solubility in water at 25°C is 6.21×10^{-15} g/L.

Silver Oxide, however, is not desirable because it forms a hydroxide ion and thus has an effective solubility in water of about 13 ppm.

The formation of dissolved metal ions with organic ligands is a process known as chelation and is central both to the take-up of heavy metals by a living organism, as well as the purging of such metals from biological tissue.

I find the old stories about the deposition of copper or other metals upon dead leaves and nuts, especially oak leaves, nuts and galls as most suggestive of the activity of gallic acid, and or its polymer tannic acid or even the product tannin.

The molecular formulae of Gallic Acid is $C_6H_2(OH)_3CO_2H$; that of Tannic Acid $C_{76}H_{52}O_{46}$; Tannin has a molecular weight between 500 and 3000; and the molecular formula of Xylose is $HOCH_2(CH(OH))_3CHO$.

I noted Lovering's observations about weakly alkaline pH being optimal and remembered that peaty moorland water is often weakly acidic. Accordingly I surmised that any formulation involving tannic or gallic acids, or both, might usefully be balanced by weak alkalis, preferably resident against flowing water, such as calcium carbonate ($CaCO_3$) or even the rather more soluble sodium bicarbonate ($NaHCO_3$). All of these reagents, I felt, would be of little avail as silver scavengers unless firmly adsorbed onto some chemically-inert high surface area substrate such as rock wool, sheep's wool or perhaps builders' vermiculite. The cuticular scales of ungulate wool, especially coarse wool, might provide a superior lodgment for chemical treatments, I surmised, to smoother fibers such as cellulose and indeed rock wool.

In view of these considerations I thought I should attempt to determine the extent to which an admixture of these ingredients might capture stream or pond silver, whether held in solution or suspension. "Suspension" in these terms includes solids held in still or moving water without settling due to molecular kinesis, i.e. colloids and "nanoparticles", sometimes denoted as AgNP or something. It was not clear to me to what extent the precipitation of silver colloids was dependent upon sulfurisation. I made no attempt to add sulfur.

The active part of this mixture was a cocktail of chemicals I called Lovering's Solution and I designed it to be an aqueous solution of five relatively cheap and simple chemicals, each at slightly less than saturation concentration at 20°C. (Bear in mind that UK stream water at 350 meters altitude and 55° latitude has an average temperature adjacent to 9°C).

Table 9.3 details the Lovering's Solution quantity required in liters, based upon the dimensions of the sample tubes and the number of sample tubes to be filled. Only five sample tubes will be required for trial purposes. The solution is a little below 0.1 of saturation levels. With respect to acorns, there is evidence that they can gather copper when they contain 5-6% tannic acid.

Table 9.4 presents the details of these five Lovering reagents, and the resulting Lovering's Solution as designed. The Gum Arabic is not an active constituent and is not present at steeping time. The Gum Arabic is only available to augment pellet competency at pellet formation time. Remember that scavenged *mass* is not of itself critical to these experiments: Only the *relative proportions* of gathered elements. Glucose has been employed instead of xylene.

Table 9.5 is, on the design basis, a costing per liter and in total for about 0.25 liters of Lovering's Solution as based upon UK prices as they were in February 2021, the date of my catalogs.

Sample Tube Length (meters)	0.1200
Sample Tube IntDia (meters)	0.0229
Number of Trial Types	1
Statistical Copies	5
Sample Tube Capacity (L)	0.04942448
Make-up Quantity (L)	0.24712239
Design Multiplier	0.10000000
Tannic Acid Fraction Achieved	0.19313357

Table 9.3
Sample Tube Numbers and Dimensions
and
Lovering's Solution Required Volume

Chemical Compound	Molecular Formula	Empirical Formula	Molar Mass (g/mol)	Molar Mass (g/mol)	PSD (M_{wiki}, M_{comp})	Saturation Quantity (g/L)	Temp. (°C)	Saturation Molarity (mol/L)	Raw Design Molarity (mol/L)	Diluted Design Molarity (mol/L)	Design Quantity per Liter (grams)
			(wikipedia)	(computed)							
Gallic Acid	$C_6H_2(OH)_3CO_2H$	$C_7H_6O_5$	170.1200	170.072	0.028215377	11.9	20	0.069950623	0.06	0.006	1.02072
Tannic Acid	$C_{76}H_{52}O_{46}$	$C_{76}H_{52}O_{46}$	1701.1900	1700.79	0.023512953	250		0.146955954	0.14	0.014	23.81666
Sodium Bicarbonate	$NaHCO_3$	$NaHCO_3$	84.0066	83.99776928	0.010511936	96	20	1.142767354	1	0.1	8.40066
Calcium Carbonate	$CaCO_3$	$CaCO_3$	100.0869	100.086	0.000899219	0.013	25	0.000129887	0.0001	0.00001	0.0010009
Glucose	$C_6(CH_2OH)(OH)_4O$	$C_6H_{12}O_6$	180.1560	180.06	0.053287151	909	25	5.045627123	5	0.5	90.078
Gum Arabic											
Total						1266.913	90	6.405430942	6.2001	0.62001	123.31704
Mean						253.3826	22.5	1.281086188	1.24002	0.124002	24.663408

Table 9.4
Lovering's Solution Formulation

Chemical Compound	Molecular Formula	Reagent Requirement (kg)	Supplier	Supplier catalog Number	Supplier Pack Quantity (kg)	Packs Required	Pack Price (£UK)	Cost (£UK)	Notes
Gallic Acid	$C_6H_2(OH)_3CO_2H$	0.000252243	Acros Organics	410860050	0.005	0.050448553	£18.70	£0.94	98%
Tannic Acid	$C_{76}H_{52}O_{46}$	0.00588563	Acros Organics	419995000	0.500	0.01177126	£49.20	£0.58	95% ACS reagent
Sodium Bicarbonate	$NaHCO_3$	0.002075991	Acros Organics	424270250	0.025	0.083039647	£13.70	£1.14	99.7% ACS reagent
Calcium Carbonate	$CaCO_3$	2.47337E-07	Acros Organics	437190050	0.005	4.94674E-05	£29.50	£0.00	99.999% (trace metal basis)
Glucose	$C_6(CH_2OH)(OH)_4O$	0.022260291	Thornton and Ross		0.500	0.044520581	£2.75	£0.12	Foodgrade Dextrose
Gum Arabic		1	Amazon		0.100	10	£4.95	£49.50	powder
Total		0.030474402			1.035	0.189829509	£113.85	£2.78	
Mean		0.00609488			0.207	0.037965902	£22.77	£0.56	

Table 9.5
Lovering's Solution Costs

<u>Dead Oak Leaves</u>

Dead leaves of some species, notably the *Quercus* genus of Old World Oaks are long known to be rich in tannic acid and its polymer tannin. Tannic Acid is a mild inorganic reducing agent and we have seen elsewhere that partially-decayed vegetable matter can sometimes function to precipitate copper from cuprous liquors in the environment. Because copper and silver are chemically closely related I speculated that dead leaves, perhaps especially oak leaves, might precipitate environmental silver that might then coat the leaves as metal at the water-organic interface.

Therefore one sunny October day I travelled to Brockton Copse and gathered a rucksack-full of dead oak leaves from the ground to use as the filling of some trial sample tubes.

It is also known that the needle leaves of the Dwarf Cypress, a conifer, are highly effective at the concentration of copper, but these are not cheaply or readily available in Mercia.

I included in this gathering a proportion of approximately half-volume of acorns, the seeds of the oak, which are about six percent tannin and thought to be able to precipitate marcasite.

<u>Commercial Heavy Metal Scavenging Resins and Gels</u>

It is possible to purchase a variety of patent chemical reagents that will capture almost all of a desired precious metal held in solution. These reagents, often sold in the form of gel or resin carriers, can then be treated to remove the valuable metal, and typically some of the reagent can then be re-cycled.

Scavenger resins comprise a chemical functional group adsorbed onto a micro-particular inert gel or resin substrate. The mixture, if resin, swells on contact with the solvent (typically water) permitting the enhanced access of the metal-bearing solution to the active ingredient.

Silia*MetS*® Metal Scavengers are typical of the class of these facilitator additives, but use non-swelling silica gel substrates to retrieve precious metals. Silia*MetS* Thiol PN: R510308 is said to be the simplest and most catholic scavenger for silver and a variety of periodically-adjacent heavy metals.

The Magpie polymer resin scavenger has been trialled for copper and reduces Cu in aqueous solution from about 60 to 2 ppm under optimal, pH-adjusted conditions. Elsewhere, the claim is made that for Au,

Pt, Pd and Rh in solution their concentrations can be reduced from 10^{-5} to 10^{-9} by this scavenger.

Magpie MPX-310 is a scavenger of choice for very low levels of Pt and Pd in the presence of very high Ag (0.131).

Of course, our need is rather the converse: We need to increase the scavenger concentration from 10^{-10} to 10^{-3}.

I made no attempt to assess commercial scavengers as potential amplifiers of heavy metal in river water.

Tea Bags

Perfectly ordinary pyramidal tea bags were purchased as PG Tips Everyday One Cup Pyramid Tea Bags Bulk Pack Of 1100, and supplied by Amazon for £18.98 and free delivery.

References

R9.1   alfa.com Alfa Aesar by Thermo Fisher Scientific
https://www.alfa.com/en/catalog/011915/

R9.2   Metaloffcuts.co.uk
https://www.metaloffcuts.co.uk/product/natural-zinc-sheet/
https://www.metaloffcuts.co.uk/product/corten-steel-sheet/
https://www.amazon.co.uk/PG-Tips-Pyramid-Bags-Total/dp/B07CJGT17P

R9.3   "Organic Precipitation of Metallic Copper"
TS Lovering
USGS Bulletin 795-C: 1927
10pp
https://pubs.usgs.gov/bul/0795c/report.pdf

AGWELL
RINGSTEAD

CHAPTER TEN
LABORATORY METHODS

Before we proceed to analysis it is as well to remember the limitations of our gathered apparatus.

In particular, we know that our best chemical balance is only accurate to 10^{-5} of a gram, and has an upper limit of about 320 grams, which however we would be most unwise to approach. Our chosen x-ray fluorescence machine, a portable model, has an accuracy of 10^{-6} ppm, which however we would be most unwise to approach.

We must not forget the most important of our instruments, for it too often forgets itself: Our human brain.

I repaired to the Forester Club laboratory in Northumberland Avenue one gray November evening in 2025. Mr McHenry the doorman greeted me in the darkling drizzle with a cheery smile as was his custom with any gentleman (or indeed myself). He knew that I was from the Lichfield and a guest of Professor Agwell, and apologised that he would nevertheless need to scrutinise my Lichfield card and note the number, and my times. Of course I happily obliged, and Mr McHenry asked if I would like him to bring me a drink and maybe a sandwich. I asked for a large Armagnac. You have already gathered that laboratory practice at the Forester is quite different from that in the universities or HMG, or indeed nine-tenths of industrial premises. For those innocent souls amongst my readers who doubt the ability of seventy-three-year-old diabetic myasthenials to manage large Armagnacs I should point out that the lab had a more than adequate supply of distilled water on tap.

The Forester Club was founded by Sir George Forester who had spied on the Turks during 1827 in the lead-up to The Battle of Navarino, though whether he was as interested in the Turks as in our esteemed allies the French and the Russians is a matter of conjecture. At any event the club and especially its laboratory looked as if Sir George might have recognised them. The scorched and scored teak benches and the ash stools were neither calculated for comfort nor planarity, whilst the darkly patinated bronze handles and fitments gave an additional air of affluence foreign to our century.

The ghostly atmosphere reminded me a little of Wednesbury Art Gallery, thought to be the only museum in the World to make no acquisition during the course of the twentieth century; or even more of the old chemical class laboratory of the Marywell Street School, Aberdeen as it was fitted during the lectureship of Mr Mustard, circa 1968.

This quality was intensified in a small antechamber which constituted a shadowy museum at the Forester Club premises. The little museum contained a disjection of nineteenth century scientific paraphernalia and natural specimens. Salient to senses were a number of bizarre homuncular skeletons, variously conjectured, but presumed by me to be the remains of pinniped foetuses or possibly the bones of small primates. Another striking relic was the alleged very piece of muslin that Sir William Crookes pulled from the person of Miss Florence Cook as the infamous Stanley Street séance dissolved in uproar, I think in 1874.

Mr Armstrong having kindly cut and prepared thirty each of 100mm square Iron and Zinc Foils and left them in the lab I set about drying operations. The pyramidal tea bags were of course unused but I thought it best to dry them together with the dead oak leaves and the acorns in three separate open dishes in the Club's oven, set to 60°C for three hours.

You can of course criticise this approach on the entirely respectable basis that when I took similar sample substrates to The Cheviots they would invariably revert to the dampness of the environment. Point taken. But I thought that at least these three substrate types would start, as it were, from a position of equivalency.

Mr Armstrong had also laid out thirty complete and identical but unfastened sample tubes. I took one and weighed it on the coarse scale. Then I filled it to the brim with builder's vermiculite taken straight from the sack and uncompressed. I weighed this simple assembly. The difference of course was an estimate of the weight of loose vermiculite in a sample tube.

It was computed that the total vermiculite required was 167 grams. So I weighed out 200 grams of vermiculite on the coarse balance, and placed it in a Pyrex® beaker which I then placed in my newly-purchased SQ-4600 drying oven that I set to the maximum temperature of 120"C for four hours. Not only would this dry the material, presumably straight from the builders' yard, but also if hot vermiculite were steeped in the warmed Lovering's Solution the latter might permeate more deeply into the vermiculite and assist adsorption of the water metals with a little absorption.

Whilst drying progressed I prepared the Lovering's Solution in the manner outlined in Chapter Nine (Organic Scavenger Reagents). The Lovering's Solution was then stored in a clean washbox. I then moved forward to roll the foils into suitable loose shapes that could be inserted into a sample tube. To assist this process I briefly immersed the zinc sheets in boiling water and formed them about a 12-mm oak dowel clenched in a vice. To work the metal I used my gloved hands. The steel sheets though stiffer were more resilient and did not require pre-heating.

By this time the oak and tea sample scavenger materials were well-dry and I removed them from their oven and sealed them in the hermetically-lidded washboxes for storage. As the materials cooled a slight vacuum helped the springs keep the boxes airtight.

At the end of that first day, I removed the vermiculite from the hot drying oven and dumped it hot into the Lovering's Solution that had been gently warmed in a microwave, and its temperature checked to be 40°C. I then tightly clipped the washbox lid back on, gently swilled the slurry and left it to cool overnight.

The water butt had its tap securely fitted, was filled with fifty liters of distilled water and left overnight to check for leaks.

The preparation of the Synthetic River Water (SRW) would of course be a protracted and tedious process best deferred to the next day.

I got out my sleeping bag, went for a shower and a bite, and returned to sleep on the laboratory floor. I am an unsociable cove, and do not enjoy other men's snoring: I much prefer my Wife's, but ladies are still frowned-upon in the Forester, and certainly not allowed overnight. As I lay I looked up at the ceiling and noticed that there was fine plaster decoration, somewhat blurred by years of repeated whitewashing and the gradual corrosion of damp acidic gases. In particular, elaborate floral bosses surrounded the plugged holes where gasoliers must once have depended, whilst incongruous fluorescent striplights hung in some discordant pattern, old Fitzgeralds I suppose of daylight 6000K tint, my preference and fitted in my own study at Bloxwich.

At that moment it occurred to my stupid apprehensions that I had parked my bedding about ten meters from the nearest lightswitch and that several obstructions intervened. So I picked up my gear and moved towards the door and the wall where the switch was fitted.

At that moment Mr McHenry looked in.

"I am about to lock the street doors, Dr Ringstead. To gain egress, please knock on Room 14, the one with the gold lettering 'Porter' near the main door. Would you like a cocoa or maybe a toddy, Sir? I can get you a biscuit or cake if you prefer, Sir?"

"No that is quite alright, Mr McHenry", I replied. "I very much doubt I shall leave the premises tonight, or indeed tomorrow".

"Very good, Sir. Goodnight, Sir"

"Goodnight, Mr McHenry"

Preparation of the 16.302 liters of SRW commenced at the crack of dawn on Day Two.

The water butt was emptied to drainage and shaken dry.

Using the pipette, distilled water from the tapped supply, and sets of weighed beakers I prepared the SRW as outlined in Chapter Six (The Weighing Machine and Ancillaries), and deposited the product in an ordinary gardener's water butt, plastic of course to minimise metallic contamination. In order to evade temperature-taking and other volumetric complications I worked throughout using weighed masses, excepting of course use of the pipette.

I started with the least present element (Gold) and proceeded to the most abundant (Sulfur) using weighed amounts of the salts obtained.

Calculated literages (dispensed as *weighed quantities*, as explained above) were prepared for sulfur (mostly as ferrous sulphate) and the metals; and then dumped into the butt, with the natural turbulence and convection being relied upon for mixing.

The Lovering's Solution was filtered from the vermiculite and the latter placed in a Pyrex beaker and put in the new oven for six hours at 120"C.

This completed the activities of Day Two.

The minimum number of samples for the statistical viability of a chemical reconnaissance study is five. This is because it is the minimum number accessible to a chi-square test. If tests of Gaussian Normality were desired, then the minimum number would be thirty. Both sample populations have nearly intolerable standard deviations even under the most controlled circumstances and much larger sample sizes, indeed in thousands, are to be preferred. The very best that could be expected of my antics in Northumberland Avenue is that the most efficient of the six test scavengers could be identified for applications in the field.

I also needed a coding system for the labelling of the sample tubes with their serial number, their contained substance, and date of exposure. I decided upon a simple alphanumeric code of the form I-X-00MMM00, for example 3-B-16NOV25 for the third sample of Iron Foil immersed on 16 November 2025.

The scheme is outlined in Table 10.1:-

	Number Required	Graphical Captions	Substrate Code	Date Code
Number of Washboxes	6			
Number of Sample Tubes				
1 Zinc Foil	5	Zinc Foil	A	16NOV25
2 Iron Foil	5	Iron Foil	B	16NOV25
3 Gallic_tannic Acid on Vermiculite	5	Acid on Verm	C	16NOV25
4 Dead Oak Leaves	5	Dead Leaves	D	16NOV25
5 Whole Acorns	5	Acorns	E	16NOV25
6 Tea Bags	5	Tea Bags	F	16NOV25

Table 10.1
Coding of Sample Tube Labels

Accordingly, Day Three commenced with the loose-loading of five sample tubes with each of the six substrates and the careful printing-by-hand of the code identifiers on the outer hull of each tube using a yellow permanent marker. The arrayed tubes were then sealed and bound with fluorescent tape and the end-plate holes checked to ascertain that they were not obstructed.

The five tubes of each substrate species were then placed in separate dry washboxes, the lid of each of the six washboxes encoded X-00MMM00, and the washboxes filled with SRW until all tubes immersed. Tubes that floated were weighed down with clean river cobbles, as they would be in the field.

The lids were clamped down on the washboxes, and the boxes each gently agitated.

The assemblies were left together on a bench for fifteen days.

This concluded work for November.

On 2 December 2025 I returned to the laboratory in the Forester, carrying my brand-new x-ray fluorescence spectrometer. I intended to unroll the metal foils, dry at 60″, and fold them into 25×25 mm squares before testing. With regard to the pelletised organic materials including the impregnated vermiculite careful readers will have observed that the pellets are of only about 22.9 mm diameter. Accordingly, fluorescence machines with a one-inch width window are barely practicable. Therefore, I chose a one-centimeter window appliance that I intended to apply to the samples over some ten overlapping areas in order to improve statistical reliabilities.

Figure 10.1 shows how a 10 mm diameter window can be applied by hand over a 25×25 mm surface of folded foil, and Figure 10.2 similarly shows how a 10mm diameter XRF window may be applied over the surface of a 22.9 mm diameter pellet. To increase our five partly-overlapping readings to ten readings we simply repeat the process after turning the sample pellet over. In such a context it is helpful though not essential to set the XRF apparatus to 0.5mm penetration. I made sure that the samples were placed upon a flat, wooden surface.

So note two important points: Strict quincunciality or any other particular geometry is not necessary; both the folded foil and the pellet may be turned over and irradiated five times again to obtain ten partially-dependent analyses from the same sample.

Please further note that handheld XRF windows do not need to be and seldom are perfectly circular or perfectly square, and they do not need to be so. Also with modern collimation and other technology windows may be very much smaller than 10×10mm square or 10mm diameter.

Therefore, we record fifty separate but not statistically-independent readings for each substrate type.

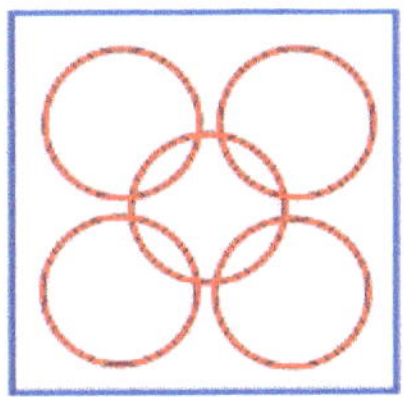

Figure 10.1
Schematic Diagram of the X-Ray Fluorescence Sampling
of a Twice-Folded 100×100 mm Metal Foil

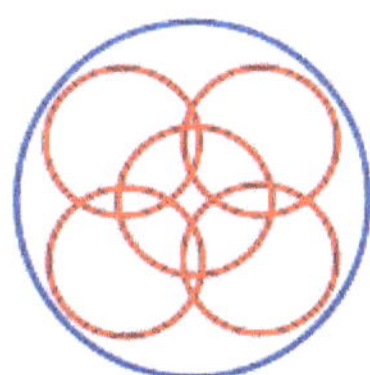

Figure 10.2
Schematic Diagram of the X-Ray Fluorescence Sampling
of a 22.9 mm Diameter Pellet

Firstly, however, the samples needed to be placed in thirty separate and code-labelled glass dishes and placed in the 60°C oven for four hours. So I poured the SRW back into its butt, retrieved the sodden samples from their tubes, and placed them in the drying oven. At lunchtime they proved still to be damp, so I applied gentle convection to another four-hour drying and went away. Thus ended Day Four and I went to dinner.

The next day, Day Five, I emptied the oven, folded the foils hot, and applying x-ray analyses in the said manner noted the results in a previously-structured spreadsheet.

I then used the pellet-formation apparatus as manufactured by Mr Armstrong to form pellets of the vermiculite and the loose organic materials. I used a rubber-headed mallet to gently tap the stainless steel piston, and reversed the loose upper platen by turning it through 180° with my fingers before expressing the pellet through the lower platen aperture. With some of the organics, especially the tea leaves, I added a trace of distilled water and gum arabic to consolidate the mechanical coherence sufficiently for pellet formation.

Before they were x-rayed each pellet or foil was accurately weighed using the fine balance.

AGWELL
RINGSTEAD

The relevant laboratory test results concern the Amplification of Concentration, z, by the six trial substrates shown in Table 11.1, together with their graphical captions:

	Number Required	Graphical Captions
Number of Washboxes	6	
Number of Sample Tubes		
1 Zinc Foil		**5 Zinc Foil**
2 Iron Foil		**5 Iron Foil**
3 Gallic_tannic Acid on Vermiculite		**5 Acid on Verm**
4 Dead Oak Leaves		**5 Dead Leaves**
5 Whole Acorns		**5 Acorns**
6 Tea Bags		**5 Tea Bags**

Table 11.1
The Six Tested Metal Scavenger Substrates
With their Graphical Captions

The (Arithmetic) Concentration Amplification of the Scavenger Substrate, sub, with respect to Chemical Element x is defined by:

$$A_x = \frac{z_{sub}}{z_{river}}$$

Equation 11.1

where z_{sub} is the Concentration of Element x in the Tested Scavenger and z_{river} is the Concentration of Element z in (simulated) River Water.

In view of the dramatic dispersion of the power of various substances to gather and concentrate elements in their environment it is convenient, especially for inspectional assessments, to transform Amplifications to their logarithms.

Accordingly, the Denary Logarithm of Concentration Amplification, $\alpha_{x,sub}$ is defined in the following manner:-

$$\alpha_{x,sub} = log_{10}(A_x \times F_{sub})$$
Equation 11.2

where F_{sub} is the Efficacy with which the Scavenger Substrate sub concentrates the Element x.

Therefore it follows that:-

$$F_{sub} = \frac{10^{\alpha_{x,sub}}}{A_x}$$
Equation 11.3

Take the case that the Concentration of Silver in Ordinary River Water $z_{Ag,river} = 6.5 \times 10^{-10}$ and the Concentration of Silver in Vermiculite steeped in Lovering's Solution and then dried before immersion ("Acid in Verm") $z_{Ag,sub} = 5.5 \times 10^{-7}$. We then compute that the Arithmetic Amplification $A_{Ag,sub} = 846.1538462$.

If by independent means (experimental results) we can measure the Efficacy of the substrate as 400 then it follows that the plottable $\alpha_{x,sub}$ is 5.529509324. This result may of course vary with the statistical dispersions consequent upon error and perturbations, and vary very widely. So the utmost technical care is required.

Table 11.2 is a presentation of $\alpha_{x,sub}$ computed from the available laboratory experimental tests from which the presentational plots are printed for study, and Figure 11.2 is a three-dimensional column chart of the same results.

Certain unexpected facts are apparent at once:-

A		The Anomalous Behavior of Sulfur
		Counterintuitively, sulfur does not attack and tarnish the iron or zinc foils to any large extent, and is not reliably concentrated by the organic scavengers.

B		Platinum, Palladium and Cadmium do not Leave Solution

		Broadly, none of these metals, already very lacking in river water, will attract to any substrate. Indeed, platinum shows a positive tendency to travel from scavenger to river.

C   Nickel, Copper and Zinc Dominate Concentration

Nickel, Zinc and to a lesser extent Copper are the most strongly concentrated heavy metals in vegetation by orders of magnitude.

D   Iron does not Dominate Silver

Regarding the marcasite argument it is notable that vegetation is about eight times more efficient at concentrating Silver than it is at concentrating Iron, and that that applies both to metal foil scavengers and the real and simulated organic media.

In terms of a simple appreciation of the concentration of metals by vegetation Figure 11.1 presents certain results.

Figure 11.3 shows how all the substrates, whether metallic or organic, show an approximate eightfold concentration of silver over iron.

I am unable to stress too often that these laboratory results must not be accepted as Holy Truth. Experimental findings can be, and are, vitiated by a hundred adventitious things, not least the technical skill of the researcher and the many preconceptions and prejudices he brings to his bench, many of them subconscious cultural implicitudes.

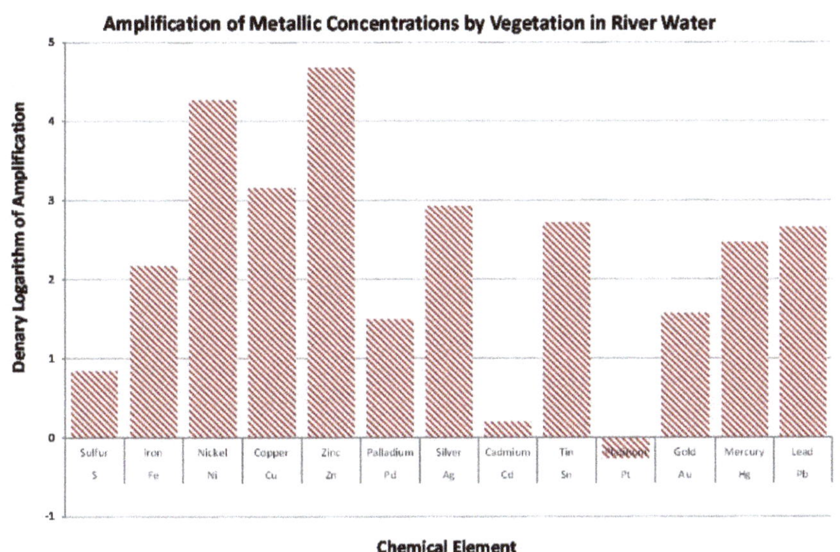

Figure 11.1
The Concentration of Metals by Vegetation from
River Water

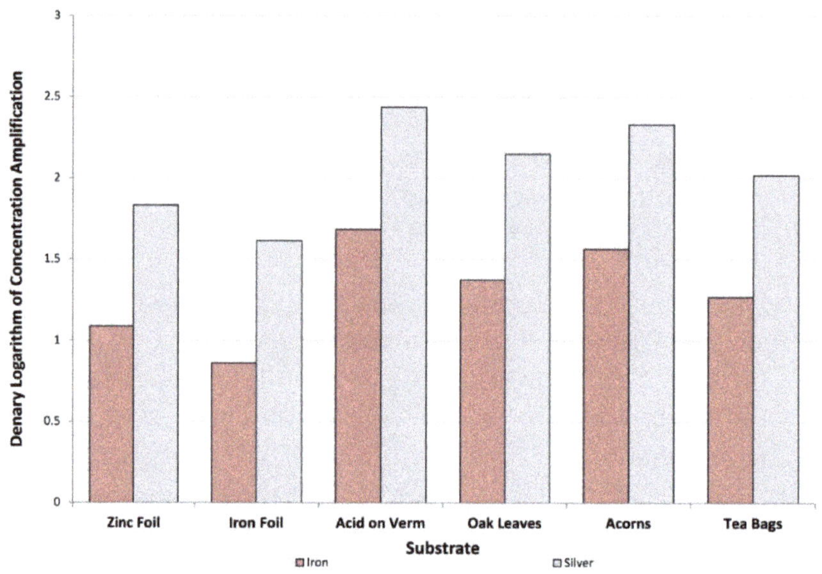

Figure 11.3
The Relative Amplifications of Iron and Silver

Atomic Number	Symbol	Element	Wikipedia Atomic Weight	Amplification, A of z (Dry Organic, River Water)	Log10 (A)	Substrate					
						1 Zinc Foil	2 Iron Foil	3 Acid on Verm	4 Oak Leaves	5 Acorns	6 Tea Bags
						0.082644628	0.049586777	0.330578512	0.165289256	0.247933884	0.123966942
16 S		Sulfur	32.06	6.984127	0.844112	-0.228197211	-0.46142586	0.36435362	0.062126226	0.237589294	-0.0583187
26 Fe		Iron	55.845	146.666667	2.166331	1.088101668	0.860525399	1.684137698	1.374081789	1.564160452	1.270047852
28 Ni		Nickel	58.6934	18333.333333	4.263241	3.188875965	2.968001859	3.789650705	3.490633554	3.661688126	3.349362339
29 Cu		Copper	63.546	1453.703704	3.162476	2.071038897	1.856616373	2.687258827	2.379968737	2.548898607	2.245344053
30 Zn		Zinc	65.38	48000.000000	4.681241	3.590170559	3.369130599	4.208710497	3.901420808	4.085128544	3.775211758
46 Pd		Palladium	106.42	31.250000	1.49485	0.415952325	0.195770395	1.01006214	0.713306913	0.879403498	0.59708282
47 Ag		Silver	107.8682	846.153846	2.927449	1.834632756	1.613763011	2.436971922	2.150312339	2.332117747	2.019781746
48 Cd		Cadmium	112.414	1.584158	0.199799	-0.880975314	-1.106548902	-0.279323936	-0.582308223	-0.411925586	-0.697967833
50 Sn		Tin	118.71	521.739130	2.717453	1.629607918	1.41450109	2.246195238	1.939919626	2.109531405	1.803860539
78 Pt		Platinum	195.084	0.547945	-0.26126	-1.339329558	-1.555380319	-0.7421639	-1.040441542	-0.869492241	-1.174479718
79 Au		Gold	196.96657	37.121212	1.569622	0.495264796	0.265853012	1.082854223	0.783775646	0.955235948	0.666427562
80 Hg		Mercury	200.592	296.000000	2.471292	1.395869984	1.165681105	1.989988003	1.691065196	1.872472868	1.566966023
82 Pb		Lead	207.2	454.545455	2.657577	1.584569286	1.348120075	2.187154239	1.878455099	2.0588907	1.745199974

Table 11.2

$\alpha_{x,sub}$ **Computed From the Available Laboratory Experimental Tests**

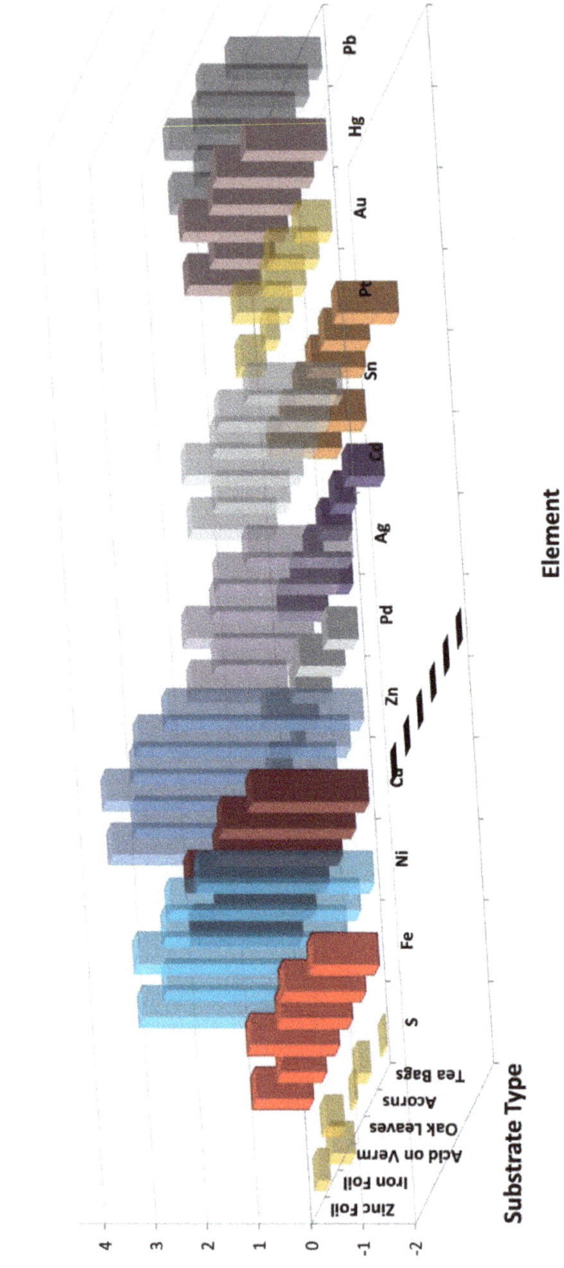

Figure 11.2
$\alpha_{x,sub}$ **Computed From the**
Available Laboratory Experimental Tests

CHAPTER TWELVE
RECONNAISSANCE

My Interview with the Kolonelleitnant

The dawn of the day 15 October 2027 saw me at the tombs. A wind had got up and the landscape was in a leaden twilight whilst the sky was a uniform and unnatural pearl-white. The air was wet and to an experienced islander it was obvious that snow threatened.

I had a brief breakfast of store-bought mineral water and salted peanuts. There were a few miles of stiff walking ahead of me and hereabouts Dere Street was hardly a line of grassy puddles between two tussock banks, so I forbore to take insulin, only taking my bisoprolol. I rolled up my sack and stowed it in my chest-bag. I lifted my rucksack onto my back with some arthritic difficulty but I had the aid of my two sticks and gingerly attacked the track. It was only a matter of a hundred and fifty meters to the curtilage of Bremenium that nestled its still-inhabited little hamlet of High Rochester with its old peel and its terrace of old cottages. Notwithstanding that the old road anastomosed to a maze of farmer's tracks in a little declivity, and I was old enough and silly enough to refer to my GPS and heading compass. I hoped that I would not encounter Bourbaki or indeed any casual shepherd who may wish to pause and pass the time of day in the wind.

I wondered idly if in the howling blizzard of the winter's nights the few folk of High Rochester feared the wraiths of the long-lost legionnaires with any of the atavistic terror that had perplexed my bivouac. Or if they viewed the ghosts as occasional wildlife or winter migrants to be tolerated, even expected. For sure, such visitors would no longer demand any vital, material, succour.

I rounded the North-East bastion and trudged past Gallow Hill and the other marching camp, long lost to the turf. Following the sheep track I passed the North-West bastion at some meters distance. Old maps marked an extramural Gallow Well at that point. I thought it prudent not to look for it but instead to scrutinise the ground ahead. I wondered if it was Roman or even older, perhaps a grim vestige of some Celtic cranium-cult. What was at the bottom, and had anyone ever essayed to find out? Within a mile I thankfully came to the modernised, macadamised Public Right of Way, and could make speed, such as I could. I was seventy-five and in poor health but was determined to die with my boots on, if die I must, and I surely should.

Within three and a half kilometers I had passed the military checkpoint and arrived at Points A and B flanking the putative Roman culvert. The checkpoint was deserted. No flag flew. I had seen or heard no creature on the entire yomp.

The wind had died down. I was well satisfied.

I placed my planned sample-tubes at point A and then at Point B, before passing without yet addressing the intermediate stations to Point E, where I was frustrated to find no direct access to the Well House or even (for an old man) a safe way to surmount the fence. Instead I had to content myself with placing the tubes in the trickle of russet water that issued from the enclosure.

Then I was surprised to hear a motor on the road above. A large black civilian-style SUV parked. It was shiny-new, well-polished and expensive: Nothing agricultural about it. It reminded me of one of those Japanese or American Chelsey-tractors. It parked above me.

Presently a trim figure in woodland combat fatigues alighted and carefully picked his way downslope. He did not appear to be accompanied or armed but somehow presented a mincing, effeminate approach. But here was the incredible thing. With my eyesight it was difficult to be sure but he seemed to have an enormous gray rat on his right shoulder!

The figure approached, and stood some three meters before me. It proved to be a woman, no longer young, with silver-flecked blonde hair swept in a bun and an officer's peaked cap, without badge, but in a vaguely European style. Neither dress nor hat made any concession to femininity.

Yes, it was indeed an enormous gray rat. He was no stripling either. His soft gray fur seemed simultaneously to be moulting and yet trim and short. He, for I assumed it was a he, stared directly into my face, stock-still in every muscle, except for two fine sprays of frantically twitching black whiskers that later proved blond in reflected light. He maintained his stare with an unblinking and inscrutable superiority, his round black eyes startlingly fimbriated with a blue margin, like a setting of jet in a hieratic figurine.

Amidst his gray intelligent face a spreading smudge of pink sensitive flesh comrade to a piercing brain denoted, as it were, the rat's questing essence, like the radome on a Gannet.

A creature total and austere like the Divine conception he was.

The lady paused expectantly. I wondered if she expected to be saluted. My storm suit bore a camouflage design, and I was wearing a camouflage peaked kepi, none of which of course bore identifying marks. It must have been very manifest, however, that I was not a serving military man.

"What are you doing, soldier?" asked the lady.

Perplexed and not a little nervous I replied:-

"I am no soldier, Madam, I am a retired scientist and I am doing a geochemical reconnaissance survey around the well and the burn".

"Pass", the officer said abruptly, as she stepped forward within arm's length, "Don't try anything stupid. I have armed men surrounding us". There was nothing macho or triumphal about her expression or her bearing. Rather her face betrayed a certain pity, admixed with a sort of bored, day-at-the-office uninterest.

"Madam, I am Kenelm Ringstead. I am not carrying my passport, but I have an old UK Driving Licence with my photograph on it".

"You have a right to be interviewed by a British Officer, should you so wish", added the lady soldier. I immediately thought that this was a *pro forma* and perfunctory invitation, done entirely to satisfy legal and administrative regulations. I replied:-

"I wish you to continue this interview meantime, Madam"

"That driving licence must do for now", she loftily responded in her faultless English idiom, as she took the card and began carefully to inspect it, photographing recto and verso with what appeared to be a cellphone, and also copying numbers into her notebook.

At this range I could better inspect my scrutineers. Her accent I fancied sounded East European, but not Russian, or not quite so anyway. I looked for Polish insignia but could see neither the crowned eagle nor that distinctive four-square design in red and white. Instead she bore epaulettes with a single pip with a squiggle and a curious emblem on her upper arm, a bit like a castle impaled by a sword, and bearing three passant lions. This was obviously no British rig, but I wondered whether other foreigners might mistake her for an English fighter. But I idly concluded that any foreigner educated enough to know that the English emblem was three passant lions would be intelligent enough to realise she was no Englishwoman. I reckoned without football.

The rat had grasped her right epaulette and adjusted his head to meet my face at the new range, and I could now see that he wore a little gray harness bearing a carabiner clip and some figures or letters on a little bronze plate. He wore a grave expression, almost distinguished, with a hint of curiosity kept in well-trained check. And those febrile whiskers continued their disconcerting twitches.

I was now thoroughly intimidated, and wondered if I could break the ice with a little levity.

"Madam", I commenced, "There is an enormous rat on your shoulder!"

"That is Kolonelleitnant Varandus and I am Major Aitamah Kask of The Army of the Republic of Estonia. Salute him", replied the woman seriously, without looking up.

I could of course see where this was going, so I dissembled:-

"Major Kask, I do sincerely admire and respect your gallant companion but I was never trained to salute and I do not wish to alarm or offend the kolonelleitnant".

"You could not alarm a rice pudding", replied the blonde scribbler.

"I think that discourteous, my lady" I said.

"One discourtesy warrants another. I ask no respect for myself. Only for a creature of innocent and luminous bravery who has saved four hundred human lives".

"I am sorry Major, I mis-spoke", I said, "tell me, do you take his orders?"

"At every instant", replied the lady dead-pan.

"I sincerely hope he draws a Lieutenant-Colonel's pay", I continued in my slightly patronising, slightly stupid, very scared way.

"He is retired", replied the Major.

I somehow formed the idea that the Major was waiting for something or someone to arrive. As she pocketed her cellphone and started to fold her papers away a slight gust of icy wind ruffled the pages of her notebook. The rat's fur waved fitfully in the breeze and the animal seemed agitated and peered over the Major's shoulder at the short heather scrub below as if assessing, in a slightly circumspect and fogyish way, whether he could risk a leap into the void. Kask gently lifted her right hand tenderly to cup the rat's snout.

Thus holding him on her right shoulder she softly whispered in English:-

"Go on soldier. See what he's set".

As the lady took a very slow and deliberate deep curtsy, and neared her crouch

she removed her restraining palm and Varandus the Hero Rat leapt into the heather and raced for the spot, some twenty meters hence, where I had set a sample-tube. He quite belied his elderly state taking care to hold his tail above the snagging scrub as only rats can do.

I watched aghast as he bounded from the outflow ditch bearing a sample-tube crosswise in his jaws.

He leapt back onto the Major's shoulder, and resumed his seat of judgment, still grasping the tube like a gatekeeper lion with a key in his maw.

Kask gently removed the tube and placed it in her pocket, from whence she withdrew a whole hazelnut in its case and offered it to Varandus who providently stashed it into his pouch.

"That was incredible. What is he trained to detect?" I asked

"That is confidential", said the Major, in a matter-of-fact way.

Varandus poked his nose into the Majors right ear, whispering his words of thanks, or perhaps imparting some morsel of tactical intelligence that only the rat and his batwoman could comprehend. There was manifestly some tender, loving, trusting rapport between the individuals, delightful to behold.

"What is in the tube, Dr Ringstead", asked the Major.

How could she know my honorific or was she just guessing?

"It is on your driving licence", explained Kask telepathically.

"It may be zinc or iron foil, chemically-treated insulation granules, or it may be natural seeds or leaves. By the ease with which the Lieutenant-Colonel held it I should guess the latter".

Kask held the handwritten code label before my eyes.

I said, "Harmless tea leaves".

"Come with me", said Major Kask. Silently four camo-clad men with automatic rifles emerged from the rear as we climbed the embankment towards the car. One of them expertly divested me of my rucksack and carried it himself.

It was silently, softly starting to snow. We entered the car. Kask and an armed man sat on the rear seat and proceeded to make a bed of it. The man with my sack placed it in the front passenger footwell, and started the motor; a third man, a young, self-conscious looking individual positioned himself in a middle bench seat with his rifle trained upon my thorax. A man with a single stripe sat beside me and glowered.

There were two peals of thunder and a flash of sheet lightening followed instantly by a raging gale. Gobs of wet, white snow hurled themselves on the West-facing doors and windows. The landscape became an undifferentiated mass of howling, whistling whiteness. Kask said to the driver, in English, for it may have been their common language "turn off the engine". The soldier obeyed. She then inexplicably said "Code X230: Purple". The driver lifted a radio receiver from the dashboard and spoke in what sounded like a Yorkshire accent, "Y30 remaining at Point Glory until 0830". "Romeo-Alfa-Uniform", came the reply. The storm raged on and the snow started to drift about the bodywork.

The gloaming was already setting-in. I wondered what Lusitanians, Numidians or Lycians would have thought as they marched this frigid league; whether they longed for their lost; whether they resigned their struggle, enemy unsighted; whether bronze was a good conductor of body heat.

Two wire cages were set behind the rear seat. Kask gently placed Lieutenant-Colonel Varandus in the one. The adjacent cage harboured a much younger animal.

"That is Captain Mary, she has not yet completed her training. She is Varandus' daughter", explained Major Kask.

The two animals kissed through a gap in the wire and Varandus tenderly spat the nut he had won against me into his daughter's mouth.

"We will leaguer here until 0830, or until rescue. A snow plough is being sent. In the meantime this is our bivouac", said Kask in English, presumably to anyone interested. "I expect a rapid thaw".

Kask said something to the youngest man in a foreign language. He lowered his rifle and rummaged in a bag. He found whatever he sought and handed it to me. It was a 500ml bottle of civilian fizzy water and a pack of cold rations, which I consumed ravenously.

Kask and the men unpacked food and drink and enjoyed an extempore cold collation. One or two men had switched on their headlamps the better to see their snap. Kask said something and they switched off their personal lights and switched on the car's map lamps instead, a much dimmer light.

"May I have my pack, please, Major Kask" I asked.

"No. Your clothes and belongings will be processed at base and returned to you in due course".

"I am an insulin-dependent diabetic. May I have my insulin set please"

The driver appeared to understand this, and uninstructed he opened my rucksack and found the cold case with surprising ease. He passed it back to me.

Kask stated "When we wish to urinate we shall use bottles, but you will use this plastic cup, wind down a window, manually if you please, and cast the contents onto the ground. Then wind the window up again".

She proffered a pint disposable beer tumbler. I accepted and said:-

"Thank you, Major Kask"

"Where are we going, Madam?"

"That is confidential, Dr Ringstead. When rescue arrives you will be blindfolded and asked to lie in the footwell. Base should be attained in less than six hours".

I marvelled again at her command, not only of her detachment, but of the English language and wished that my Estonian, or at least my Russian, was half-as-good.

Aside from the driver with the "Yorkshire" accent and the sallow young man with the rifle there was a heavy, rough-looking character with the plain three stripes of a vanemveebel and an equally severe individual with a single stripe. The latter took out a half-bottle of spirit and proceeded to swig it, rather selfishly I thought. He glowered at me, and had intently been glowering since we reached the car. He had undone his gear and exposed his hirsute chest. I wondered that he would do this in such weather, and that neither the officer nor the sergeant-major had reprimanded him.

This corporal sidled up and roughly punched my bad bicep with the heel of his hand in a mock-comradely, mock-confidential way.

"We know who you are!" he confided in my face with his draught of alcoholic breath, "You are Professor Bourbaki, master spy of the AFI"

"Don't worry", he chuckled "We won't give you to the Brits. Fuckers"

Kask shouted something in a foreign language. The sergeant-major roughly grabbed the bottle and threw it from a window.

The corporal resumed his surly silence.

My heart sank.

I took a chocolate biscuit from its foil and broke the morsel in half. The previous example had proved disgusting, possibly because it was protein, salt and vitamins enriched. I proffered one to Varandus and the other to his daughter, who both consumed avidly.

"Don't feed the animals. You'll give them diarrhoea", admonished Kask.

"Sorry, Madam", I murmured with false contrition.

But I was too tired to care. I took my sleeping-sack from its chest-pack, drew it over myself and fell asleep.

Around three in the morning I woke and wanted a pee. I used the cup and carefully opening the window and assessing the draught (the storm I mean) I cast the contents to the snow. The snowfall had in fact remitted somewhat and the wind had dropped to the merest freezing vesper. I did not re-wind the window immediately, because I thought I heard a faint drumming type of sound in the distance, about half-a-hertz, and I wondered if it was the plough, or a small pile-driver operation miles away. The sound seemed to fade and re-strengthen is if perturbed by squally winds or perhaps topography. Sometimes it was like an eighteenth-century military drumbeat, or otherwise like the soft soughing chuff-choof of a boyhood coal-train as it laboured up a distant gradient.

My sleeping companions tossed fitfully as they slept. The two rats seemed more perplexed, very awake, fidgeting and squirming in their cages with lots of frantic squeaking most uncharacteristic of this father and daughter. I became re-agitated myself. Whatever vehicle this was, possibly a Chieftain, it was going to crush us in the dark. Suddenly a full moon passed from behind an icy cloud and lit a transcendently beautiful moorland scene of soft snowy hills nestling the little valley, and beyond the coruscating cohort of Northern stars and their strewn galaxies. Surely even in a Chieftain or Centurion, with its dreadful view of the road ahead, the driver could not fail to see our black car blocking the white lane in the snow ahead?

The drifting rhythm seemed gradually to be getting louder and I wound the window till only a tiny slit of exposure remained. Presently the cadence became more distinct, like the sound of a company of hobnail boots pounding a gravel parade ground. Then without warning an eerie pure white light suffused the sleeping cabin. I was now terrified. The rest slept on. The rats were frantic. I could not see its lamps. Then a host of little balls of feint russet light like the sheen of burnished bronze bouncing together with rhythm in the moonlight processed *through* the car. Sudden as a switch it became icy cold. It was beautiful and then it was gone. The rats simmered down, sucked some water and groomed themselves.

Some of the sleepers stirred. The Major shouted at me:-

"Ringstead, what the fuck do think you're doing? If you attempt another escape I will shoot you personally. There's two meters of snow, man. I thought you were intelligent"

"I am very sorry, Major Kask. It will not happen again, Madam. Sorry"

The woman tossed in her bag and faced the opposite direction, like a sulky wife in my bed.

A little later I felt a gentle tap on my arm. A gruff male voice with a very thick accent and hesitant English addressed me in a whisper:-

"English..., I also saw. When I was little boy I lived village avec grandpop. A Roman road pest through little town. Autoroute now. He told me...very serious...you know, spanky stern, clip round ear time. My English not good, I only soldier, I old man like you, understandi, Señor? Never sit by, he said, never sit by a Roman road enjoying the winter moonlight, ... not even when you big, ... avec your femme. Never, son. The Lost Legions they come by, you see them, you hear them, you sad, sad time ahead. Grandpop say 'we had war enough now'".

This reminded me of the lore of the Anglo-Saxons, who would never site a dwelling beside a Roman road, only at some half-mile away from one. They too believed that ghosts marched, and knew that bandits trafficked by night.

"Is this a Roman road", I asked deviously.

The man drew away across the bench.

"Oh, English, am I ass? I old soldier avec map".

And then in an astonishing display of academic English, perhaps remembered from a newspaper or a lecture, he said:-

"It presages war".

For some reason, which you may find silly, even naive, this witness convinced me that this was no hypnopompic hallucination, but some kind of genuine external event, supernormal as they say these days. And since that time it occurred to me that Kask's extreme reaction may have occurred from an instinctual need not to admit her experience, even to herself.

AGWELL
RINGSTEAD

CHAPTER THIRTEEN
CATCHPOOL GOES FISHING

The next thing I remember I was sitting on a hard wooden chair, apparently an old mess chair, in a brightly lit room. There was an advanced blue dusk and bare trees in the courtyard beyond the windows. On the other flanks of what could have been a small parade ground where functional military huts of a semi-permanent design and an obvious twentieth-century vintage.

The place was silent but for the susurration of the breeze and an annoying fifty-hertz hum from the fluorescent lights on the ceiling.

There was something ghostly, something archaic about my predicament, something that could have been of any time, something that reminded me compellingly of distant toddlerhood in the triste gloom of post-war England long, long, a long lifetime ago.

If anything, the bawled command of someone in the courtyard to unseen auditors intensified rather than humanised the silence. Although these gross features of the beyond were discernable, even to my poor eyesight, detail was frustratingly elusive because, I suppose, of the clear reflection of the desk before me and the room behind in the highly-polished glass of the window panes.

But as I roused I knew instinctually that it would be fatal to look about me or to show any other intelligent interest in my surroundings. I knew that invisible cameras and microphones invigilated every moment. So gingerly I clocked the several wooden doors behind and beside, set in the whitewashed wall like the portals of a Restoration theater. And in this chamber there was no token of modernity: No microcomputer, no idly-mislaid cellphone, no coffee paraphernalia. No touch of femininity or metrosexuality: No potted plant, no charity calendar, no sweetie tin or yellow or pink memo sticker. But atop the solid pre-war desk which could easily have been a hundred years old there were two Forties-vintage GP 332L hard-wired landline telephones one black and one red, a cheap crystal ashtray, a couple of Admiralty pencils, a pusser's foolscap notebook (yellowing and dog-eared) and inexplicably one of those old square protractors sometimes resorted to by field officers confused by their maps. At some time, some philistine had covered the desk top with a sheet of Formica and secured it at the edges with chrome clips.

I leaned forward and placed my head in my hands as I rested my elbows on my side of the desk, simulating a greater despair than I actual felt.

I do not know how long I affected this posture; maybe an hour, maybe less than a minute. At any event a burly man in his mid-sixties entered and sat in the seat opposite. I slowly leant back in my chair and looked at his face. It was as pasty as mine and even less distinguished. He had a stupid little Hitler moustache, but blond unlike its infamous archetype. He wore an expensive civilian bomber jacket above a non-descript white cashmere pullover. He had no insignia and in British military terms he was "wholly undressed".

"Good evening, I am Commander Lons Catchpool. Tell me about Freeman Fox". I wondered if I had heard right: Either his name or the question.

I was utterly astonished. I had not worked for the long-gone London consultants' partnership for nearly fifty years, before even my doctorate had been ratified, and had been employed in virtually the most junior post among the professional staff.

"Yes, Commander Catchpool. It was a Westminster civil engineering consultancy, bridge designers basically, though they had advertised under the heading of the Computation Research and Development division and I was hired as a..."

"Stop!" interrupted Catchpool.

I stared at the man. He stared at me. He seemed to keep staring for minutes, but of course it may only have been seconds.

Suddenly a gust rattled the windows in stormed surprise, the twigs outside quivered and what sounded like a discarded cardboard coffee cup skittered along a gutter outside.

He continued his stare in what I surmised was an intentional attempt to intimidate. He reminded me of one of my old bosses, not at Freeman Fox, who had been a Major in the Sally Army and was a bit of a psychopath.

Suddenly, he swiftly spanked the Formica top with his right hand. His wedding band, worn eccentrically on that appendage, made a nasty sharp click on the hard plastic and it seemed to my fancy that the humming lamp tubes missed a beat. The commander, if such he was, maintained his silent stare, but his over-controlled face flushed and anger and hate began to betray his eyes.

Then, very quietly and slowly he said:-

"We have tanks and mud, and bogs where bodies have vanished for a thousand years, Señor, and I am not a man to take the piss out of, you cunt". That last gratuity was spat with such venom I fully expected violence there and then.

Now I really was scared. My head took on the involuntary shaking and dipping that distresses it during violent altercations, and my hands and body had begun to tremble.

His moustache now took on the hue of a nicotinic toothbrush bristling upon the surface of a prize tomato. He took out from his pocket an old-fashioned sharkskin case and removed an expensive-looking corona which incongruously he lit with a cheap disposable lighter. I stopped smoking decades ago but somehow enjoyed the soothing aroma that settled me a little. I was, however, not invited to share a smoke.

At length I said:-

"Commander Catchpool, would it help if I told you how I came to be here?"

"Go on", he replied cautiously in the idiom of another of the hated bosses of my past, the boss of the boss who stared out of the Sally Army.

"I trained as a geologist. I never practiced as one, but knowing my interest in matters of recondite science, Emeritus Professor Ernest Agwell of the Forester Club and Durham University drew my attention to a controversy that had arisen about the nature and origin of mineral precipitation in certain British springs...."

"Oh, do shut up", interrupted Catchpool with a remarkable if discourteous gentility.

Catchpool took out an expensive silver pencil, a Yard-O-Led®. It was chased with a manly Classical pattern.

He placed it very carefully upon the Formica desktop, perpendicular to the long sides, pointing straight at where my thymus had once been.

He looked along the pencil, as if sighting a rifle, until he had the point, the finial and his right eye co-linear.

He closed his left eye. He slightly adjusted his head to re-establish coincidence.

Then he closed his right eye and opened his left.

He would have perceived a slight shift in the instrument's background and a slight rotation of its azimuth. At least if his eyesight was aligned. My eyesight is not aligned. If I attempted the experiment I would merely get double-vision.

Then Catchpool said:-

"Tell me about parallax"

I instantaneously if subconsciously elected to pitch my little lecture as I would to the youngest classes of college students.

"Most certainly, Sir" I commenced.

"Parallax is an elementary optico-geometrical effect of great utility in the sciences and in medical and military procedures. During your brief experiment just now you saw how a potentially-measurable angular displacement might assist the estimation of objects' distances with appropriate calibrations. In 1676 Felix Roemer used this effect in relation to the four moons of Saturn in order to estimate the speed of light and to establish that light's celerity was finite."

"Later astronomers used the effect habitually to measure stellar distances etcetera. Dispensing opticians used it and the refractive properties of glass to design eye-glasses and opera glasses. In summary, scientific and technical applications were manifold."

"Early in the last century a young Swiss geologist and theoretical electrician called Albert Einstein asserted that mass differentials bend light, and in particular that the stars and the Sun diffracted light at their edges in an infinitesimal but measurable way."

"The great German professors and the other high authorities of European Science laughed at the uppity young Jew and said:-

"That's just Parallax!"

Catchpool's fat countenance seemed to turn like litmus from red to purple whilst I watched.

He said nothing. He rose.

He took a plain officer's ebony baton from one of the desk draws and I "knew" at once that he was going to break my head with it.

Instead Catchpool rose and smote the edge of the desk with such a speed and force that I could not see the rod's arc. The baton split in half and a fast-rotating fragment spun into one of the ceiling's metal luminaires. The fitment swung biliously as the fluorescent strip flickered and died.

A length of the Formica edge broke with a crack and a chrome bracket dove floorward and made a tinny clatter on the concrete.

Catchpool just stood there like a thwarted magician holding his splintered wand.

At length, Catchpool cooled down and resumed his seat.

"It was not Felix: It was Ole" he corrected, with surprising pedantry.

"And it was not Saturn: It was Jupiter".

"I do beg your pardon, Commander Catchpool. You are entirely correct, Sir. Sorry" I grovelled.

I could not remember whether he was right or not, and of course I cared even less.

"Wait here", he added, perhaps a little redundantly, as he rose impatiently from his seat and strode from the room, streaming cigar smoke and all.

I was still enjoying the fragrance of the cigar some minutes later, when Catchpool resumed his seat bearing a yellow sheet of stiff A4. Somehow it subconsciously registered that this was modern paper, but my overwhelming sensation at the time was a remarkable sense of personal triumph I suppose compounded of stress-fatigue and a resigned contempt for my interlocutor and all he stood for.

Catchpool held the sheet on a slope before his face as he leant his elbows on the desk in front of me.

Catchpool resumed the silent treatment, affecting closely to study the contents of the A4 sheet, and repeatedly flicking his gaze from it to my eyes with a look on his cooling visage something between hauteur and blimpish disapproval.

At length Catchpool observed:-

"It says here that you were born in a caravan in the corner of a farmer's field on the Cardurnock Peninsula".

I relaxed into bliss which of course I could not express, because I now knew that whatever painful fate awaited me it would not be because I was mistaken for an Argentine spy or saboteur.

"That is not my information", I replied softly, "but I shall not dispute your finding".

Catchpool continued to flick his eyes up and down portentously.

I could not of course read the paper or even see its printed surface, but in the reflection that usually manifested in the polished window, continuously enhanced by the nightfall, I perceived what appeared to be a photograph of a well-beaked wading bird, possibly a curlew or a knott, and at the bottom of the sheet of paper was another picture which appeared to me to be a panoramic shorescape or at least a bluish stripe above a yellow-tawny one. The actual text seemed to be divided into two columns and at the top of the sheet, impossible to read in reverse, was a bold, underlined and centered heading whose word-lengths could have been consistent with the phrase "Northumberland Wildlife Trust".

I had to be careful not to stare fixedly at the window pane behind his shoulder.

Catchpool continued with his histrionics.

"Tell me, Professor Bourbaki, how far are we from Carlisle?"

"If we are where I think we are then I would say sixty miles?" I offered tentatively.

"And where do you think we are, Don Nicolas?"

"Otterburn Camp"

"We are at Spadeadam, and 19.7 miles from Carlisle, Señor. Otterburn Camp is 64.5 miles from Carlisle. And it is pronounced Spad-ede-am, not Spade-adam. You are on the wrong Roman road!"

"Sorry, I was not aware I had mentioned Spadeadam", I shrugged.

I do not know even now what Catchpool thought he was doing or what he intended to achieve, but I was starting to enjoy myself, and that of course was most dangerous.

Another indeterminate episode of this stupid acting ensued.

Presently I said "Commander, do you mind if I visit the lavatory, Sir"

Catchpool laid the sheet in a draw face down, rose and escorted me to one of those peripheral doors. He opened the door and a light came on automatically to reveal an old-fashioned impulse pan with a high-level cistern. Anomalously, a modern washbasin was also provided. Catchpool locked me in from the outside.

I had some difficulty and it was minutes before I knocked on the door to return to the interrogation room. The patient Catchpool was standing outwith and ushered me back to my station.

"Commander, I am still rather nervous", I simpered "Please may I have one of your fine cigars, Sir" I begged. Catchpool appeared to enjoy my faux submission and his plenteous face briefly broke to a smile. He handed me a smoke and shoved the lighter across the table.

I lit the known carcinogen and never enjoyed a smoke as I enjoyed that smoke, more even than the stolen smokes of boyhood.

Catchpool sat back in his chair, in real or affected relaxation, I could not say which, and flicked his ash onto the concrete floor.

"It said in my brief that your mother was reputed the camp whore", observed Catchpool with casual equanimity.

"My Late Mother was a Petty Officer RN" I replied.

Catchpool paused.

Then he smugly dispensed "An Englishman would have known that such a postnominal was only permitted to commissioned officers of the king". He said this with that air universal among old men who overestimate their acuity, or think that their percipience solves all dilemmas and dispels all doubt forever. It is the doctrine of Masons, Communists or others of the terminally bigoted.

Catchpool seemed to have expected a reply.

"Is that not the case, Professor?" The man leaned forward with a smile. I was going to write "the toadish man" but of course toads are honorable and I am not about to libel they who cannot sue.

When this sordid interview began, three minutes ago? three days ago? Catchpool seemed to me to be simulating a local accent, always very difficult in Geordie land, and never advisable.

Now the mask was slipping it seemed somehow to betray an Old Carthusian if I've got that right. The only Old Carthusian I knowingly heard often was Miss Cathy Newman, the journalist, and of course she was only briefly at the school and was a soprano.

"She was a deserter, and your father was a coward and a traitor"

"Those are your words", I replied coldly.

Catchpool rose from his chair and left the room. Moments later he returned and sat once more in his chair. His cigar had gone out and he reclaimed his lighter to re-ignite.

His color had gone and he seemed to relax, perhaps genuinely. He was another serviceperson who seemed to be waiting for something: Perhaps superior orders, perhaps a tactical advantage too arcane for lay observance, perhaps a breath of wind, perhaps the Return of The Eagles of the Ninth. Perhaps he thought, workmanlike, that he had just done his job and was now simply waiting for the clock to turn seven. Perhaps, with the patience of the seasoned professional, he was only awaiting the enemy capitulation.

My cigar, too, had gone out, but I too enjoyed a sense of victory and was becoming sanguine of survival.

"Oh, sorry Commander Catchpool. I forgot something" I said.

Catchpool leaned forward, all ears.

In a new act of the surreal Aitamah Kask entered the room without knocking bringing a tray of drinks and biscuits like a stewardess. "My, you two look like real clubmen!" she observed with matronly aplomb as she served Catchpool a large frothy cappuccino and helped me to an equal measure of hot chocolate. She set a mound of luscious chocolate biscuits between us, and it morbidly occurred to me that this might be the Prisoner's

Last Meal or else a witches' eucharist. Considerately, she also laid before me a fresh, cold syringe of Humalog 25 and couple of needles.

"Dolly wants to see you", said the Major to Catchpool with I thought not mere familiarity, but a mixture of confidentiality and contempt. She walked out briskly, leaving the refreshments.

"There's something in this drink" I remarked to Catchpool.

"Whiskey" he replied.

"No, something else"

"Xylocaine, I suppose, or whatever they bloody use these days"

"Are you trying to poison me, Catchpool?" I answered.

"Hell no: I don't like you enough. Tell me about Condor", said Catchpool.

This caught me seriously off-guard. Of course I could have told him a lot about Condor, and American attempts to thwart it, but I knew that even if I hinted that I might conceivably have heard of it, then I would not leave the room alive.

I shifted nervously in my chair, spilling a little chocolate.

"Why did you shift nervously in your chair?" queried Catchpool.

"Sorry, I don't know", I lied, "I am a lot on edge, and this chair is beginning to hurt my backside now. I suppose the mention of the Nazi regiment and the thought of its attributed atrocities gave me the wobbles".

It seemed that Catchpool was not overly excited though I tried to be careful not to notice whether he was curious or worse.

"That point about my late mother", I resumed with blatant deviousness, trying to discuss anything other than Condor, Argentina or the Southern Oceans.

"Yes?" said Catchpool with a hint of boredom.

"She was a keen bird-watcher" I replied.

There was no immediate nibble at the float.

"Is Hitler still in Bariloche?" asked Catchpool.

I had no idea and did not know where or possibly what Bariloche was.

"If Hitler is still alive he must be pushing one hundred and fifty" I observed.

"Not impossible with the right medics" asserted my interrogator.

"I appreciate how stressful it is for you, Bourbaki, or whoever you are" tacked the Commander, leaning over the desk to re-light my cigar "I am no chicken myself and I want rid of this shit".

Notwithstanding his earlier profanity I thought it odd that a man of Catchpool's age and class would choose that expression.

"Look, I'm sorry about the drugs old man, but you really were nervous, very understandably. And I want a full and frank discussion as they used to say in our day".

It seemed there was no limit to this man's mendacity and duplicity. As I said, it was difficult to define his motivation or even to whom he was loyal, if anyone. I began to yearn for my gentle companions at Point Glory, hardly friends of course, but loyal and loving to their simple comrades, especially the true rats among them. Good companions in a storm, as ready to cuddle you warm as to put a bullet in your brain.

Suddenly there was a muffled explosion somewhere outside, and a broad streak of fire stormed skywards into the night. The glass panes vibrated but did not shatter and a slab of biscuit scree slid from Mount Teatime.

"What in fuck's name was that?" I exclaimed in genuine surprise, the more so as the wilderness silence resumed and, in the smogless skies of Northumberland, or was it Cumberland? the sparkling stars resumed their freezing watch as the vapor drifted away from a cloudless firmament. It occurred to me that Catchpool may have been truthful about Spadeadam, for whatever devious reason. Or maybe the fireworks had been laid on for my entertainment. But silence after this event was not total: In some distant forest canopy a parliament of rooks convened a raucous complaint and I took this as some sort of scholastic proof that I had not hallucinated.

"That is nothing, and does not concern us" assured Catchpool.

"Finbarr Larne"

I pretended to think he was thinking aloud and continued assiduously to munch and swig my funny cocoa.

"Finbarr Larne", he repeated, louder.

"What?" I replied, as uninterestedly as I might.

"The Anglo-American dingle-dongle or whatever it is".

"Sorry, you have me at a disadvantage, Catchpool".

I needed to change the subject, and fast. Larne was long dead but he had sons at large, one probably on UK territory.

"Oh, Commander Catchpool, I forgot to mention. I think it is the smoke and the xylocaine. I can take my whiskey".

"Yes?"

Catchpool leaned forward on his elbows in what appeared to be becoming a Pavlovian response.

"Perhaps I am just getting senile. It is irrelevant, come to think of it" I dallied.

"No, go on, Coronel Mayor"

"It is something about the activities of my Late Mother", I declared.

Then I was startled by Catchpool's sudden and inexplicable rise from his chair as if I had mentioned The Queen. He stepped aside and picked up his chair and, holding it by the varnished front seat strut with his left hand and the wooden chair back rods with his right hand he proceeded to pump the thing up and down in an almost onanistic way. I did not know what to make of this performance. I sat there fascinated. As the chair's five loose castors met the concrete of the floor there was a sickening castanet-like report.

Catchpool had colored again, and as he bowed and dipped about this business I studied his jowly profile, his Bibendum neck and his slightly parted lips and intent expression. There was something of the well-fed toddler lad about him, more than a little infantile, in a slightly autistic sort of way I suppose.

"Go on. Now we're getting somewhere. Now we're getting somewhere. After all this Freeman Fox bollocks I can tell we are reaching the heart of the matter. The real nitty-gritty of this".

Then Catchpool said "When was it you decided to spy for the Argentines. Was that at Freeman Fox with the nancy boys". I mentally breathed a sigh of relief. I was back in command. Catchpool had passed me the baton.

"Commander", I commenced, "I was only at Freeman Fox fifteen months, nearly fifty years ago, and I was the most junior employee, except for the post-room staff. I did not encounter any 'nancy boys'. I was a FORTRAN programmer, but I was often told off to take packages to other firms in Westminster or the City, and I enjoyed that. Many of my colleagues were married men and I married myself in their service".

"You married yourself? Was that legal in 1980"

"No, Sir" I explained carefully, "I married a woman. Not a Fox woman, Sir"

"Oh, I see"

"Yes, Commander Catchpool"

"You mentioned Parallax to one of them"

This was getting stupid.

"Yes, Sir" I responded, "I was having a difference of opinion with one of the girls about the weight of a parcel for postal dispatch. She maintained that it was 503 grams and I thought it was 498. In those days the cost was significant and I suppose differed across 500 grams. She said 'no, look, that reads 503'. It was one of those old-fashioned spring contraptions, circular with an enclosed mechanism and a sweeping brass pointer. That hand stood a good five millimeters proud of the calibrated dial. I said to the young woman 'That's just parallax'".

"Bourbaki, there is no fathom to the depth of your stupidity, or your treachery".

I did not comment.

"Miss Semple thought you were Hilda's confidential messenger because she often glimpsed you vanishing in the direction of Whitehall with that pompous little absolite case you used to sport. She ran for a taxi as hard as she could. She could have no idea you were tipping Featherstonehaugh at the FO. There were none in Tothill Street but as she ran into Petty France, she took off her heels and discarded them, running ahead on bleeding feet. She knew there were four minutes and eight seconds warning but rather than take refuge in the tube or a basement she sprinted along till she reached London Centre. As you know it was in Petty France in those days. Before she could reach the switch room and scramble A-force, a drunk driver rammed her in the arse and her cranium split on the kerb. She died on the spot in a fountain of blood. I saw it. Mathews came in and said it was another false alarm, and everyone stand down. You should have been shot on the spot".

"I don't know what to say Commander, but there must have been something seriously wrong with your protocols in those days. I thought the young woman lit out for a better job. You should remember that CRD was a commercial firm and we were not privy to your codes and tried to keep that sort of thing at arm's length. I am very sorry, Commander, but the world has moved on and so must we".

"Yes, you money-grubbing bastards are always moving on, leaving honest patriots to pick up the pieces".

"Before you ask, Catchpool" I replied with calculated insolence "I have no idea who Fanshaw or Mathews are or were and though I thought MI6 was probably in Petty France or at least some bloody agency was I did not care and did not want to know. When I left the premises it was nearly always to taxi or more often tube magnetic tapes to a mainframe computation agency in Leonard Street, Shoreditch, because our machine was too small. I did not ask what was on the tapes and I did not wish to know, but I assumed that they related to transportation network planning, and that was as much as I was paid for. Semple died because you and your mates could not and had no inclination to do your jobs, and you are as incompetent now as you were then, and my country, yes my country, will never prosper as long as you and your cavalier class are in charge".

Catchpool had been holding his chair off the floor, but he settled it back carefully behind his desk. Then he proceeded somehow to attempt to align two of the foot castors with the edge of the desk right pedestal's inner margin. The desk had a modesty panel. I could not see exactly what he was trying to accomplish. I did not especially want to look.

I am not psychiatrically-trained but it seemed to me that this behaviour went beyond the neurotic and trespassed the ground of clinical psychosis.

I said "Can I help you with that, Sir?"

Catchpool gave an exasperated sigh, slammed the chair in the floor ill-temperedly, picked the thing up again and carried it over to my left a good four meters from where we had been sitting. I suppose if I had not realised that we both were under continuous recorded invigilation, than I would have been tempted to determine if he had a concealed pistol, on his person or in the desk; to relieve him of same; and attempt a run for it. Of course, that would have been quite stupid, but this was my pattern of critical thought at that juncture.

Catchpool just stood there, open-mouthed, cradling his chair.

In this Dadaesque clinch I suddenly clocked that just behind him on the whitewashed wall was one of those white sheet-steel Rowntree's Kit-Kat dispensing machines of the sort you used to get in student canteens and was marked with a big bold "6^{D}" sign.

"Do you think there are any chocolate biscuits in that?" I asked.

"What?"

"Aren't ours good enough for you?" queried the Commander "Wouldn't they be a bit stale?"

"Got a tanner?" I asked.

Catchpool set his chair down at that spot and marched to his desk. He started to rummage through the draws, exposing the back of his neck to me. "Don't try anything stupid" I counselled myself in my drugged and very severely tempted state.

"Tell me, Lons, if I may call you that. I am Kenny. Tell me, did they bully you at Charterhouse?"

"Don't try any of that balls on me, you arse-fucking little traitor. Do I seem like a man who can be bullied?"

"There is no need to be rude, Lons"

Catchpool retreated to his chair before the vending machine and cradled it again, this time sort of defensively I thought, as a child, woken by a nightmare, might have cuddled his teddy-bear.

Just at that psychological moment a man in steward's whites marched in without knock or ceremony, but when Catchpool turned to face him directly he saluted very smartly and said:-

"It has turned 2015 hours, Commander Catchpool, shall I take the cups and trays, Sir. Would you like anything else, Sir. What about Dr Ringstead, Sir. Perhaps something a little stronger given the hour, gentlemen?"

"Doctor Who? No, I bloody wouldn't" snapped the Commander.

I noted the three stripes on the man's arm, and the oak leaves and acorns on his collar.

"Could I have a stiff bourbon, please, Purser, and a treble Armagnac for the Commander".

I put a twenty-dollar bill on the tray.

"You can have several for that, Sir!" the Chief Steward answered breezily, with a smile. "No excise here!"

"Treat the mess, and have one yourself" I said.

"Thanks a million, Sir. We'll make a weekend of it!"

CHAPTER FOURTEEN
DUTCH COMFORT

A little while later the steward returned with our drinks. Not to be shamed, Catchpool gave him a fiver. I suppose he still thought a pound was four dollars, I could not resist telling myself.

Then a most curious figure abruptly breezed in, and parked himself standing to my right about a meter or more to the left of the now sitting Catchpool. The new man must have been over seventy-five, lean and tanned, but dressed in deciduous woodland camouflage combat fatigues. There were no insignia. I took an instant dislike to him, as I had to Bourbaki, and for much the same reasons. This person also had that ingratiating grin and that swaggering bonhomie about him of the kind sometimes affected by Scots and Continentals, especially when they do not like you.

He stepped forward towards me proffering his hand. I rose and shook it:-

"Hello, Freeman Fox man!" he bawled at me with false bravado "and how is Freeman Fox man this fine and balmy vernal vespertide?" he added sarcastically.

I resumed my seat.

"I am very well, thank you Sir" I replied.

"Good. Excellent. I am Admiral Piet Van der Trump of Dutch Naval Intelligence. We want to talk to you about my favorite subject, and I know one of yours too. Antarctica!"

"All my friends call me Pete"

"I am Kenny Ringstead" I replied

"We know"

Who's "We" I wondered.

Pete took something from his pocket, and threw it spinning into my crotch.

"What is it, Kenny?"

"It's a geochemical water sampling tube" I stated

The introductory smirk was vanishing little by little from the confessed spy's face.

"Give it to the Commander", he ordered.

I picked it out of my lap and placed it on the cleared desk in front of Catchpool.

"Admiral Van der Trump" I said formally "On this mission, are you representing NATO or the European Defence Force?"

"Those are neither exclusive nor preclusive categories as you are well aware, Dr Ringstead".

I was not sure that this was a valid statement of either logic or English grammar, but I thought I understood what he meant. It reminded me of a very high jest I had once heard at a Strathclyde University lecture, one dark wet evening in the Glasgow of long ago. Both my Father and Ian Barr were in attendance. The speaker referred to something the nature of which I have long forgotten but would have related to stream hydraulics. Some wit in the audience asked, "Do you say that in the nominative or the vocative, Professor". The whole theater burst into laughter.

I was not otherwise answered.

Pete turned his face fully to the sitting Commander with a full scowl.

"Take it apart, Danny"

I did so hope that Daniel was not his birth name, or my days were done, though like the Prophet of old I hoped that whatever torments or tribulations lay ahead I should endure to a Greater resolution.

Lons Catchpool had been sitting dejectedly with his head bowed and hands visibly trembling even though he rested both arms on the desk surface. He was obviously in no mood, nor perhaps condition, to effect analysis.

"Bu, ... , But Dolly" the Commander stammered "it might be charged with azide or nerve agent"

Pete leant over and snatched the thing from the desk, and then brutally tore off the gaffer tape seal. He threw the tube back onto the table and said to Lons:-

"Pull it apart"

There was hate and menace in the command.

I now realised, vain Fallen man mortal that I am, that this was not about me. This was about much bigger problems, and the settling of old scores, clearing the decks of dead wood, and perhaps the preparations for Armageddon.

Lons started to cry

"Please, Dolly, we'll all die"

"How old are you? How many fine men and women have you killed in the prime of youth? Ringstead isn't scared. I'm not scared. Even the fucking rats aren't scared. Who has a right to be?"

I wasn't scared it was true. I was beside myself with terror. I knew the dark device would not blow my face off, or infect it. But there was no knowing what these two clowns might do, or order.

Pete took out a pistol. He did not point it at me.

"Pull it apart"

Pete turned his head to me and sneered:-

"British Intelligence. Not very intelligent as they say in the old films".

Lons was still snivelling.

Tentatively, slowly, unsteadily he grasped the terminal flanges and gave a sudden two-handed tug.

With a load pop of broken vacuum three sodden pyramidal tea bags plopped onto the Formica.

Van der Trump dissolved into a storm of demoniacal laughter. He lowered his weapon, unwisely I thought, turned around, and beat one of the window panes with the butt of his pistol. The glass shattered.

Then he turned back to me his face red with glee, his nose running with mucilaginous discharge, and tears streaming down his cheeks.

Lons was also weeping uncontrollably.

He seemed to be a quivering wreck of a man.

"Now. Freeman Fox man. Christmas has come two months early for Freeman Fox man. Here we go *Homo Vulpensis*, we will have a cracker of a Christmas!"

Van Der Trump removed a second sample tube from his pocket. Either the tape had been stripped from the junction, or this was an apparently identical device, not of my manufacture. Keeping hold of one of the terminal flanges himself, Pete offered me the other.

I took it in hand. This device was distinctly heavier than the last. I pulled briskly and threw my end to the floor.

A metallic impact sound coincided with the hollow, plastic pipe clatter. I looked down and saw one of my rolled-up iron plates.

Lons jumped in his chair.

"What's that Kenny" Pete asked casually.

"It's a high-purity iron plate of a type supplied to chemical analysts and assayers", I said, unaccountably promoting the credentials of my substrate.

He picked it up and polished away a thin film of limonite that had formed during its brief submersion.

Pete threw it on the desk and said:-

"Hear that, Danny? It's O point eight millimeter iron foil, ANALAR®"

I was not sure Lons any longer understood or cared.

"Danny, your duties are now surplus to requirements, old man" said the Dutch Admiral, if indeed he was. Certainly it was a (British) Royal Navy form, but of a far remote idiom, pre-Fifties.

Van Der Trump ostentatiously pushed a button concealed under the desk, if indeed the button was there, and the "purser" strode in, acorns and all.

The NCO put a brotherly arm around the Commander's shoulder and helped him from his chair, as he offered him a Kleenex®.

"Come on, Sir. Cheer up, Sir. We don't want the troops to see you like this, Sir. Bad for morale. There all sorts of rumours, Sir. Would you like a snort, Sir?"

As he gently led Catchpool away, like the broken geriatric that he was, the "purser" turned to Van der Trump and said "Tea and cake, Sir? And what about The Prof, Sir? Shall I bring the drinks trolley, Sir?"

Van Der Trump stiffened into a pompous upper-deck posture and replied:-

"No thank you, Parker, that will be all for now".

Van Der Trump sat in Catchpool's chair opposite me. He was expressionless but pre-occupied and did not seem to know or care that I was still sitting opposite him. He took a small mobile telephone out of his inner pocket and dialling a number selected from its memory said what sounded like "telepromp-doudle-bol-o-bont-vent-seed" and then switched off without awaiting reply.

Then he opened the desk draw and I wondered if I was going to be treated to another display of littoral bird-life.

Instead Pete removed two seemingly-identical printed yellow sheets of A4 from the draw, and placing one before me said:-

"I want you to read that through whilst I read mine. It is important to get our stories straight, and know exactly how we will handle the civil authorities if it comes to that. If you agree to the terms you shall sign both documents, which are identical, with the same style. I will retain one copy. No clause may be added or removed. You may ask points of clarification".

We took our time despite the advanced hour.

Six or seven of the brief clauses grabbed my attention:-

(a)   I have not been tortured or otherwise mis-treated, my medical needs have been supplied, and I have had timely and adequate food and drink. I have been treated with courtesy and respect by all authority and its delegates.

(c)   I have not suborned nor have I ever intended to suborn any serviceperson, nor have I intended or executed any act of espionage, sabotage or sedition in any state or territory.

(d)   I am a civilian. I have discharged my contract to the entire satisfaction of NATO Forces and its agents and allies meantime. In consideration I have received the sum of US$25000 in regard to services and supplies, in full and entire discharge of mutual financial obligations. I may request equivalent payment, in whole or in part in Sterling, Euros or Gold, subject to exchange differentials or controls. The Officer Commanding in Locus is not obliged to secure such conversions. All sums shall be rendered to the Contractor by 30 November 2028.

(e)   I agree that any report, or purported report or disquisition, or communication of kind, or lecture, film or similar production, or private discourse, said to have arisen from events near Otterburn or Spadeadam or anywhere in October or Fall 2027 or sometime, or the environmental properties of the same or similar places, or of alleged military or security proceedings, is or are entirely a work of literary fiction and intended for purposes of serious entertainment or secular or religious instruction only. I may present the whole or part of any such story on my authorised website or in literary or private media, but not on "social media" or with any agent of the press or broadcasting. Such alleged events may not be editorially-traduced or vulgarised in popular "conspiracy theory" productions or third-party literature.

(g)   Translations into languages not Standard British or American English must be approved by The Minister of Culture of the Kingdom of the Netherlands.

(i)   Any dispute arising regarding the validity of this Notice, or part of this Notice, must be referred at once to the nearest Embassy of the Kingdom of the Netherlands.

"This seems fair" I said to Van Der Trump.

"May I ask two or three points of clarification", I said.

"By all means, Kenny"

"First the very mundane. How am I going to get out of here?"

"You can pick up your bags and walk out now if you really want to, but there is further snow forecast, and the buses are terrible. I anticipated several questions or even perplexities and I have planned for us to grab a few hours' kip, and leave in daylight. I have ordered an Allied driver to put your kit in the back of my old Continental, sans your sample tubes of course, and at 1030 drive us to Newcastle Station, where you could hopefully catch something, and hopefully not COVID!"

Pete giggled at his own comedy and looked at my eyes as if for expert approval.

"Thank you, Pete. That is very good of you. I gratefully accept your offer"

"I won't be able to linger. I've got a ferry to catch"

"Thanks, Pete. Can I ask something about Clause (a)"

"Fire away"

"Was I drugged at any point during custody?"

"I am sorry, Kenny, really I am. But you were very understandably very scared:- Which is no reflection on your courage or resolution in any way. We have seen enough of both. I asked Professor Kask to give you a small shot of lidocaine, first in the car whilst you slept and again in your cocoa. She is a registered pharmacist both in Europe and the UK and a perfectly genuine Estonian army officer and animal handler. She is not involved in any Circus nonsense".

This was the first time I had heard that term outside of the pages of Le Carré (the late David John Moore Cornwell).

"We had ascertained that you were a seventy-five year old diabetic myasthenial who had had three heart attacks and a triple by-pass. The very last thing we wanted was a corpse on our hands. They are very difficult to explain. Remember Kelly?"

Yes, I did. With a chill of my blood.

"Anent courtesy and respect, Catchpool called me a 'cunt' and an 'arse-fucking little traitor'. I am a heterosexual loyal Briton, and I hope a clever one".

Van der Trump giggled dismissively

"Of course you are Kenny, all of those things" he replied ambiguously.

"Catchpool was also most insulting about my parents. He called my Late Mother a 'reputed camp whore' and my Father a 'coward and traitor'"

Van Der Trump sobered up.

"Shall I make him apologise"

"No. I do not want an apology unless it is heartfelt. It would dishonor us all, as if there is not enough dishonor in the world".

"Quite right, Kenny. Let's move on"

"Can you fill me in about 'Parallax', Pete"

The man seemed suddenly troubled.

"Oh, Kenny" he sighed "this is known world-wide in the trade as The Semple Affair or *L'affaire Semple*. It is as notorious amongst the community as Skripal among the news-viewing public".

"I've never heard of it"

"No of course not" Pete agreed

"Cast your mind back to the Seventies and Eighties of last century"

I could do as bidden, too easily and too well.

"Intelligence was an analog industry in an increasingly digital world"

"In MI6 the young turks were eager to get with it and embrace the new dawn of informatic and data-driven espionage: Narcolalia as it came to be known. They had little taste for the tedium and soil of plodding through the cold, literal or otherwise: Hilarity or Miranda as it variously was called. Meanwhile the 'old guard' and especially 'The Board' of senior spies, were literary men, usually classicists, who were comfortable with wordy ways"

"Meantime, Hilda and Joseph were dead keen on anything public sector being sold-off or floated on the Stock Exchange. Hilda was most suspicious of anything which looked or smelt 'Circus'. She wanted 'suitable' private outfits to bid for Government work".

"Sometime around 1957 the Triple-Trigger System was invented, or at least introduced to spying circles. This was supposed to be a fool-proof way of initiating crisis responses and in particular nuclear retaliations. Suez had accelerated adoption, and, being a kind of literary and mathematical hybrid process Triple-Trigger was a compromise system acceptable and accessible to both the human intelligence tendency and the increasing numbers of technicians. The theory of the thing was that you had three lists each of two thousand English words, giving therefore six thousand different words. Technical or other unfamiliar words were to be favored but nothing so obscure as to be impossible of recollection. Clerks were tasked with selecting three words from each list, by perforce different words, to serve as this month's passcode for field operatives to use. On the last day of each calendar month all the operatives world-wide who strictly needed to know were encryptedly-wired with this month's code, which was intended for verbal identification and instruction only. Obviously, it had to be 'impossible' for the triple to arise in the normal course of conversation".

"As Kenny has no doubt already discerned there are eight billion different possible combinations of these three word choices. According to the doctrine of classical British Goodenough Theory, an accident with a probability of occurring on one occasion in very nearly eight milliard is an accident impossible of commission. But as Kenny discovered long ago, this is Britain and Sod's Law applies at all times."

"The Americans hated this system from the outset, and many agencies, especially the French and the French-influenced refused flatly to have any participation in it. The Israelis naturally pointed out the theoretical limitations of the method and pressed for something mathematically more rigorous. Of course, messaging is almost wholly cybernetic today and the Duel-Key System is used both in diplomacy and commerce".

"Fatally, the method depended upon the ever-vulnerable human linkage. The method could only be made to work, sort of, where couriers were physically capable of running or driving from source to sink before the action they were to initiate became irrelevant or impossible. For example, the British had four minutes maximum of warning between a Russian thermonuclear ICBM being detected at Fylingdales and the thing actually detonating over London. In the meantime, the Prime Minister was supposed to decide upon counterstrike or not as his or her fiat; tell a messenger; and he or she run, scoot or taxi to the Switch Room at London Centre where the switches would be thrown to get A-force safely skyward. To pre-empt fraud or sabotage, the messenger would tell the driver (if any) the magic three word formula and the three words would serve again to validate the order to the Switch Room. After that, the code was of course useless, one way or the other".

"This could just about be practical where all the relevant Agencies were within half-a-mile of one another, as in Victoria-cum-Whitehall, but was quite meaningless in places like Washington, Buenos Aires or Wellington, to choose capitals at random: Even places where there was 16 minutes strike warning".

"I remember, Kenny, attending a CIA seminar at Langley in I think 1982 just after the Falklands when the speaker was referring to the Callaghan initiatives of 1978. Callaghan had taken a team of aides to Buenos Aires to try and explore the possibility of making an Anglo-Argentine condominium of the Falklands. The British were experienced in imperial politics generally and condominium in particular. The junta hated the very concept, but the British, always with an eye to the dollar, saw nothing especially sordid or dishonorable in such an expedient. Neither did the junta see anything especially sordid or dishonorable in stealing another man's land or patrimony, and in any case they did not want the Falklands. They wanted the Falklands Islands Dependencies and their millions of square kilometres of mineral and marine resources. After a hot and humid morning of negotiations in Spanish that got nowhere a young man called Freeborn went into a nearby air-conditioned bar-restaurant for a cold beer and took a seat by the window in case colleagues or even adversaries happened to pass and he could beckon them in. It was evidently a very costly joint but Freeborn was on expenses. The triple today was "Homer Apse Maud". Presently a couple of middle-aged female friends (strangers to Freeborn) happened along and studied the menu in the window, cheerfully pointing out to each other dishes they might order inside. To Freeborn there was something slightly odd about this couple. They looked and were dressed in cashmere and other slightly out-of-fashion smedleywear and somehow looked more British than Argentine. Freeborn hurried outside and accosted the ladies with a smile. There was much pleasantry visible through the window, and although the ladies almost certainly thought he was the manager or head waiter they went in and took a window seat next to his. Freeborn resumed his study of the street outside, whilst listening to the ladies' private chatter. They spoke a kind of patois of Spanish, Italian and English. Freeborn was fluent in all three. Suddenly one of the women said "Homer asked Maud" before pattering on in Italian. Was it "asked" or was it "Apse"? Freeborn was not sure, but he suspected an Argentine surprise strike was being betrayed. He must alert Centre. He went to his car parked outside and the driver let him in. Freeborn took the "satellite" telephone, and dialled London Centre. It is not known what he said to the duty officer or whoever he had at the other end but presumably it was "Freeborn, Rosio: Homer Apse Maud". For one thing, the satellite was not overhead, so the Argentine telecom firm (thought to be the American ATT) automatically routed the call through the cable to Ascension. But that had been savaged by a shark (no, really) and was awaiting repair, so the thick-film router in the ATT apparatus at Buenos Aires automatically defaulted to an obsolete Strowger array routing through Rosario (where, incidentally, the Argentines intercepted it, and scrambled air defence). But by the time the automatic analog technology had routed the call to its own satisfaction eight minutes had gone by."

"Satisfied at last that the message was received and understood Freeborn returned to his seat in the lounge bar and triumphantly reported to the astonished ladies 'Homer Apse Maud: RAU". The hubbub in the restaurant briefly stilled and then normal conversation resumed".

"Two or three minutes later a slim man in a well-tailored gray suit..."

"Secret police", I interjected, as excited as a schoolboy.

Pete continued his narrative, "A slim man in a well-tailored gray suit slid of one of the stools at the bar, went over to Freeborn, and gently tapping him on the upper arm, said a few words. The two men left the premises and entered Freeborn's car. Freeborn, mystery man, driver, car and all vanished from history".

"The mystery man turned out to be the Russian Trade Attaché"

"I suppose Lami Dozo dropped them in the sea" I speculated.

"Anyway, how do we know all this?"

"A yank was sitting three tables back toward the eating area, and was following developments closely".

"CIA?"

"No. Navy"

"Fancy a snifter?" said Pete

"Don't mind if I do"

"Can I have that excellent cocoa as well, preferably without the lidocaine this time"

"'Course you can"

"You can have the lidocaine as well if you want it, or even coke, we're not prudes in Holland"

"No, I'll give that a miss, I think, cheers Pete"

Parker entered, this time without any pretence or theatrics. The muted sound of a late-night television football match drifted in as Parker came through the door.

"Snifter time then, gents. Feyenoord v Arsenal, Dr Ringstead, Sir. Want to know the score?"

"No thanks, Parker. They immunised me at school"

The "steward" giggled socially and said "Nicely put, Sir. We play a greater but more sanguinary game".

"Brits win, tonight, then, Dolly!" shouted the "pusser" with a very un-naval familiarity.

"Don't they always" responded Van Der Trump diplomatically.

Presently Parker brought in some sandwiches which proved fresh and excellent and put them on the desk. Then he fetched the trolley with the hot drinks, a selection of fine spirits and another mountain of biscuits.

When he had left and closed the door (not that he was not listening all the time of course, one ear for us and one for the footie) Van Der Trump resumed his reminiscences anent Triple-Trigger.

"There was another junior, let's call him Tommy, who was working in the Cabinet Office a bit later on in history. Tommy was a devout Catholic but he was going through a contested separation and as you may surmise he was rather stressed and distracted. And it was late at night. Despite that, a driver in a standard black cab was parked outside with his engine ticking over. Hilda came out of her office and baldly said 'two Russian H-bombers, Bisons I think, are coming for a probe patrol over the North Sea. ETA 0945 tomorrow. Ring Air-Commodore Wilkins' and went straight back into her sanctum. Tommy did not know Wilkins or how to contact him but he knew where London Centre was and thought they could handle it, which of course they could. The triple was "Bismuth Chestnut Snoring". Tommy sat in the back seat and the driver said 'Where to, Gov' or words to that effect. Tommy put his head in his hands, and then straightened his sitting position, and exhaled a sigh of stress and fatigue. Then he quietly specified "Fuck knows Mate". The driver floored his pedal and tore off up Great Charles and allegedly hit eighty along Birdcage Walk, and screeched through Buckingham Gate. It was two o'clock in the morning".

"Why didn't he just drive round Parliament Square and up Tothill Street"

"God knows, Kenny, I suppose it was some subconscious arcane cabbie knowledge about jams or one-way systems".

"Anyway Tommy entered London Centre within 120 seconds which is some sort of record and he stormed into the Switch Room. The P750 was calmly humming away on its cushioned anti-static lino in its dust-free air-conditioned atmosphere and the duty operator and his mate fell back in astonishment almost spilling their coffee. Fortunately they were not smoking. Breathlessly, Tommy announced in clear and in English, 'I've just come from Hilda's. The Russkies are sending some Bisons over the North Sea tomorrow morning. Tell Air-Commodore Wilkins' which of course they did. That instant. Tommy was given one calendar month's unpaid suspension, both operators got three month's unpaid report-for-duties for breaking machine-maintenance protocols and for permitting or allowing unauthorised entry, the Met door guard was sent back to Met beat duties, and the driver was given a final warning".

"A final warning? I did not realise Civil Servants could be dismissed" I queried.

"Well they can be released for criminal conduct, but what I meant is a final warning before suspension. Centre-related staff can never retire and never be dismissed. They can only die" clarified Pete laconically. "Not that it affects a foreigner of course".

"And what did the fuzz think of these capers" I said.

"They weren't asked" replied Pete.

"Anyway, I digress" continued Pete, "Parallax".

"Ground rules, Kenny: I am not allowed to name any civilian or any non-commissioned person or any officer not relevant to the Circus operation in question. These are NATO rules not British or Dutch. For our purposes 'The Circus' is MI5, MI6, Special Branch, SCD7, and cognate British or Foreign secret state intelligence organisations, especially the CIA and GRU (properly the GU), not forgetting the actually important Intelligence Hierarchies of the three armed services and their foreign counterparts!, or indeed GPO Intelligence, ATT, etc. Controversially, we might also include, Kenny, the private 'contractors' of the present and the past, firms like CRD, Serco, Halliburton, even Barr and Stroud and firms at that sort of geographical and organisational remove, or the relevant parts of them."

"For clarification, Kenny, Centreland is those parts of SW1 between Piccadilly street and the river, often known in Britain as St James's or colloquially Clubland, extending to Mayfair, Soho and the City only where relevant. Devon House was at the geographic center of Centreland. Centreland includes any cognate district of a relevant foreign capital, and clandestine strategic intelligence anywhere that is not openly military in the public sense".

"Yeah. 30 November 1980. As soon as the printer spewed-out 'That's just parallax' the duty operators didn't like it and they demanded to see C in person. He made the immediate decision there and then that they must broadcast "Phasor Phillips fraction" as next month's triple. He summoned 'The Board' that night. Most of them didn't like it either and some of them smelt treason. The Old Guard made a big fuss about the new computer and the vulnerability of such things to tamperers. Someone pointed-out that the CRD also had a Pr1me 750 or were planning one immanently. Someone said that there might be some kind of telephonic liaison between the two machines, either arranged by the Soviets or the Argentines, or more likely by Freeman Fox itself in order to garner industrial or commercial intelligence, provided gratis courtesy of MI6. Someone else said it was funny that no one in Devon House actually appeared to be designing bridges, but that they had advertised for computer boffins to join the staff. Someone else this this was normal in finite-element engineering. And so the night dragged on..."

"Some eager-beaver of the back-offices decided to trawl the engineering press and broadsheets for the original "advert for boffins". Eventually someone found a half-page advertisement in the Autumn 1979 edition of some very obscure civil engineering news-sheet that was headed 'Computation Research and Development' in big bold capitals. Not Limited, Company-Incorporated, BV, SA or nothing. Freeman Fox was nowhere alluded to. I cannot remember the exact nature of the call, but FORTRAN was certainly mentioned and remuneration certainly was not. An executive's name was printed and Devon House mentioned in the address for applications".

"Pete, I give you my personal assurance, and I will swear to this in court if that is what you require, that neither I nor any colleague, at any institution, participated in clandestine activity of any sort, or in statute crime. And that covers my personal enemies as well as my friends".

"Kenny, I appreciate your candour and your offer and your loyalty. This is not about conscious treachery by anyone or about criminality, rather is about good men and women, and occasionally very brave ones, who sought to serve their country *and* at the same time the causes of peace and progress" said Pete gravely.

"I impugn nor accuse any person" added the Admiral.

"I know it's late and that you are very ill. Are you okay to continue..." added Pete solicitously.

I think I have already mentioned the "time warp" atmosphere of this situation. Then a thought suddenly occurred to me. There was no snow: Not on the rooves, not in the sky, not it sounded on the parade ground.

"I've got a pain in my chest" I complained.

"Yes, I'm really sorry about that" said Pete

"Why?"

"When the helicopter extracted you, you had a fourth heart attack. Aitamah gave you a shot of adrenaline and when we got you to base we performed emergency surgery. You were placed in an induced coma for 98 hours. This is the first occasion in which you have marginally been fit for interview. Would you like Major Kask to come in and give you a shot of something? Perhaps more lido if she agrees? Perhaps just some codeine pills? Here, what about I pour you a Jack Daniels!"

"Can I have the Jack Daniels, please Pete" I replied.

"That's Kenny Ringstead! Never known to refuse!"

"Are you sure you can go on, Kenny? I can delay the ferry if you like?"

"No, that's, okay, Admiral Van Der Trump"

"Piet?"

"Yes, Kenny?"

My eyes began to water.

"Is there going to be a war?"

The Admiral suddenly started simultaneously to straighten and relax at the back of his chair, as Tommy, Thatcher's messenger, had been recorded doing in the Centre taxi all those decades ago.

"Oh, Kenny, Kenny, Kenny...." he sighed, leaning forward with his face in his hands "I don't know, I don't know, I don't know. I doubt the Presidents and the Prime Ministers know either. We can do what we can do and we can do no more".

"The Netherlands are Britain's closest ally and we too are a little country but we will stand by you" he added.

I wondered what about the US, Canada, Australia, above all New Zealand. And as a nationalist I hardly appreciated my country being thought "little".

But of course I valued his sentiment.

I said:-

"Thank you, Admiral. That is greatly appreciated".

"Major Kask accused me of trying to escape" I complained worse for wear

Van der Trump laughed.

"Surely, as a British Officer, it is your duty to escape!"

"In truth, I am no officer, Pete. All I did was piss in a cup and open a car door to throw the contents on the snow".

"Kenny, let me tell you a little story"

I thought he had done nothing else all night.

"Kask radioed for a helicopter to airlift herself, her detachment and her prisoner from her snowbound vehicle. Yes, her personal SUV, not any Army pool vehicle. The Romanians sent a Lynx to airlift personnel back to base winching one-by-one in a ten-knot breeze with wet snow flying. After all, the Romanians had a man of their own trapped. Kask herself touched-down at 0546 that morning. She was soaking wet and freezing. She stormed into the CO's office absolutely livid. She shouted and swore at the CO, said that some bastard had fired a Sidewinder at her and missed, and something black had torn off her wing mirror. And the bloody prisoner had tried to escape in the confusion. Then the old bugger had had a heart attack. She was going to be court-marshalled if she returned to Europe. She was going to send a report to the Estonian Military Attaché about the CO's incompetence and slack ship. Her new car was on top of a bloody foreign mountain. She held him financially responsible for her car..."

"Surely Kask is only a Major..." I objected

"Kask is a lioness. And she is a bit more well-connected than most majors, even here in the UK".

"And since I know you wonder, Kenny, both rats were winched first. They were harnessed to the winchman. They are trained to tolerate air operations. They were awarded high ranks for a reason".

"So what did the CO do?" I asked.

"He did not do anything. He sat at his desk in his underwear eating his muesli and without looking up he said 'Take off your clothes, Dear'. She stopped raving. I don't know whether she expected a spanking or what. She complied in silence. The CO shouted 'Batman!' His male valet trotted in at the double and the CO said 'Get the lady a set of clean dry fatigues and dry boots'. The order was instantly obeyed and Kask dressed and flounced out".

"That kind of thing is very dangerous these days" I counselled.

"Of course it is Kenny. But there are a lot of HOs and old men, service retirees and civis like you, around these camps. He does not have to worry about his career or even his freedom. Anyway the War will sort things out for everyone, many think complacently".

"It was ever thus" I acknowledged gloomily.

"Why didn't the plough come through?" I asked.

"One was dispatched, Kenny, but the snow was falling in buckets, and the driver and his mate had never used one before, only military trucks. They reached Point Arthur just North of Silloans Farm where there are two turning loops. They turned with some difficulty and began to head back. As they did so something bright, fiery and loud seemed to pass through their cab and the mate thought it was a missile but at several hundred feet range, whether vertically or horizontally he was unsure. The driver thought it was part of a meteor. He had seen a programme on the telly about someone in Russia who had recorded such a thing on his dashcam".

"It was that night's sensation in the gunroom and doubtless the lower-deck where, at least in the former, the general consensus was that Spadeadam was up to its old tricks and that the thing was some sort of exotic acoustic weaponry on trial".

"Sometime around midnight the next day the local Police rang the CO to say they were holding a foreign NCO with poor English on a charge of drunk and disorderly. Apparently this character had gone into the de Percy, got pissed, and shot off his mouth about Night Marchers, the spectres of doom, and his grandfather. He then went up to a farmer sitting with his wife, and regaled them with this nonsense. The landlord called the local fuzz and they picked him up as they said in our day. He found his way into the CO's office at two o'clock in the morning with two of Northumberland's finest, plastic jackets, checkered caps and the works. The CO was in his usual state of undress. He asked if the constables would drop the charge if the man apologised. The NCO did so most abjectly:- In French. The police officers left and that appeared an end of it".

As I sat there I wondered how any event that happened fifty years ago could possibly bear upon the current global crisis, this peripheral mobilisation, or even the most trifling contention current.

The World is a different place, and times had moved on as I had attempted to explain to Catchpool, with whatever grace I could muster.

Almost as gloomy in its own way was the thought that if Miss Semple had actually made it up those long-vanished Passport Office steps this planet may long have been a cinder and these fatal consultations never pursued.

"Sorry, Kenny" said the Admiral unnecessarily.

"I must return to the mission I never consummated" he added.

"I was just a young bloke, newly graduated, with a short service commission. I liked the sea, and my countries gallant marriage to it, and one morning my Commander called me into his office ashore and said 'Van Der Trump, the British are complaining about shedloads of computer data being sent over from some engineering firm, all of it about strategic road and railway plans and even tram services here and they wonder what we are playing at. Frankly, I don't know. Go to London, contact RN Intelligence and see if they can help you get in control of things. Send me a report by 0900 23 December 1980'. I saluted and said 'Yes, Sir'. That Commander is long dead. Of course I submitted the report but it was inconclusive".

"Anyway when I arrived, I was invited to talk to people at the 'Passport Office' in Petty France. The place was completely demoralised and in an advanced state of confusion. I was invited to another nocturnal 'Board Meeting'. Whether it was laid on for my benefit I don't know. Anyway there were all manner of speculations, and conspiracy theories, and just plain old-fashioned ill-informed bollocks".

"I discovered that the vast majority of Centre staff, around 230 personnel at London Station were based in offices behind the Passport Office, and on military land between Petty France and Birdcage Walk. There was a strong body of opinion among MI6 officers that whatever, if anything, had happened in Devon House was a carefully-engineered Hilarity stratagem designed to get someone, (not necessarily an actual Centre operative), somewhere in Centreland, to voice the magic formula in order to licence real action to kick-off. This was later to become Warsaw Pact orthodoxy."

"The collegiate atmosphere was very much like that of *Tinker, Tailor, Soldier, Spy* except that few thought that the mole was in MI6, and no George Smiley stepped forward to save the day. Technical people drew attention to the fact that both London Centre and Devon House were within five hundred meters of one another; both had PR1ME 750 minicomputers; and that it was technically-possible to arrange communication between these machines using either line-of-sight infra-red or the ordinary GPO voice telephone system".

"One of the experts aired that if *one* of the machines relied upon acoustic coupling then there was a mole *both* in MI6 *and* in CRD. On the other hand, if each machine was electronically hard-wired to the GPO system then *one* human mole was required and he would *have to be* an expert electronic and software professional. And if infra-red was used then acoustic mediation was most unlikely. C ordered the Technical Office (Le Carré's 'lamplighters') to get to the bottom of these questions immediately".

"Kenelm Ringstead was named and some cast doubt on his personal ability to corrupt the system. Motivation was always a difficult question whoever was culpable. I suppose in English Common Law motivation is forensically irrelevant".

"Minority opinion spanned a range of plausible or outlandish theories. Some thought that the CRD was either Hilda's private listening-post, equidistant and co-linear as it was between Downing Street and Petty France; that it was some kind of Chilean station; or that it had been penetrated by the Argentines; or even all three! Someone interjected that the Chilean Embassy was quite literally round the corner from Devon House, fifty or sixty meters on the other side of the Chairmen".

"It occurred to no-one at London Centre that CRD was a purely commercial outfit ready to hire a desk to anyone willing to pay his subscription. Such was the mentality among Civil Servants in those days".

"I think I can throw light on this, Sir" I answered officiously.

"We had two major contracts at the CRD. We were involved almost exclusively in transportation planning. We used the P750 to model different outcomes, as forecast by our alternative infrastructure models. I was employed to re-draft scientific software programs for the new machine, but we still required the services of a mainframe computer elsewhere, and sometimes I was ordered to transport physical magnetic tapes to or from that Shoreditch establishment. I did not know the source of the original code, and neither did I ask. To modify other men's code to work on a new operating system is a far more technical, more difficult, task than writing computer programs *ab initio*".

"In those days computer programmers, especially scientific computer programmers, were scarce, and they could state their own terms. I did. I was a practiced practical mathematician, but the work was not trivial, and apart from trifling errands which anyone could have run, though a trusted man was required, I had little time for anything else and certainly not the kind of things that Commander Catchpool has implied or stated that I achieved".

"Now by Christmas 1980 I had accomplished what I had set out to achieve for my employer, and whether by co-incidence or otherwise the CRD lost its two contracts nearly simultaneously. Those contracts were to lay-out roads and roundabouts for The Milton Keynes Development Corporation, and more comprehensive work for the Netherlands Ministry of Transport".

"Dutch specialists worked at the CRD to facilitate the comprehensive multimodal Dutch planning and it is clear that relevant data was intensively shared with Dutch technical agencies using computer telegraphy, as well as physical dispatches".

"This was an entirely commercial, technical proceeding and there was nothing 'Circus' about it".

"In March 1981 I and others were dismissed our posts at the CRD and at Freeman Fox in Victoria Street. But in 1980-81 British engineering and industrial posts were being lost by the million in factories and consultancies all over the UK".

"That just about summarises my rôle at the Computation Research and Development division or any other manifestation of the Freeman Fox partnership. I was not a Partner, did not regard myself as 'on track' to become one, and was not knowingly acquainted with any of the Partners".

"I had no complicity in or gained any advantage from any dishonesty that may have occurred around me witnessed or unwitnessed".

"To address Commander Catchpool's post-room allegation specifically:-"

"I do recollect a dispute that I had in the post-room. There was a certain amount of jealousy and false proprietorship between the professional grades in Devon House and the clerical grades, including post-room operatives. The young woman concerned, I never learned her name, on this occasion felt she had to defend her determination of a certain parcel's weight in a slightly huffy manner, as they say. I contradicted her. I do not know for what reason, certainly not to save my employer cash, probably as a matter of pride. We specifically addressed the position of the pointer indication. The weighing machine pointer stood well clear of the calibrated scale. At length in relation to her interpretation I said 'That's just parallax'. Suddenly a gentle smile of feminine satisfaction spread across her face which I considered most odd since as far as I was concerned I had 'won' the argument. I left the post-room and resumed my duties elsewhere".

"Until today I have been wholly ignorant of the subsequent events and developments that may have devolved from this encounter" I terminated.

"Thank you for your frankness and you truly do have the astonishing memory often imputed, Dr Ringstead, but your testimony differs from the witness of several in crucial particulars" replied Pete with a double-edged formality.

"First of all a dispute at Board level in MI6 arose about whether you had said 'It's just parallax' or 'That's just parallax'. Then there was the constituency who thought that you did not qualify as 'Circus' and that by tacit extension anything you said was irrelevant. A third overlapping tendency considered that CRD itself did not qualify. Many reminded C that no reference to 'parallax' ever was a trigger-code because C himself had personally defined an entirely different triple for December 1980. Following the official Special Branch position another not necessarily exclusive cohort thought that nothing had happened anywhere in St James's, but that either Hilarity or the coming computational systems or both were inherently dangerous".

"Danny just happened to be idly gazing from a window in the actual Passport Office, of itself a security breach that would never be tolerated today, when his fiancée was creamed by the drunk driver. Nothing would shift him from his position that you were either a Russian or Argentine agent, that you had somehow corrupted MI6's PR1ME 750 computer from your desk in Devon House, and that you were therefore ignorant of the fact that C had countermanded the broadcast of 'parallax'".

"MI6 knew this was a classic Triple-Trigger problem, but they also knew they were helpless to resolve it. There were nine people in the Devon House post-room that afternoon, including you. It so happens that one was a Special Branch plant ostensibly investigating mis-directed or stolen dispatches. He entered in his Site Report that day that no suspicious items or incidents had been detected and of course that went straight to New Scotland Yard".

"New Scotland Yard was in Broadway opposite the St Ermin's Hotel a mere two hundred walking meters from Devon House" I interjected.

"Correct" agreed Admiral Van Der Trump.

"So obviously, when the Semple accident started to look like a state-security event The Yard hauled him in for interview. This person was shown a photograph and agreed you had visited the post-room at the relevant time but had 'assumed' you were one of the professional engineers and claimed that you had dropped off the parcel without incident".

"The Met immediately took the entire Devon Street cohort, some thirty people, across Tothill Street for interview. Most people were clearly elsewhere in the three-or-four story building but their locations were noted, and the post-room staff interrogated separately and closely. Specialist police officers attempted to ascertain if there was a clear electrical route from office monitor-keyboard remote terminals to the GPO system and established there was not, but that there was an acoustic couple in the Machine Room that required manual intervention for each use. Of the seven relevant witnesses, three claimed there had been no discussion about parallax or weighing by anyone, two had noted some temperate dispute about weight, and only one said that the word 'parallax' had been uttered. One was not sure. All interviewees were told that Kenelm Ringstead must not be signalled or informed about 'Parallax' in any manner. Those who maintained they did not know the person were shown a photograph taken of you drinking in the St Ermin's Hotel, seemingly awaiting a contact".

"Back at London Centre, C was very active. He had the accident site cleared and cleaned within fifteen minutes using some Circus janitorial staff. He forbade any photographs and had uniformed Met officers posted around Petty France accosting photographers and moving-on known or suspected journalists. The cover story was that the American Ambassador was scheduled to visit the Passport Office. Actual passport applicants who acted normally were allowed to come and go at will."

"Then C drove himself to Bayswater in a hired Escort to meet some BBC big-wig guy or gal who allegedly had the power to suppress that sort of news. When he got to the relevant address he found it stood on a double-yellow line. He parked the car half on the pavement, turned the flashers on, and the tango met him and showed him inside. About fifteen minutes later C came out only to discover that a warden had shoved a ticket under his wiper. C had a little tantrum. He started shouting for "the bloody warden", along with sundry profanities and so-on. Pedestrians studiously ignored him. Some householder called the Police. C sped off, ticket and all".

The Admiral continued his breathless narrative as I sipped my bourbon and water.

"When he returned to his office, C made a call via GPO landline to Dollis Hill".

"Who was Dollis Hill?" I interrupted.

"Oh, sorry Kenny. I meant the GPO Telephonic and Telegraphic Laboratory at Dollis Hill, a district in North London. It was already four-o'clock by the time C insisted on seeing their Head of Operations immediately. He got back into his hired Escort, now sans ticket, but with a professional driver and a telegraphy expert, and zoomed off to Dollis Hill. He asked this Head of Operations instantly to tap the line from Devon House to the Passport Office and to send him transcripts care of that department. The Head refused. He alleged he could not read the data content anyway, the technology was impracticable, but he could record the *fact and duration* of relevant inter-connections if such utilised GPO wires and he had a licence from Special Branch or the Cabinet Office. C strongly objected to such contact, and left frustrated. Whilst he was away some zealot had ascertained that neither the 'Passport Office' nor Devon House had line-of-sight gear at any frequency".

"The weeks rolled by and no-one had discovered anything that would positively incriminate Kenelm Ringstead or indeed anyone else. Also voicing three random words, not of themselves obscene or seditious, was an offence in no jurisdiction. Indeed, in December 1980 neither was computer hacking".

"Then in the summer of 1981 it was discovered that the current whereabouts of Kenelm Ringstead were unknown, at least to London Centre. Discrete enquiries were made at Freeman Fox but all record or knowledge of the individual were denied. This in itself raised suspicions among some of the more naive traditionalists, but what really set the henhouse fluttering and eventually attracted Circus attention world-wide was the discovery by some unknown investigator, thought to be Special Branch, that the very white escort that Ringstead had hired from a Mayfair showroom in September 1980 for the purpose it was thought of touring on honeymoon, was the self-same car hired by C on his personal account three months later. New Scotland Yard immediately suspected foul play, indeed criminal conspiracy if not treason was afoot, but there was still no evidence anywhere that an event had even occurred, much less anything that would stand-up in court, or even be CPS approved. Special Branch seized the car and literally took it apart. Nothing suspicious was found. Special Branch nevertheless decided to re-classify the case as a formal Metropolitan Police Murder Enquiry. The absence of a *corpus delicti* was of course no impediment in England and had not been since the days of George Smith and The Brides in the Bath".

"At about the same time, and remember this was at the height of 'Evil Empire' hysteria, the Romanian Ambassador sent someone to the FCO to enquire about the whereabouts of 22-year-old Romanian national Elena Salariu or Salara who had not reported to a Romanian consulate to confirm her current address and occupation. Scotland Yard was informed and thought the matter either a casual defection, or else a possible criminal abduction, or possibly the young woman had become a prostitute. The matter was shelved pending developments but a routine notice was sent to MI6. At London Centre some underemployed functionary wondered if there was a connection between this and the mystery woman killed so bloodily in *L'affaire Semple.* Somehow or other the Romanians got wind of Circus interest. Their staff made very discrete enquiries and established that the drunk driver was a young lecturer and researcher at the Department of Astronomy in Queen Mary College, Mile End, a very tidy five road miles from Petty France. Both the Romanians and MI6 made the 'Parallax' connection straight away of course and Special Branch enquiries established that Kenelm Ringstead had been interviewed for a research post at The Department of Astronomy in Queen Mary College, but it was not known whether or not he had been appointed, or even if he had a history of involvement with astronomy or optics. No-one of the right description seemed to be at Queen Mary and the trail went cold once more".

"Of course, within Petty France, C called Danny into his office and asked if his fiancée had been a Romanian. He said "No". She was a Frenchwoman called Salome Paguits. Instantly, one of the crosswords and acrostics specialists pointed out that this was a pun on the phrase 'silver well' or 'silver fountain' and there the matter rested".

"Military intelligence were informed and placed a permanent watch on one of the two literal Silver Wells in England, the one in Northumberland that happened to be on MOD property".

        "C was still very much interested in 'Parallax' and remained so until his retirement, even when Hilarity became purely a matter of historical interest. In 1984 he decided to place the trigger 'That's just parallax' back in the field if only to excite Circus initiates and perhaps incite Gerald to poke his head over the parapet and have it duly blown off. Foot operatives, usually Special Branch or even uniformed Met, were asked to visit the learned societies and retail opticians in St James's and Mayfair, as well as any other relevant concerns to ascertain whether they used the word 'parallax' in the course of ordinary activity, or whether it was likely to be uttered by patients or customers. The Royal Institution and of course The Royal Astronomical Society both said the word was quite likely to be pronounced in any month of the year, but they had no relevant statistics and in any case the word was much more likely to arise in writing. They were told that an educated murderer was at large and they were trying to map where the expression had been overheard. All outlets and institutions agreed to co-operate and were told to record all utterances of the slightly recondite term during December 1984. Records would be collected and staff interviewed early in the New Year. There were a surprising 34 instances reported but none were significant. A cluster of 11 utterances were recorded in Great Charles Street, literally round the corner from Devon House. It transpired that these occurred in The Institution of Civil Engineers and in two cases the Institution of Mechanical Engineers. Special Branch returned to these premises and ascertained that all the pronouncements related to theodolites and other surveying topics".

        "It is not known whether this exercise had excited the interest of codename Eastleigh, a well-known spy writer and sitting MP. He started to try to interest his publisher in a putative non-fiction tome about 'Parallax' and the other mysteries of Hilarity's dying days. The Special Branch visited both Eastleigh and his publisher and warned them off".

AGWELL
RINGSTEAD

CHAPTER FIFTEEN
SORDID INNOCENCE

Operation Charrington in Dagenham

In those days there were three distinct civilian state security services.

Perhaps the best known was the internal state surveillance organ MI5. This organisation was viewed with some contempt in Circus circles, and others. Many of its agents were female, or feminine, though not necessarily homosexual, males. The British abhorred secret police, more than they do today, and the conventional stereotype of the MI5 agent was of a devious, somewhat manipulative, middle-class lady of a certain age, often harbouring a silent hatred of Communism and Trades' Unionists: An underemployed local busybody. The sort of gal who would have, and probably did, join the BUF before the War.

Then there was the almost equally infamous and if possible more disreputable overseas state intelligence agency, MI6. This comprised a rag-bag of seconded Armed Forces officers, diplomats, linguists, cipher specialists and academics, almost all of whom were public-school and Oxbridge educated males in an age when less than four percent of the British could claim such distinction. They, too, had a reputation for slackness, harboured several ideological Communists, and were prey to exploitation by foreign powers.

In my humble opinion, expressed of course as a mere onlooker, by far the most professional of these outfits was the so-called (Irish) Special Branch, a truly secret organisation comprised mainly of experienced civil policemen and their hand-picked specialists. The Special Branch liaised closely with The Metropolitan Police ("[New] Scotland Yard") and was utterly impenetrable and incorruptible. Like normal police anywhere they were law-focused rather than ideological or political. Their only public manifestation was when they swooped with surgical precision to effect the arrests of spies or other organised criminals.

Pete commenced a long chorological, or perhaps I should write topographical, monolog. He seemed to want to set a scene. Not a scene from any respectable drama, certainly not Shakespeare or Schiller. Not indeed a scene from the television work of Mr Michael Portillo. But a scene perhaps from an early Victorian melodrama, though seasoned with sex and farce.

"From the outset, Scotland Yard CID and uniformed staff saw The Circus purely through an organised crime prism. They were only interested in the national and international state intelligence communities insofar as they committed or incited statute crimes: Wounding, Breaking and Entering, Demanding Money or Services with Menaces:- the usual rigmarole of gangland infractions".

"The vast majority of allegations made to the civil police, in any context, were motivated by interpersonal malice and upon investigation found to have little or no basis in fact. This was also assumed to be true of 'Parallax' and other spy fantasy, as the Police saw it".

"In the case of Circus activities there was found to be a considerable overlap with upper-class 'Clubland' crime like gambling, bullion offences, financial irregularity and the higher reaches of prostitution and extortion".

"As early as the late winter or early spring of 1980, Kenelm Ringstead was photographed or reported in several compromising contexts. In late February or early March he was pictured emerging from an expensive brothel in Shepherd Market, also frequented by figures from the Hungarian and Romanian Embassies. Around the same time he was, on the other hand, reported from much more sordid situations in the East End gangland haunts of Rainham in Essex. (Not to be confused with the very similar but unrelated settlement on the opposite side of the Thames: Rainham in Kent)".

"Rainham, the nucleus of which was a quaint seventeenth and eighteenth-century village of some splendour, with large houses and many old taverns, sprawled into salt-marshes and heavily industrialised riverside zones. Rainham was technically in the jurisdiction of Essex Police, but was acknowledged to lie in a twilight zone between London and the Met in the West, and provincial administration in the East."

"Especial difficulties centered around the suburban intersection of the Old A13 New Road and the A125/B1335 Rainham Road, and its immediate environs, including the waste land about the flood plain of the Ingrebourne River (forgive the pleonasm: That is the way the OS specifies it)" continued my very expertly well-informed foreign interlocutor.

Pete paused for a swig. Never to be outdone in such exercises I immediately emulated. Admiral Van Der Trump continued:-

"This particular carfax of ill fame had a number of licenced premises, a number of lay-bys and the said wasteland and various semi-disused gateway aprons. It was a meeting place for smugglers, mobsters and cruising homosexuals".

"The epicenter of this activity, to use the modern misnomer, was the long-vanished Ingrebourne Hotel. This sported a large and well-furnished lounge bar, the sort of tavern where in other contexts or other places a woman might drink unmolested".

"Your crew were very well remembered when Special Branch interviewed the landlord", clarified Pete.

When interviewed, the landlord of the Ingrebourne Hotel said we were invariably well-spoken and dressed in Mayfair suits and club ties, therefore he "presumed" that we were either ganglords at the top of the North London crime tree, or else we were precious metal couriers, or more likely both. At any event, he was disinclined to enquire. Special Branch said nothing and did nothing regarding the Ingrebourne Hotel landlord's flagrant breach of Licencing Laws.

I remember that on one of these tedious winter's nights we were holed-up in some entry at the junction with our lights off and our heater off. It was about two in the morning and there were four of us in the car. There was a lull in the lorry traffic and we had to keep alert to remember to actuate our clicker-counters if a lorry passed which looked Tilbury-bound.

It was not my trick but at some moment I looked up and saw a car parked very conspicuously upon the central lawn of the roundabout under the full yellow glare of the intersection's sodium lamps.

I remarked on this to my colleagues. Another junior said it was another CRD crew, which I thought unlikely, and then a consensus developed that it was employees of the London Borough of Havering who were spying on the spies to check that we were doing the job the ratepayer was paying us to do. I wondered what that ratepayer, or indeed the redoubtable Dame Margaret Hodge of Dagenham, would have thought of local government functionaries on treble time invigilating private contractors performing a nocturnal exercise any reasonable person would have thought meaningless. I wondered why they had not been warned-off by uniformed patrolmen.

I have had fifty years to think about this one and I have concluded, rightly or wrongly, that the car on the roundabout was MI5.

At any event a rumour trickled through around that time that two old biddies, a retired private-school headmistress and a lady crime writer had been the personnel in the mystery car when they spied a trucker pull into a lay-by a hundred meters down New Road. They roared off the island and parked right up against the truck's front fender. The trucker promptly backed, turned out and stormed on before they could do so much as write down his number plate. The next night they thought it sensible to park in the actual lay-by with two uniformed officers. Presently, a driver pulled up in an unmarked blue Transit (or at least it looked blue beneath the sodium lamps). He got out and made his way through the scrub of the patch of flood plain seeming to carry something in his left hand.

A hand torch or hand torches (flashlights) were seen to flicker behind the bushes and a short while later the driver emerged to the lay-by carrying a small box and a bound document. Aha! A dead letter exchange, thought the good ladies of MI5. They got out and intercepted the driver. On challenge, he averred that he had gone into the bushes to defecate. His burden proved to be an opened box of Kleenex® Man Size and a copy of the soft-porn magazine *Mayfair*. The nesh spies did not feel inclined to enter the bushes to check his story, so they sent the uniform. The latter did not find any excrement that seemed to befit an adult human male, but they found fresh tissues with traces of semen. The driver was sent on his way.

Readers unfamiliar with the history of Hilarity idiocy possibly wonder why any of this ever took place (if it did). The answer is that in the pond life of fieldwork, spies and criminals often appeared in a combination of clothes or personal effects that would convey a pre-arranged signal to those to whom they wished to communicate a secret warning or direction.

Such were the entertainments in the lower reaches of Circusland.

Further to set his scene and provide much needed light relief Pete continued:-

"I remember hearing allegations substantiated by some of my Dutch colleagues of the time that uniformed Dagenham and Essex officers started to haunt the general vicinity in the small hours after numerous public complaints and local newspaper articles had made further ignorance untenable".

"One night, a constable on foot had a nasty encounter. He found four men drawn up in a Ford on an access apron with all lights off. He approached the driver who wound down his window. 'May I assist, Sir' enquired the policeman. A man with a falsetto voice or possibly a woman in the back seat screamed 'Fuck off' and brandished what could have been a pistol. The officer beat a hasty retreat to the Albion, and commandeering the landlord's telephone rang Dagenham nick. By the time armed officers arrived by car, the target had vanished. The unlucky constable was disciplined for failure to note the registration".

"They had nothing to do with us, Pete", I assured, I think truthfully "We never went armed, and I do not think public-sector agents did either. Firearms have been very tightly controlled in the UK since the days of Peter the Painter, and possession is always highly incriminating".

Pete received this assurance without verbal or facial response. He was of course armed, but would have been most foolish to be so in an urban place in peacetime.

"The brothel in the Market", said Pete.

There was a lacuna.

"What about it?" I said.

"Tell me how you found it" replied Pete with I think intentional ambiguity.

"By the time I took up my duties at Freeman Fox I had already submitted my doctoral thesis, but it had not yet been approved by the competent authorities. My own supervisor, the late Professor Ian Barr was naturally very supportive but the external moderator RI Ferguson insisted upon a viva, which I duly attended at Glasgow on 15 February 1980. Dr Ferguson required certain changes. The existing typescript was set in IBM Diplomat and this greatly circumscribed the number of typists and machines that could perform the adjustments, even in London. The first, Glasgow, typist who had started in Diplomat gave up due to the complexity of the material, and therefore I had to purchase a Diplomat golfball for myself, before I returned to Aberdeen to find a typist who could finish the thesis. On Sunday 17 February I returned to London and searched for a typist. I found one in Conduit Street, but she did not seem to relish the commission, so she pointed me at a typing agency in Shepherd Market. Now remember, I was very much a Highland laddie, and a virgin, and I never suspected that Shepherd Market was a red-light area. I duly trotted over to the address she gave, and there were several well-spoken and very well groomed ladies there who seemed surprised to see me and even more surprised when I explained my need. They quoted £30 per page, or part page, of A4 typescript. I lent them my ball and the relevant pages of very mathematical manuscript. I came back the next day. The three pages of typescript were absolutely faultless. The typist of the Professor of Physics at Glasgow University had thrown in the towel, after making a compete cods of the script I lent her. These women had typed a scientific manuscript perfectly. In 1980 £90 was £90 but I had no complaint. I received my doctorate in civil engineering".

"Well, Kenny." commented Pete doubtfully, "You always had your stories straight and you have had fifty years to perfect this one" said the cynic.

CHAPTER SIXTEEN
DEBATABLE LANDS

The End is a New Beginning

The state of bereavement is bitter.

Grief is like a cold and sallow furrow ploughed through a fallow field of winter. Grief is a scar covered by time but unforgotten, the seed of guilt, and the bed of regret eternal. Grief is as the gall that blasts the spelt of spring and like a dining skeleton reminds us of the privations to come.

The Romans who marched these hills so long ago and built their homes amid the soughs and tussocks, blasted by the eternal wind and caressed dead by snow, these Romans knew these things, as they marched into the frigid forests where Rome's extrapolation lost its argument.

Parker led me to the car. He opened a rear door and ushered me in. He opened the trunk and placed my gear within, but placed my chest-sack with water, snap and insulin beside me on the seat. I fitted the sack in case I was re-directed or worse.

I relaxed into the soft plush leather and its smell of lavender admixed with the sweet indolic stench of the excrement with which leather is tanned, and with the human pheromones of years of countless sitters. Van der Trump and the driver seemed to be unaccountably delayed. Idly, I wondered what Varandus would make of such a loud cacophony of scents. I am told that Gambia giant rats have eight thousand times the sensitivity to smells that men have, and about 60% more olfactory discrimination than dogs.

I had never before sat in a Bentley. It reminded me of the splendid Armstrong-Siddeley owned by a professor in Glasgow, who one sparkling winter's day of 1978 drove my friends and me to Ben Cruachan and up to the dam, where the road-side icicles shimmered in the skulking sun with the colours of the rainbow. That car, too, was a wonder of comfort and silence.

My mind wondered to Nickolas Bourbaki and his fate. I did not like the man or his country or his presumable mission but I could not help a certain admiration for the lonely courage of this man or devil at the opposite pole of his planet, on land so much like that his covet, armed with nothing more than a camera, binoculars and an Argentine passport, without so much as a proper jacket to put them in. I did not know where he was or what he hoped to achieve though I feared that he and I were destined to be nameless sacrifices upon the altar of other men's malice and cupidity. I hoped he was free, that he stayed free, and that I would not betray him. I did not know whether I should pray for him. I elected not to, but God knows the mere question may have been a sufficient imprecation.

Suddenly the far door opened and Aitamah Kask placed a wire cage on the seat beside me. The cage accommodated none other than Kolonelleitnant Varandus. Kask did not acknowledge my presence. To Aitamah Kask I was just another foreign spook to be neutralised or controlled before The Next War kicked-off properly, an exasperating distraction from her research and teaching career.

Kask disappeared as abruptly as she had arrived. Sitting up in my feather-soft seat with some aged difficulty I took a furtive look around the lot, which was set at some distance from the nearest building. No one seemed to be about. I turned to Varandus and saluted as smartly as I could, Navy style of course. The hero rat lifted and lowered his head briskly about the neck, whether in acknowledgement of my courteous subordination, or in his idea of a returned salute, I could not tell.

There was a kind of small cupboard or cabinet set into the floor half-way across the footwell which seemed softly to be purring like a kitten. I wondered if it was a refrigerator. If so it was a small one. I had difficulty finding the catch-release to open it. I could not ask Van Der Trump or the driver because there was still no sign of anyone. It had clouded up again and a squally breeze threatened rain, but only a heavy shower, I surmised. Leaves and debris skittered disconsolately in the wind as they had during the Catchpool interview, making a discordant series of desolate hollow reports on the tarmac.

Eventually I managed to open the door or lid I suppose to disclose an unopened half-bottle of Armagnac, a liter bottle of fizzy water (only ASDA own-brand), a can of full-strength Fanta®, a can of (sugar-free) Pepsi Max®, a full syringe of Humalog 25 with appropriate 8mm needles, and a packet of chocolate biscuits. There was also a stack of plastic cups of the sort you get from coffee vending machines. Some considerate person, Kask I suspected, had obviously anticipated me. Curiously, there was also a half-consumed small packet of cheese-and-onion Hula-Hoops®. I am childish enough to favour these also, but thought it strange and slovenly of whoever to have half-eaten the crisps and discarded the rest in the icebox.

There was still no sign of anyone so I took out a potato crisp morsel and offered it to Varandus. He ate it with relish. I gave him another, likewise lustily consumed. Perhaps he was hungry. Perhaps he wanted the salt. I gave him a third, entire, hoop. He stashed it in his pouch for later. "It will go soggy" I advised him. If he replied it would have been at a frequency inaudible to human ears.

I opened the fizzy water. I thought about giving some to the rat, but decided against since it might make him ill, he presumably not being inured to redundant luxuries. Instead, discarding all pretence at breeding, painfully aware that this might well be my last Earthly hour, I poured myself a very large brandy and mollified it with a little of the water.

I took a deep draught and topped-up the plastic cup.

Suddenly there was action.

The front doors opened simultaneously and Van Der Trump dove into the passenger seat and I recognised Vanemveebel Alexandru Enache, he of the Night-Marchers in the snowbound SUV. Enache of course took the driver's seat.

"Sorry we're late, Kenny, there was some sort of contretemps with the animals. Kask has flown Mary back to Tallin but the pilot did not know he was to take Varandus too, so took off without him. I have been deputed to fly him from Amsterdam. Whilst we are on the subject, and at the expense of anility Kenny, please do not feed the rat. Do you want your friend to spew his guts out on the long, fraught voyage to Tallin? Is that recompense for all he has done for us? Kask would have kittens".

"I am dreadfully sorry, Pete. I was stupid. I wish and pray Varandus has a safe and serene voyage".

"*C'est le guerre*" commented Enache bleakly.

I tried to imagine Kask bearing her feline offspring.

I wondered whether the kittens would prove friends to the rats, as predators and prey raised from infancy are apt to be. Perhaps the rats, creatures of age and the World, would prove sound tutors or even Dutch uncles and aunts.

Kask was the only senior woman I had happened to meet for many years. She reminded me a little of Mother. Serious, even intellectual, but with a soft side, leavened with an incendiary temper. Both were scientists but I guess that both exemplified the virtue of Woman: The Three C's: Compassion, Courage and Cheerfulness. Whatever the shortcomings of The Sex the cruel unsmiling female coward is a rare beast. When Woman is narcissistic, her self-regard is purely superficial, preferring to borrow her prejudices and her bigotries from a male partner and mortgaging her soul to him, without losing sight of the irony of her predicament or even its comedy. This has nothing to do with politics or fashion. It is a fact of human nature visible in all but the most inceptive societies.

They say that the male of the species is cruel, but males are not so much cruel as indifferent, except where the cruelty is of a type to give a lascivious thrill. But indifference is first cousin to disinterest, and the Male is the victim of science and circumstance.

"Fancy a brandy, Pete?" I asked.

"No thanks, Kenny. It's a bit early for me. But Alex might like a small one"   I poured Alex a few milliliters of Armagnac in a plastic cup and offered it round his left arm.

"*Non, merci, amiral. je conduis*"

"Oh, for goodness sake." I thought "We will probably be dead tomorrow". I withdrew the cup, but was nevertheless flattered and gratified by my sudden and unlooked for high commission: But in whose navy!

I took the Fanta can out of the icebox, tore off the tab and handed it to Alex, who took a sip and stowed it in his console can-holder.

Alex Enache turned the key and the engine started almost silently. The old automatic gave the slightest buck and pulled away. I was still confused about my location: Whether I had returned to Otterburn from Spadeadam, whether I had ever been to Spadeadam, or indeed whether I had visited either place. At any event, the Sun was trying to break through and it tended to our offside beam so if it were early morning we were travelling East. If we were making for Newcastle-upon-Tyne, then this was consistent with either base, or of course many other places. Sometimes the Sun was dead ahead, but this did not necessarily mean we approached from the North-West. I looked for signs that said either Jedburgh or Carlisle, but could see neither, even at considerable junctions. Perhaps the inane practice of removing road signs had already been progressed, as on the eve of The Second World War.

After a while we turned left off the contraflow road which I provisionally identified as the A68 and on to a much narrower road, probably a B.

"It will be quickest if we continue down the A68" I essayed at Alex.

His entirely predictable response was:-

"*Je ne comprends pas, monsieur*"

"Nice try, Kenny" replied Pete for him "we are passing through a small village to pick up another passenger. It is a little out of our way".

Presently we left the hills behind and passed through a beautiful and largely deserted little valley which I have since thought might have been Coquetdale. I had never been there before, but it reminded me somewhat of the Blackwater Valley in County Cork, another lovely drive though the Irish valley is much wider, longer, lonelier and infinitely more ghostly.

Piet turned in his seat and asked baldly:-
"Where does your loyalty lie, Kenny?"

"Piet Van Der Trump", I commenced, slightly portentously, "In 1997 I became a convicted Christian, and my conviction has remained, at least intellectually. If I were glib enough, or stupid enough, or lazy enough I could reply 'God, Country, Family. I am a God and Country man!' But you are intelligent, and I shall not insult you, neither debase myself, nor blaspheme the Name of God".

"If, Piet, I said 'I am loyal to my friends and family' you would rejoin 'then why did you desert your friends when they were no longer useful? Why did you desert your father in his final hours?' If I said 'I am loyal to my Country, you might say which is that, Chile, Mercia, Scotland, Britain?' If I said 'I am loyal to my God' you would say 'Which God is That: The God of the Friends, The Catholic and Universal God, the God of the Rosy Cross and Golden star, or the God of your own conception'".

Pete replied:-
"And yet, Kenny, you have managed withal to insult me, for in rehearsing a congeries of alternatives you have evaded the question. Precisely that which a good existentialist is supposed to avoid".

"I have done my homework, Kenny, and I know that you have developed an instinctual aversion to privatives, and the definition of things by their defects. Nevertheless, I wish to put this to you".

There was another of those unaccountable pauses in proceedings, so unnerving.

Pete then did something most unexpected. He opened the glove box on the walnut fascia in front of him. A feeble yellow light only deepened the shadows within and disclosed nothing. I wondered if he were about to retrieve his pistol and donate me the benefit of a little lead. As he ratted around inside I thought 'if he shoots here he will puncture the fuel tank and all four of us will immolate'. He eventually retrieved a small, tattered black book with thin pages. The pages were edged with gold leaf. The ancient spine was sliding from its buckram binding. The book was embossed with the words "Het Statenvertaling", a phrase which, like Vienna, meant nothing to me.

Pete opened the book and flicked through the pages as if looking for a favourite quotation. The lunging motion of the car on the uneven country road made such activity bilious. Pete turned to Alex and said "arrêtez-vous". Alex turned the car into the entry of a farmer's field and turned off the engine.

I felt suddenly oppressed in the silence, and the pastoral desolation around me. I wound down the window. The wind fitfully blustered about the bodywork and into the cabin. A little river to our right bubbled over rocks and rapids beneath its ashes and willows.

The argentine remains of my head-hair ruffled. The rat's incanous fur ruffled. The golden pages ruffled.

"Why quest for silver when you can hold gold in your hands?" Pete said enigmatically.

Pete turned awkwardly in his chair to face me, holding his book open at the page he had found.

"Kenny, the text was written by someone who said he was the son of a king, and yet he nominates himself in the feminine, as a speaker who addresses a fellowship, perhaps as a Quakeress might, or some other priestess. What do you make of it, Kenny? Was he a princess?"[R16.1]

"I have no idea, Pete"

"I don't know how to put this in English and do justice to the prose. Why search for silver when you can search for gold?" Pete almost repeated, whether distractedly, whether in age, like myself, he forgot he had already said things, whether in wonder at the aptitude of his utterance he thought the thought bore repetition. I could not decide whether the slight variation was careless or intended.

"He or she says that he sought for knowledge and wisdom, possibly not the same thing, and came away dis-satisfied. Then he turned to works and labours, and there was no novelty in his designs and inventions, and he was appalled. Then he sought gaiety in sex, drink and laughter, and this also failed to satisfy him. Then he amassed gold silver and property, but this too palled and he found himself jealous of his own posterity, and this too dis-satisfied him".

"I am sorry, Pete, this is above my level. I do not see how this relates to my allegiance to anything", I objected.

"As I said I know and think I understand your aversion to negatives, Kenny, but this becomes semi-intelligible if we examine the converse of loyalty: Treachery. For the traitor searches for his idol that turns to dust in his hands. He is dis-satisfied, fundamentally, subconsciously, wilfully and cannot settle in the Hand of God. Does that make sense, Kenny?"

"I do not know, Pete, it is all too deep for me. I may or may not be an existentialist, but I am no philosopher, for I lack a philosopher's equipment".

"Kenny I put it to you that whatever our best or worst intentions or our brave strivings, or our cowardice, we are all idolaters. The beauty of a woman or a river is an idol: Beauty itself is an idol: The Truth of Science is an idol: Science itself is an idol whilst Truth unknowable; Nation, Fathers, and the Fathers of Nations are idols: Armagnac and sex are idols, however low and derivative they are. For Ideal and Aspiration themselves are idols, mirages spun and shone by Satan for the distraction of Men".

Then I became aware of the very strangest thing. The rat was following this conversation, almost risibly turning his head first to follow Pete's obscure disquisition, and then to assess my reaction. Did the animal understand English and if so how? Surely, I thought, though his senses, all so much sharper than a man's, might hear the sound of men's voices, surely the contouring of the frequency-intensity spectrum, the Fourier spectrograph if you will, would have a wholly alien conformation? This "ought" to render humans unintelligible, perhaps in the way, and you appreciate this is only an analogy, perhaps in the way an elder when asked "Would you like a cup of tea?" hears "Wood Jew like a cupel tree?" but deconvolves the sound neurologically to make sense of the message from its context?

"Pete", I replied "I am no ontologist but to me altruism lies at the heart of Evil. My Late Mother often said to me 'The Road to Hell is paved with Good Intentions'. My Mother fought the Nazis using Science. The Nazis sought an improved humanity, fitter, stronger, cleverer, happier and braver than the old Sons of Adam. What they achieved was consummate Evil, earning a special and perhaps private circle in Perdition. Their Communist enemies sought an improved humanity, kinder, gentler, braver, more communitarian than the old Sons of Adam. They achieved Futility and Evil. Ideals and their idols meet at the extremes as a continuum, for in religion Quakerism and Catholicism merge at their frontier and in politics fascism and communism blend at re-entry so that they become identical in practice if not in theory. As I see it loyalty can be a perversion when assigned to such traducements, just as treachery is the cankered fruit of ambition".

"They say, Piet, that imitation is the sincerest form of flattery, so to borrow your contrapositive rhetoric I should say that the opposite of treachery is Fidelity. Fidelity is an active and considered election rather than the feudal dumb passivity of Loyalty. Fidelity is the cheerful prosecution of help to a beloved thing whether it is a wife, a village or a rat, keeping he, she or it safe from harm, healthy and prosperous, without surcease or desertion, keeping faith in the inherent goodness of the thing regarded, as the ideal woman and wife of chivalry loves a husband, without selfishness, without rancour, without pride, but with selfless humility and forbearance, in loving disinterest".

"You have still not answered my question, Kenny"

"No. Nor can I"

"When is ignorance a disability, Kenny, and when is it a depravity?"

This was a completely left-of-field avulsion. I struggled to understand the tendency or even the sense of the question. As usual, I sought refuge, or at least thinking-time, in historical abstraction.

"If religion is the inceptor of civilisation, Pete, then preception was its first weapon and the quest for knowledge its lantern amid the darkness".

"Are you using your language correctly, Kenny? Or are you intentionally ambiguous?"

"I don't know, Pete. I suppose I am fumbling my way forward. I find your question very difficult"

"I think", I continued, "that somehow ignorance is a qualified evil and a related failing, judgment, an unqualified one, for to judge is blasphemously to usurp the office of God and to seal, so to say, an experience frozen as prejudice".

𝔉𝔬𝔯 𝔊𝔬𝔡 𝔰𝔥𝔞𝔩𝔩 𝔟𝔯𝔦𝔫𝔤 𝔢𝔳𝔢𝔯𝔶 𝔴𝔬𝔯𝔨 𝔦𝔫𝔱𝔬 𝔧𝔲𝔡𝔤𝔪𝔢𝔫𝔱, 𝔴𝔦𝔱𝔥 𝔢𝔳𝔢𝔯𝔶 𝔰𝔢𝔠𝔯𝔢𝔱 𝔱𝔥𝔦𝔫𝔤, 𝔴𝔥𝔢𝔱𝔥𝔢𝔯 𝔦𝔱 𝔟𝔢 𝔤𝔬𝔬𝔡, 𝔬𝔯 𝔴𝔥𝔢𝔱𝔥𝔢𝔯 𝔦𝔱 𝔟𝔢 𝔢𝔳𝔦𝔩."[R16.2]

"We inherit the sins of our fathers and my Late Father was as his Father and too often myself a very judgmental man. My Father's father was immovable in his adherence to communism, even when its cruelties and hypocrisies became a matter of notoriety. My own Father despised his Father's views and himself adopted the polar position, so co-incident, embracing a debased coin of fascism that ossified into anti-Semitism and other pointless or perverse opinionations. My paternal grandfather, notwithstanding his communism, had little objection to Anglican rites at his own funeral. My Father, on the contrary, insisted upon an atheistic oblation, without regard to his survivors who may have wished instead a bog-standard Church of Scotland ceremony in which they might offer thanks without demur. Such is such when judgment hardens to prejudice, and prejudice congeals to narcissism, for in spiting the son, we mortify those whom we might have served".

"There is a certain irony in what you say", observed Pete.

"Of course there is", I replied.

"Sometimes", I continued, "ignorance is a wilful choice, congratulated by its suffering practitioner, and sometimes it seems not. On the last day we passed on this Earth, my Father said to me that not only did he not know things he needed to know when a young man, but he did not even know what he needed to know. It was one of his flashes of wisdom, as rare and as splendid as a breach of sunbeams through an overcast. Whether this wisdom was as glorious as the freedom he afforded me to make my own discoveries, and my own errors, I must, Piet, offer to your judgment".

"It seems to me, Kenny, that you are trying to say that you think naivety a crime".

"I do not know what I am trying to say, Pete. I am confused myself. For sure, naivety, or perhaps you would say innocence, is an ornament delightful in a four-year-old, a suspect danger or an affectation in a twenty-four year old, a fraught liability in a thirty-four year-old, an evasion in a forty-four-year-old, and rank cowardice in the hypocrisy of a seventy-four-year-old".

"For example" I continued, "the pacifism commendable in an eighteen-year-old savours of idealism in a twenty-eight-year-old, smells of ideology in a forty-eight-year-old, and stinks of fear in a man of eighty-eight, whose contemporaries so often use their mouths to consign younger and better men to an early doom".

"Ignorance is as often a choice as an imposition, for like all ills ignorance is a spawn of cowardice, the father of all evils".

"For whilst the co-incidence of three words might be fortuitous, the association of folly, wickedness and ignorance is determinate", I concluded.

"You are a hard man, Kenny. I am glad I did not have to work with you".

"Not really, Pete. But I have known some bad men and some heartbreaking circumstances".

Pete closed his book and put it back in its glove box. He turned to Alex and said:-

"*continuer*"

Alex started the engine and pulled out. We continued our stately progress down this sequestered little valley. A cow and a donkey looked over a wide field gate on the opposite side of the road. It suddenly came on heavily to rain, a fitful squally onding typical of a North Country autumn. Circular wens of gin-clear water disfigured the greasy windscreen. The Vanemveebel turned on his wipers. Somehow the desolation seemed to be heightened, heightened beyond the natural loneliness of a lush valley, somehow prescient and ominous beyond reason, beyond expectation.

It was not many minutes before we entered a pretty and interesting-looking village, or maybe a very small town, whose buildings of rough ashlar had an unnaturally dark look that intensified the dour mood of the day. I could not make up my mind whether the building material was a sort of carbonaceous sandstone, or whether a much lighter rock that darkened when wet. Alex pulled off the main street onto a higher and parallel road that was terraced on one side by expensive-looking country shops and a large pub-type hotel called The Turk's Head.

I asked myself if these were the same Turks that we were courting for allies, or the Turks our ostensible enemies at Navarino, or even earlier Turks who took us to slavery in the Maghreb. Or even the Turks who so grievously defeated the combined forces of The British Empire at Gallipoli.

A stout disconsolate figure stood in taurine lassitude beneath a large black umbrella before the hotel entrance. Alex drew the car beside him and, elegantly closing his umbrella, the figure opened the rear door beside me and sat on the opposite side of the rear bench uninvited.

"Where the fucking hell have you been" the newcomer shouted at the back of Pete's head, "I've fucking missed the bus now".

I was not sure whether the man spoke literally or figuratively or perhaps both, but this little vignette put me in mind of Geoffrey Household's spying novel, *Rogue Male*, the scene where Quive-Smith taunts the hero with this accusation, as well as the alleged comment of Mr Neville Chamberlain with regard to Adolf Hitler, after the former had landed at Heston. Come to think of it, there was something old-fashioned and a touch forensic about the dress of this abrupt entrant that put me in mind of the notoriously prim and dapper premier though I rather think that Chamberlain omitted to qualify the little Austrian's loss as *fucking*, and it could not have been Vansittart who spoke as of course he was a tram man.

"I am very sorry, Paddy" Pete replied with admirable self-possession "we had a puncture. I have got your Chilean for you".

"He's an Argy you cunt"

If they were speaking of me I was neither. Another lacuna. The newcomer turned to me. His red pasty face reminded me of Catchpool, but this man was clean-shaven and had a West Country accent. I turned my head to meet his gaze over the intervening rat in his cage, a fellow-traveller I should have found curious, but who did not seem to interest the newcomer.

"I am Sir Hugo Patrick Lysand. I am a Major-General and President of the Supreme Court of Justiciary". The man was not in uniform. There seemed to me something plebeian and defensive, not only about the utterance of his rank and honorific, but about the whole tenor of his approach. He seemed to think that I was either too foreign or too stupid to know that the current President of the Supreme Court of Justiciary was Sir Reginald Mouncy. To resort to another literary allusion perhaps this person was not, in civilian life a painter but perhaps a BBC man.

"Hello, I'm Dr Kenelm Ringstead" I replied with intentional discourtesy, "and for clarification I am an Englishman, born locally".

I quickly resolved to go on the offensive, in both the tactical and the social senses.

"Tell me, Mr Lysand" I commenced "Is Major-General a British rank?"

"Of course it bloody is"

"Thank you for lightening my ignorance. I am told I am an admiral" I replied emolliently and of course truthfully, turning awkwardly and proffering my hand.

Lysand did not see fit to shake it, so I withdrew.

"Mr Lysand" I re-commenced "As a South American I am understandably confused. Please tell me what country we are in."

"As a spy and a traitor you know perfectly well where you are" rejoined the self-alleged President of the Supreme Court of Justiciary.

"Does the President of The Supreme Court of Justiciary have any jurisdiction in this country, or indeed any business in any?"

Lysand coloured in just the same amaranthine way that Lons Catchpool had done in the recent interrogation at Spadeadam, or was it Otterburn?

He did not reply. He turned to face forward and fell silent. I do not think that he was sulking childishly. I think he was genuinely confounded to have been derailed from his prepared script, and was pondering a way forward.

Suddenly a vagrant thought crossed my tired and rather drunk mind. Surely this person could not be Lons Catchpool coming back for another try? No, it was just too stupid to contemplate, even in my advanced state of paranoia. But if they were not the same man, then more likely, I thought, two superannuated thespians who had joined MI5 on a HO basis for the beer money.

Reminding myself of my inebriation and taking full advantage of Dutch courage I decided to press home my attempted humiliation of this thoroughly unlikeable character.

Turning to Lysand I said:-

"You're not that cunt Catchpool are you?"

Neither Pete nor Alex could resist a brief snigger. I was mildly surprised at the latter's grasp of English idiom. I even wondered if the Kolonelleitnant understood and enjoyed a private laugh.

Lysand looked offended, but it was impossible to know whether at being unmasked; whether at being unmasked and accurately assessed; or whether at the outrageous thought of being Catchpool. At any event, he betrayed no curiosity to know who Catchpool might be.

Not to be defeated so early in the passage of arms Lysand turned to me and said:-

"Tell me about Narcolalia"

Well, if he was not Catchpool he had surely been briefed at the same silly spy school and of course I recognised the danger. If I professed not to know what Narcolalia was I would fall into the same elephant-trap that yawned below the common criminals you sometimes see interviewed on TV, the ones who respond to every question with "No Comment". As Van Der Trump and I seemed earlier to agree, few things are as incriminating as wilful ignorance, except perhaps a firearm.

It is always much better to elaborate your answer in tedious and protracted detail *even if you are talking complete nonsense* and your interrogator knows it.

"Well, Lysand" I commenced, "I went up to read geology. In those days, computers were exotic beasts and few knew what to do with them and that included me. In my first year my subsidiaries were physics, chemistry and compulsory crystal optics, something about which I was and am completely clueless..."

"Get on with it, we haven't got all bloody day" interrupted Lysand impatiently but very helpfully.

"Er, sorry, where was I?"

"Your bloody university"

"Oh yes. Well in the second year a junior lecturer called me into his office and reminded me that I had to choose a single second-year subsidiary and in a rather arrogant tone told me I had to elect for computer science. To his surprise, I acquiesced without protest. The computer in this institution was said at the time to be the largest in Europe and occupied the entirety of an enormous deep-plan building specially built for it across several former streets that in the innocence of youth I thought had been demolished to accommodate it, but that I have since realised were cleared by a parachute mine. Professor Rohl and his staff taught me to program the machine, not for geology (that came later) but for miscellaneous scientific purposes. I took to it like Prometheus Unbound. I thought 'this is a poor boy's route to a doctorate' and so it transpired. My whole professional career, or you may say, careers, became computer-related. When after a further six years of intensive computer-based research and study I joined Freeman Fox I had a sound foundation in the application of computers to data science and computerised telegraphy".

"Did you use an acoustic coupler?" asked Lysand. He was obviously well briefed, at least about things that ceased to be of any interest fifty years ago.

"No. We had one in the teleprinter room, but they smelt of trouble to me. Others used them to route processing to a similar ICL1904S in Newcastle, but I could tailor my work to use only the local machine, so I had no cause to employ tenuous links".

"The machine at Manchester was a 1906A" objected Lysand.

"Goodness, who has been a busy boy?" I thought sarcastically.

"Yes, sorry. I am speaking of the machine at Strathclyde University in George Street, Glasgow".

I thought involuntarily, "If British Intelligence is *this* obsessed with the past, then we are sure to lose The Next War". But of course we were all well beyond working age, and the young brains were already at the intended fronts, or in industry.

This man seemed a bit more intelligent than Catchpool and seemed to have no particular axe to grind about Parallax.

We slowly entered a small village, or rather hamlet, another of those curious Border settlements that seemed to comprise a grove of retirement bungalows plus Something Else, and in this case Something Else was an empty stockyard of galvanised iron pens and a curious round Victorian building in their midst, which I assumed to be an auction ring.

The whole place appeared deserted.

Alex turned a corner and unexpectedly drew up by a bus stop. He kept the engine ticking over.

"Dr Ringstead" tacked Lysand with unexpected courtesy "are you the kind of man who passes by on the other side?"

Suddenly, I realised with horror that I was being interviewed for a job, English-style. And yet I could not make up my mind whether he wished to employ me as a spy or as a traitor, and why if the former a President of the Supreme Court of Justiciary could not more conveniently hire one of the numerous and doubtless superb private detectives that Edinburgh affords?

So now it was clear that my interlocutors had made up their minds that I was a spy (I was not) but seemed to be in doubt about whether I was a traitor, and wondered whether even if I was a traitor I could be exploited as a double or even triple agent during the course of The Next War.

"One of my employers of the last century, Lysand, made persistent attempts to get rid of me but I was a married man and a good trades unionist and cleaved tenaciously to my employment whilst, with assistance, augmenting my income at each accessible juncture. I shall not name this shady organisation, for I believe it still trades at a much reduced level".

"Quite right too, Ringstead!" interrupted Lysand with a sudden blimpish agreement. Strange. Maybe a sort of flattery or encouragement he had been trained to deploy?

"On one occasion, I fought three years for a major promotion with back pay and with the assistance of altruist idealists I won, though to obtain the back pay I eventually had to resort to the services of a celebrated gangland solicitor. I felt obliged to the altruistic honorary union executives and agreed to serve the Cause myself as a steward. So I in turn represented my colleagues in disputes with corrupt managers, and I always succeeded on their behalf. But I felt dirty. I was dis-satisfied. I told myself that the people I defended and empowered were almost invariably drunks, or slanderers, or idlers, or other disreputables. So I gradually excused myself from further participations and eventually resigned my stewardship. I was dismissed within eighteen months, and all my helpers with me or very shortly thereafter. I may or may not pass by on the other side, Lysand, but for sure I am careful where I cross, and why".

"So you washed your hands?" asked Lysand, somewhat mixing his Scriptural metaphors.

"I never need to feel dirty in the sense you imply, Lysand, in order to wash my hands, but for sure I wash my hands when they are dirty, as I wash my hands of you, Lysand, and the filth you canvass".

There was a pause. Lysand stared into my eyes across the rear seat in the same way that the Sally Army man had in his office all those decades ago. That office and his building has been a small housing estate for over thirty years now, and his firm the merest shadow of its former self. That man sought to intimidate me without, perforce, the threat of violence. This Lysand was also trying to intimidate me. This time I felt that anarchy and violence were very much on the menu: Whether to choose to dine thereon was a matter of personal choice.

Suddenly and quickly Lysand put his right hand in his jacket pocket. I feared he might produce a small pistol. I was unarmed. I was in an awkward defensive posture, slumped in a deep soft chair with a large wire cage between he and me.

Before I had time to react he had taken a strange little purse from the pocket and offered it to me. It was one of those vulgar little pouches of purple velveteen that are sometimes issued in casinos etcetera if the staff wish to present your dice or chips. It was closed with a black draw-cord. I took the package suspiciously. Was it radioactive? Was it poisoned with ricin or sarin or something? It did not seem to have injured Lysand.

I loosened the cord and started to pour the heavy contents into my palm. Three or four threepenny pieces emerged. They were of white metal and only slightly worn, but they were all dated with years of the late Twenties or the Nineteen Thirties, the Depression Years. My Late Father had often described them to me, usually when disparaging Britain or especially the little brass twelve-sided coins of my boyhood.

I did not know what to make of this new unreason. I looked up to Lysand's eyes. He gazed back at me. He said nothing. I said nothing. Pete and Alex said nothing.

There was still some kind of stuff in the pouch. I poured the rest of it into my palm. It was all little pre-war threepenny bits. I counted them eidetically. Then, so to say, the penny dropped. There were exactly thirty.

I was beside myself with anger.

I did not really know what to say or do. The hellish tableau was beyond objection. Beyond rejection. Indeed I resolved as if by a subconscious Volition not my own not to compound the curse, if that was what it was, by casting the coins back at their donor.

So I put the coins back in their pouch, and put the pouch in my pocket.

"You have cheated me, you arse-fucker" I said quietly and calmly to Lysand in a lover's tone, but with the hate that abuts love at its continuum.

"How so?" said the nasty major-general and President of the Supreme Court of Justiciary, self-alleged.

"These coins are only half silver. You owe me thirty more".

With that Lysand opened the nearside door and leapt out with a sprightliness surprising in a man who must have been in his early eighties. I opened my door and jumped out and walked round the trunk to meet him in the middle of the empty road.

I do not know what I had in mind. It was certainly hostile intent. I did not stop to think about whether the two Europeans would simply drive off and leave us there. I suppose I would have punched or kicked him or something. I could not believe he expected to catch the bus he had complained of missing.

Lysand and I stood there looking at each other in I suppose mutual astonishment.

Lysand reached into I thought a breast pocket, withdraw a pistol and pointed it in my direction. At that instant a report rang out and Lysand crumpled, clutching his right wrist and dropping the weapon on the road. Lysand was still standing, but in obvious pain and groaned or whimpered slightly. Then unaccountably there was another sharp crack sound and Lysand fell to the road and was still and silent.

Someone roughly grabbed me and pushed me back into the car, slammed the door and sped along the road in the opposite direction.

The rat Varandus had wisely, albeit with an old man's inefficacy, taken refuge under his blanket.

"What the fuck was all that about?" I asked of no one in particular.

"You almost started World War Three, that's what the fuck it was about", shouted Van Der Trump from his sedentary position.

I felt something heavy resting in my lap. I looked down and saw that it was a small pistol. I picked it up and examined it stupidly. I had not held a pistol since, I don't know, 1955 or 1956. I would have been seven or eight and my Father took me to Bisley. He was training to be an officer at the time and whether the event had something to do with that or not I have no idea, and the whole thing is now inaccessible to history. Anyway it was a brilliantly sunny morning and someone lent me an old Webley revolver and invited me to shoot a rusty oil drum about twenty-five meters away. I surprised myself and the adult onlookers by hitting the thing with four of my six rounds.

For some minutes I was too distraught to find any interest in my new acquisition, no matter how vital. I did not know how to open the magazine to check how many rounds Lysand bequeathed me. At length I asked Piet, or in my English idiom, Pete, to unload the weapon for me. He did so with a stage magician's dexterity and passed back the gun and its ammunition clip. The clip was empty.

I put Lysand's weapon in one of the inside pockets of my storm suit.

"Have you just killed that bastard?" I asked Pete.

"No, and it is Alex you must thank for your life. And in answer to your next question *he* did not kill the cunt either".

"Thank you, Alex" I said in a contrite tone "*Merci beaucoup mon ami mon Vanemveebel*".

"*Ça va. Je dois garder ma main.*" came Alex gallant reply.

"Where did the second shot come from?" I asked.

"I have no idea. Lysand had many enemies, both personal and professional. Perhaps it was your mate Nickolas Bourbaki?" said Pete provocatively. How the hell did he know about Bourbaki? Was Bourbaki also in custody? "Whoever it was they clearly expected him, since it was a high-velocity strike fired from maybe a mile".

It then dawned on my stupid brain that we had been followed. Whether by confederates of Van Der Trump, Bourbaki or of Lysand himself I could not guess.

"Do we need to move faster, Gentlemen?" I asked naively.

"What for?" replied Pete, "We can't make the first ferry and the tide is going out. The next will not enter until the evening and will loiter overnight".

"Can't you use your mobile and ring for a delay?"

"What, and have the Brits track our position. That is daft even by your standards, Kenny. MI6 must have been proud of you".

"I was never in MI6"

"No, of course you weren't", agreed Pete sarcastically.

"What about a plane?"

"Don't be silly"

"What about the police?"

"Oh, you are such a bloody worrier, Kenny" remarked Pete with a tone of dismissive impatience. "We are trying to prevent

Armageddon and you are worried what you will say to lads in chequered hats".

By now we had entered an urban area that could have been the outskirts of Newcastle-upon-Tyne. We entered a slip road and as I saw Jesmond Church flash by on the left it seemed from that and from the changed direction and the play of the light, together with our appearance on another major road, that we were bearing away from the city center.

Bearing away from *Pons Aelius*. Clearly the Roman Newcastle had had a bridge over the Tyne. Not an easy river to span. But then again the Romans had thrown a bridge more than a mile long across the Danube. I was sure Alex could tell us all about it. Now of course the city had a new castle, a thousand years old, and five younger bridges, each an engineering innovation in its time.

I said to Pete:-

"You're not going to take me to a train station, are you?"

"Look, Kenny, if I set you down here or at a train station and you intend to survive then you must immediately taxi to the nearest Police Station and submit yourself to The Northumbria Constabulary and hope they can do their jobs. Immediately you must confess to the murders that you never committed, especially the most recent you witnessed, and for preference also the 'Parallax' crime of twentieth-century Petty France. Then you must agitate, discretely of course, for a long sentence in a high-security unit, one where your many wealthy and aging enemies, both those who know who you are and those who think you are someone else, cannot find you, or cannot bribe a cellmate to do their deed whilst you sleep. But little sleep may bless you, for withal Britain is still a nuclear power, and its many enemies will waste no time obliterating its ships and its cities and their prisons with them. I did not know Lysand, though MI6 told me to meet him. But Lysand knew you, or thought he knew you. I do not know whether you knew Lysand for certain, or thought you might have recognised him. In particular, I do not think he was Catchpool, though I admit all these Brit ex-military types seem alike to me. Now as a young man Patrick Lysand and Kenelm Ringstead, if that's who you are, dreamt of glorious deaths falling heroically at the head of their admiring acolytes. What happened? Lysand died a sordid death unknown and unloved, but certainly well-hated on some God-forsaken road in God-knows where".

"On the other hand, in Europe Kenelm Ringstead or whoever it is may pass an affluent and respected old age swanning diplomatic circles, the confidant of presidents and high commissioners, perhaps even representing his beloved country in its absence. I know you have no surviving family, Kenny, in the UK or anywhere else. What have you to lose? You have lost the confidence of your people, why lose your life to their vengeance or their vanities? If you lose your pensions and you surely shall they may be replaced by some other".

"You are our last sane link with British Intelligence".

"There is a long time to the sailing, Kenny. Why don't you take your time and think about it? As you were when I presented the Contract you failed to sign, you are a free man and free to leave at any time".

Pete was a very persuasive salesman, and I wondered what else was in the bargain for him. I thought it best not to ask.

Instead I said:-

"Alexandru, you are a modest and patient man, and it seems to me a thoughtful one. What is your opinion of what transpires?"

"*que voulez-vous dire, amiral?*" Alex replied.

"*Alexandru, vous êtes un homme modeste et patient, et cela me semble réfléchi. Quelle est votre opinion sur ce qui se passe?*" I repeated in French.

There was the briefest pause for reflection.

"I old man. I old soldier. I go home. See Daughter. I die. Even rat. He go home. He see daughter. I simple soldier. You clever men. You old men. You go home. You die.

I defender of men.

I go England. I ask. Why kill our girl in Circus? English no answer.

I go back. Long, long, straight road. I march all winter. Night and day. I linger not. I go Romania. Maybe Roman soldier he fall in. He fall in moonlight. Freezy cold. He say I chatty chatty. I keep company.

Salve miles! Ego panthera

I ask Roman Soldier. Why you go Dacia? Why you kill our girl in circus?

Soldier say: *Bellum quad Bellum. Momento mori. Te Gradiar.*

Freezy cold. I march Romania. Maybe trucker pity me.

I go see daughter. I no pension. I die.

Clever men have pension. Roman soldier. He have pension. He have pension always. He Jesus earthly daddy. He Progenitor.

Roman turn to me he say:-

"*Et nolite timere. Filius meus vobiscum semper*"

The rat squeaked his acclamation.

<u>References</u>

R16.1 Ecclesiastes 1:10-2:18
R16.2 Ecclesiastes 12:14

CHAPTER SEVENTEEN
ANALYSES

The Source of Silver

[This Page Intentionally Left Blank]

AGWELL
RINGSTEAD

CHAPTER EIGHTEEN
BIBLIOGRAPHY AND REFERENCES

CHAPTER ONE

    R1.1   Page 1: Line 19: Word 10

CHAPTER TWO

    R2.1   Page 1: Line 8: Word 4
    The National Library of Scotland Side-by-Side Map Archive
https://maps.nls.uk/geo/explore/side-by-side/#zoom=5&lat=56.00000&lon=-4.00000&layers=1&right=BingHyb

    R2.2   Page 2: Line 12: Word 10
    The Silver Nut Well
    "The Northumberland Wildlife Trust: A History"
    Angus Lunn
https://www.nwt.org.uk/sites/default/files/2018-05/Angus%20Lunn%20-%20NWT%20History.pdf)

    R2.3   Page 2: Line 21: Word 4
    Witchcraft (the esoteric believe system)
    "Forbidden Rites: Your Complete Introduction to Traditional Witchcraft"
    Jeanette Ellis
    O Books; 1st Edition (31 Aug. 2009)
    ISBN-13 : 978-1846941382
    636 pp
    p77
(https://books.google.co.uk/books?id=Gr_BaAPVhMQC&pg=PA77&lpg=PA77&dq=the+silver+well+story+northumberland+otterburn&source=bl&ots=JmMUx079gR&sig=ACfU3U18VPqJ5Q-9EIJFs839rdWhQg1RqQ&hl=en&sa=X&ved=2ahUKEwi3-8GQy5buAhU0Q0EAHUGmAqk4ChDoATADegQIARAC#v=onepage&q=the%20silver%20well%20story%20northumberland%20otterburn&f=false), Jeanelle Ellis

    R2.4   **Existential Paradox of Knowledge**

CHAPTER THREE

R3.1 **Periodic Table**
Wikipedia contributors. (2021, February 20).
Periodic table.
In Wikipedia, The Free Encyclopedia. Retrieved 14:48, February 24, 2021,
from
https://en.wikipedia.org/w/index.php?title=Periodic_table&oldid=1007918501

R3.2 "The Metallurgy of Lead"
"Including Desilverization and Cupellation"
John Percy MD FRS
John Murray of Albermarle Street, London   1870
567pp (also 30 pages of publisher's advertisements)
Ex Libris University of Michigan
ISBN-13 : 978-1144223944 (Hardback)

https://ia802703.us.archive.org/28/items/metallurgyleadi01percgoog/

metallurgyleadi01percgoog.pdf

Silver in British Lead Ores
p102
Cost of the Pattinson Process ("Pattinsonization")
p139
Cost of the Parkes Process
p153
Observation on Cupellation
p203

R3.3 "Mining for Metals in Wales"
FJ North
National Museum of Wales (1 Dec. 1962)
ISBN-13 : 978-0720000214
120pp
Hardcover

R3.4   "Organic Precipitation of Metallic Copper"
        TS Lovering
        USGS Bulletin 795-C: 1927
        10pp
        https://pubs.usgs.gov/bul/0795c/report.pdf

R3.5   "Sulfate in Drinking Water"
        WHO/SDE/WSH/03.04/114
        ©World Health Organisation, 2004

https://www.who.int/water_sanitation_health/dwq/chemicals/sulfat
e.pdf
        16pp

CHAPTER FOUR

R4.1   Wikipedia contributors. (2021, January 14).
        X-ray fluorescence.
        In Wikipedia, The Free Encyclopedia. Retrieved 16:00,
February 24, 2021,
        from
 https://en.wikipedia.org/w/index.php?title=X-
ray_fluorescence&oldid=1000381618

        Picture Description
        English: Historical note: this was run as a pressed powder on the
scanning channel of the
        Siemens MRS404 at Blue Circle Cement, Atlanta Plant, in 1995. We had
no scandium, gallium   or germanium!
        Date   24 December 2006 (original upload date)
        Source Transferred from en.wikipedia to Commons by Pieter Kuiper
using CommonsHelper.
        Author LinguisticDemographer at English Wikipedia

CHAPTER NINE

R9.1   alfa.com Alfa Aesar by Thermo Fisher Scientific
        https://www.alfa.com/en/catalog/011915/

R9.2   Metaloffcuts.co.uk
        https://www.metaloffcuts.co.uk/product/natural-zinc-sheet/

https://www.metaloffcuts.co.uk/product/corten-steel-sheet/

https://www.amazon.co.uk/PG-Tips-Pyramid-Bags-Total/dp/B07CJGT17P

    R9.3   Page 6: Line 3: Word 10
           "Organic Precipitation of Metallic Copper"
           TS Lovering
           USGS Bulletin 795-C: 1927
           10pp
           https://pubs.usgs.gov/bul/0795c/report.pdf

CHAPTER SIXTEEN

    R16.1 Ecclesiastes 1:10-2:18
    R16.2 Ecclesiastes 12:14

Serial: 1
Local Filename: TheWesternGatewayAtBremeniumgeograph-
5769095-by-Russel-Wills (2).jpg
Source: Geograph
Photographer: Russel Wills
OS Grid Reference: NY 83196 98614
Latitude and Longitude: 55°16′53″N: 2°15′58″W
Place: High Rochester, Northumberland
Subject: The Western Gateway of BREMENIUM Roman
Fort

The large ashlar about (0.2, 0.2) is Roman as is the gate jamb (0.35, 0.25). The small ashlar (0.5, 0.25) and (0.2, 0.55) is modern, possibly eighteenth century. Looking East.

The position is very remote, waste and vulnerable and for centuries avoided by both English and Scottish settlers: Hence the excellent preservation of stonework.

Serial: 2

Local Filename:

RomanTombAtPettyKnowesByPeteSaundersNY8398GeographSharp12x1217322_46b63066.jpg

Source: Geograph

Photographer: Pete Saunders

OS Grid Reference: NY 83834 98166

Latitude and Longitude: 55°16′39″N: 2°15′28″W

Place: Petty Knowes, High Rochester, Northumberland

Subject: Base of Mausoleum

Roman Law forbade the intramural inhumation of humans, but respected or affluent deceased where entombed extramurally along the sides of highways. Several such tombs were constructed here, of which only this has significant subaerial vestiges. It was probably the burial-place of a high officer, conceivably the garrison commandant.

The Course of Dere Street follows the line of tussocks from (0.0, 0.5) to (1.0, 0.45). Lamb Crag is the knoll about (0.8, 0.6). The small white dots are sheep as for instance around (0.5, 0.6). The structure at (0.25, 0.65) is the remains of a modern stone sheepfold (locally called a stell).

Serial: 3

Local Filename:

DereStreetSouthOfFeatherwoodNT8203Geographgeograph-3433302-by-Andrew-Curtis (2).jpg

Source: Geograph

Photographer: Andrew Curtis

OS Grid Reference: NT 82042 01423

Latitude and Longitude: 55°18′24″N: 2°17′04″W

Place: Petty Knowes, High Rochester, Northumberland

Subject: Dere Street West of Mounthilly, Northumberland

The valley with the coniferous forest at (0.5, 0.75) is Redesdale.

The farmstead at (0.1, 0.6) is Silloans.

The tarmacadamised road that dominates the picture is a modern military road built upon the Roman military road Dere Street. Note the lateral movement of sections of the course as the ancient road has shifted on its wet peat substratum over the centuries. Note also the military checkpoint hut at (0.6, 0.6).

Serial: 4
Local Filename:
        MoorlandWestOfSilverwellByMikeQuinnNT8203Geograph37084
36_0104444b (2).jpg
Source: Geograph
Photographer: Mike Quinn
OS Grid Reference: NT 8117 0249 (camera position)
Latitude and Longitude: 55°18′54″N: 2°17′54″W
Place: Unnamed Position, The Cheviot Hills,
Northumberland
Subject:

The object at (0.95, 0.55) is a stone boundary marker. The tiny white foreground flecks, for example at (0.55 , 0.05) are the blooms of Bog Cotton also known as Common Cottongrass (*Eriophorum angustifolium*). This species of plant favours highly acidic soils, especially peat.

**The PDSA Gold Medallist Pouched Hero Rat Magawa
with his Friend in Cambodia**

The Gambian pouched rat (*Cricetomys gambianus*), also known
commonly as the African giant pouched rat, is a species of nocturnal
pouched rat of the giant pouched rat genus *Cricetomys*, in the family
Nesomyidae.
A Tanzanian social enterprise founded by two Belgians, APOPO, trains
Gambian pouched rats to detect land mines and tuberculosis with their
highly developed sense of smell. The trained pouched rats are called
HeroRATS. The rats are far cheaper to train than mine-detecting dogs; a
rat requires $7,300 for nine months of training, whereas a dog costs about
$25,000 for training.
In 2020 a Hero Rat received a PDSA Gold Medal, the animal equivalent of
the George Cross, becoming the first rat to receive the award since the
charity began honouring animals 77 years ago. 'Magawa' has detected 39
landmines and 28 items of unexploded ordnance, clearing over 1,517,712
square feet [141,000 square metres.] of land, preventing many injuries and
deaths, in his 4 year career so far.
https://en.wikipedia.org/wiki/Gambian_pouched_rat

According to the NGO the main advantage over conventional methods is
speed. They point to past studies that show that less than 3 percent of

landmine suspected land actually contains any landmines. Animals such as dogs or rats detect only explosives and ignore scrap metal such as old coins, nuts and bolts etc., thus they might be able to check areas of land faster than conventional methods. They claim that one rat can check 200 m^2 (2,200 sq ft) in around 20 minutes. In Angola, however, from 2012 to 2016 49,625 m^2 (534,160 sq ft) were cleared as part of a team including conventional equipment, indicating a 35,000% slower rate in the field. The rats are indigenous to Sub-Saharan Africa, so are suited to tropical climates and could be resistant to many endemic diseases. Few resources are needed to train and raise a rat to adulthood and they have a lifespan of six to eight years. Furthermore, rats do not form bonds with specific trainers like dogs but rather are motivated to work for food, so trained rats can be transferred between handlers. In the minefields, the rats are too light to detonate a pressure-activated mine when walking over it. Their small size also means that the rats can be more easily transported to sites than dogs.

https://en.wikipedia.org/wiki/APOPO

The PDSA Gold Medal to an Animal for his Gallantry
https://en.wikipedia.org/wiki/PDSA_Gold_Medal

Please refer to https://www.apopo.org/en for further details.